Th

Judita Šalgo

THE ROAD TO BIROBIDZHAN

Translated from the Serbian by John K. Cox

p PRESS

2022

Judita Šalgo, *The Road to Birobidzhan*

© 2022 by CEEOLPress
Originally published in Serbian as *Put u Birobidžan*
by Stubovi kulture, 1997

Translated and published in English with the permission of Ivana and Tamara Mirkovic.

Published in 2022 by CEEOLPress,
Frankfurt am Main, Germany

The publication was made possible with the support of the Ministry of Culture and Information of the Republic of Serbia.

All rights reserved. No part of this publication may be reproduced, stored in a retrieval system, or transmitted, in any form or by any means, without the permission of the Publisher.

Typesetting: CEEOL GmbH, CEEOLPress
Layout: Alexander Neroslavsky

ISBN: 978-3-949607-04-2
E-ISBN: 978-3-949607-05-9

Table of Contents

CHAPTER ONE. (untitled) 7

CHAPTER TWO. THE EASTERN
SIN OF NENAD MITROV 24

CHAPTER THREE. THE LOST TRIBES 68

CHAPTER FOUR. FRAGMENTS FROM
THE WORKING DIARY ABOUT BIROBIDZHAN. . . 97

CHAPTER FIVE. THE JOURNEY
OF BERTHA PAPPENHEIM 101

CHAPTER SIX. THE FEMALE
EDGE OF THE WORLD 109

CHAPTER SEVEN. THE WOMEN OF GALICIA. . . 135

CHAPTER EIGHT. THE BIRTH OF HYSTERIA . . . 143

CHAPTER NINE. FEMINIA 147

CHAPTER TEN. FLORA'S VISION 156

CHAPTER ELEVEN. THE SECRET LIFE
OF BERTHA PAPPENHEIM. *The hysterical circle* 157

CHAPTER TWELVE. HYSTERIA
IN THE HOTEL HUNGARIA 163

CHAPTER THIRTEEN. PSYCHODRAMA
WITH HYSTERIA 177

CHAPTER FOURTEEN. AT THE GUTMANS' 179

CHAPTER FIFTEEN. EPILOGUE:
FLORA'S VISION. *The Impression* 194

CHAPTER SIXTEEN. SUTINA 198

CHAPTER SEVENTEEN. FLORA GUTMAN 201

CHAPTER EIGHTEEN. DOCTOR SAVIĆ 212

CHAPTER NINETEEN. HAIM AZRIEL 216

CHAPTER TWENTY. FLORA
SEARCHES FOR SUTINA 220

CHAPTER TWENTY-ONE. BERTHA
PAPPENHEIM TRAVELS TO THE SOUTH
AND TO THE EAST 229

CHAPTER TWENTY-TWO. FLORA GUTMAN'S
VISION. *The Impression* 237

CHAPTER TWENTY-THREE. A DOUBLE
JOURNEY..241

CHAPTER TWENTY-FOUR. THE FOREST
OF THE MARTYRS................................249

AFTERWORD: THE BELGRADE CONNECTION ..275

SELECT BIBLIOGRAPHY........................283

TRANSLATOR'S NOTE 286

CHAPTER ONE

(UNTITLED)

According to a collateral descendant, this is what Genesis looks like in the case of the Rothschild family:

When God made man, he named him Mayer Amschel Rothschild. This man lived his seventy years and begat five sons, who dispersed into five major European cities. The London son, Nathan, called "the golden one," the financial victor at the Battle of Waterloo, begat Lionel, the financier of the Suez Canal and a British member of parliament; Lionel lived his seventy years and begat Nathanael, the first lord among the Rothschilds, or in any other Jewish family, and Walter, a celebrated zoologist. The French son of Mayer Amschel, James, a British banker in Paris, lived nearly seventy-six years and begat Baron Edmond, known to all Jews as the initiator of the fund for the acquisition land in Palestine, a philanthropist and distinguished collector who invested a great deal of money and zeal in everything Jewish that grew or traipsed across the land of Palestine. And the remaining sons of Mayer Amschel were in Naples, Frankfurt, and Vienna, men of high credit and high principles: industrialists, builders, bankers, philanthropists, produced sons and daughters who were all worthy, diligent, and wealthy, but whose doors could be smashed in, their houses pillaged, and their bones scattered in evil times.

For our story, Edmond is the most important of these, a declared collector of artwork, a lover of both art and people, to whom the first colonists in Palestine, around the year 1880, turned with a request for financial assistance. He responded, and little by little he took upon himself the care of all Jewish settlements, sending money, agricultural experts, and clerks to see to it that Jews were led back into the cultivation of wheat, grapes, vegetables, poultry, and cattle. He bought them, from Arabs and Turks, some 125,000 acres of land and established settlements across Samaria and Galilee. He died in 1934 at a very advanced age. Twenty years later, his grateful compatriots transported his remains to Israel.

The noble baron undertook, therefore, to buy the Jews a home, to redeem the land of the biblical fathers, lost so long ago. This was not at all simple, because the Turkish sultan pointedly opposed Jewish settlement in Palestine. Turkish common law, however, worked to the colonists' benefit: when a man raises four walls and plants three trees, no governmental authority can budge him from that spot, even if he bought the land contrary to the law. Thus each new bed of tomatoes, every row of onions, became a bulwark of the homeland.

Serious debates and divisions raged among Jews at the turn of the century. Emancipated, well-to-do Jews from the West were of the opinion that they should seek a homeland, receiving it or purchasing it wherever it might be: in Uganda, under a British protectorate; in Argentina, following the plan of Baron de Hirsch; in the former kingdom of the Hova in Madagascar; in southwestern Australia above Esperance; in the Amazon or in Palestine, if only the Sultan would sign a charter. Jews from the East, on the other hand, constantly victimized in pogroms, plundered and murdered, looked to Palestine, which belonged to them by historical right, and they were not prepared to compromise. Western Zionism was their tactical ally. Assimilationists on both sides, however, maintained that emigration to Palestine would fatally weaken Judaism in the diaspora and would not solve the Jewish question. Hasidim in Poland simply pounced on Zionism, and reformists did not consider themselves to be members of a separate nation but instead a religious community. Finally, spurning the lot of them, both the well-heeled Rothschild land purchasers and the Zionist conjurors, as well as bourgeois nationalists and cosmopolitan assimilationists, and the Jewish syndicalists in Russia advocated cultural autonomy within a future Pan-Russian socialist federation; they saw their new home beneath the newly minted Soviet star.

Baron de Rothschild remained loyal to his concept of history created through purchase, but all of these varied takes on the Jewish question invariably awoke in him the desire to route his tutelage and his money in different directions. And, just as is the case with every true collector and philanthropist, while paying off one obligation he was already seeking a new one; it had to be that way; and so Rothschild, buying a home for poor relatives in Palestine, was already measuring for a roof over the head also for the neighboring poor people, and then a third, and maybe a fourth, small back-up homelands for his scattered compatriots, each of them under a different sky, each of these homelands different but equally private, as far as possible from world markets and holy bonfires. For it was right that a people for centuries dispersed, without a homeland, will ultimately receive at least two. Threatened in the one, they can seek salvation in the second; driven out of the second, they will shelter in the third. And with these thoughts in mind, the baron was already seeking out suitable locations on the map of the world: swampy deltas unattractive to others, plateaus surrounded by natural obstacles, islands with steep coastlines and underwater shoals hard by their harbors, regions of jungle in which the state moved, encroached, or pulled back in concert with the vegetation and woodcutters. With a goose-feather quill in his hand, he traced on the map, romantically but intensely focused, the oceanic, telluric, and air currents that build, destroy, and alter the world. He pondered the forces that underlie the Gulf Stream and the Labrador Current; he wondered what governs the planetary winds, the migration of eels and birds, the movement of peoples, languages and money. He dipped his feather into the ink, wiped the superfluous bead on the crystal neck of the inkstand, and lowered the tapered tip to the eastern coast of the Levantine Sea. He let, as if distracted, a second drop fall onto the wood-free paper and be absorbed by the coastal blue next to ancient Jaffa, in order to that it would, suddenly, with the gesture of the artist who after long hesitation renders the first stroke, start out after his own imagination, to the West, along the coast of North Africa where it got stuck on the Rock of Gibraltar, paused at the Rio Guadalquivir, continued its path above the Pyrenees, and, in an arc through the middle of the continent of Europe, and just at the point where it dropped down to the Black Sea, or not; to the foot of the Caucasus and then closed the ellipse of diaspora through Asia Minor the way the earth completes its trajectory around the sun, just at that moment the Baron de Rothschild made a capricious, baronial, or simply artistic reversal and skipping over obscure, cheerless Asia, stabbed his quill beyond all orbits, right into the bottom of Eastern Siberia.

Every person who has ever scribbled on a large-scale map feels like Columbus, like an adventurer, a visionary and the spiritual proprietor of a new world, and Baron Edmond was all three. God and History had deployed his co-nationals across a broad swath encompassing the Mediterranean and Black Seas, propelled them on several occasions onto the path across the Atlantic, to the two Americas. Now the quivering drop of Edmond's ink was going to transmit Semitic seed to the very end of the world, and there erect a new nursery, but a safe one, God willing, a greenhouse out of which, strengthened by the harsh environment of the Siberian races, will arise a new and fortified Jewish generation. That place in northeastern Asia where the Baron's inky arrow stuck lay outside of the roads and currents along with Jewry had, up to that time, moved and suffered, outside of its desires and fears. The Baron, through thick lashes on his fleshy eyelids, goggled at the previously unknown, measly little rivers Bira and Bidzhan, which sprang forth from his quill and slithered towards the Amur. That spot was incalculably distant from Mt. Zion, to which his spirit returned with gratitude as if to a high-altitude resort, from those inland landscapes to which he compared the exhibits of his art collection, so far from the bluish olive trees, cedars, Mediterranean pine, dates, oranges — the first Jewish wetland since the Great Flood. One homeland would be in the Near East and the other in the Far East; one historical, the other para-historical; if the latter should prove to be uninhabitable, it will still serve a purpose: to be let out, exchanged, sold, or used as a temporary lodging, and as an unlimited one in case of emergency.

Then the Baron noticed that another drop of his ink had spilled on the map of the world. The blur, later named *Rotšildovo*, became the subject of scholarly curiosity; Jewish cognoscenti in the coming decades read into it important inklings. It's true, at an auction in London in 1953, at which were on offer some less well known specimens from the Baron's collection, plus a set of his personal documents, one very old gentleman, with the face of a mummy, expressed his doubts in the matter of the origin of the cobalt blue spot on the atlas, maintaining that Baron de Rothschild, despite his modern world view, did not use blue ink, then a technological novelty on the basis of aniline dye, but rather black, prepared especially for him from a mixture of ferrous compounds and coal, of which the ancient Semites availed themselves, or even, less frequently, a wondrous fluid of charred fir resin, wine yeast, and gum arabic, made from an Egyptian recipe. With such ink Moses must have written in his youth, said the friend of the house of Rothschild, and maybe he even used it to write out the concept of the Law that in the decisive hour, in the name of the Lord, he would carve into clay tablets.

The biographers of this prominent member of the Rothschild family nowhere explicitly mention his east Siberian point and the plans potentially connected with it, but the facts do show that even during the Baron's lifetime, in the first decades of this century, steps were taken towards its realization. The truth is that in Eastern Siberia, in contrast to Palestine, the Baron's money was not at work, but rather Soviet power. The planners of revolutionary changes, during their conspiratorial apprenticeships in Europe, had to follow on the heels of the Baron's brainchild; they crossbred it with the ideas of Leon Trotsky on this issue and soon after the proclamation of the new Union they set about exploring the possibility of Jewish colonization of the Amur basin. The report of the first expedition was, truth be told, not exactly encouraging: it acknowledged that the terrain in the area in question was not very suitable for living, and major preparatory work would be indispensable, but there was no giving up on the plan for the first Jewish convoy to head to Birobidzhan as early as 1929.

The aged Baron had no more influence on the real world, but there were Soviet and other exponents. Their call to the Jewish population of Soviet Russia didn't have the resonance they wanted, but in Poland, Romania, Great Britain, and the United States the Birobidzhan idea won over many champions. Money was collected for colonization; contingents of farm equipment from all over the world arrived in Moscow to be forwarded from there to the East. Along with the machinery, people were dispatched as well: according to the Soviet government's program, to the Autonomous Jewish Oblast of Birobidzhan should be conveyed in 1932 18,000 Jews, the following year 31,000, but in these two years only one-fifth of that number arrived, and the ones who came largely scattered, and this was the subject of an article in a Western newspaper.

The Jewish press followed the Birobidzhan campaign from afar, relying on the accounts of the relatively few eyewitnesses. The territory envisioned for the settlement of Jews, they reported, was a hideous marshland with an unhealthy climate, short humid summers, and long rainy winters, which impelled even Ukrainian peasants, the predecessor of the Jews in this experiment, to return to the place from which they had been brought. But the authorities did not give up. In 1934 Kalinin signed a decree on the establishment of the Autonomous Jewish Territory and announced that by 1937 there would be 150,000 Jews living there. A film from that time, *In Search of Happiness*, showed the joy of the settlers, the new Birobidzhanis. The film even swayed a number of Russian Jews and impelled them, despite all sorts of bitter experiences, set out on the road to the new promised land.

Regarding their fate, however, there are no reports. Here and there one can find in the press, before the war, some references to Birobidzhan, but not to the Birobidzhanians. In the Moscow paper *Izvestiia*, in June of 1939, on the occasion of a census, it was stated that in this territory there lived more than 100,000 people, but in an article published in the West, not even 30,000 of them were Jews. Before the German invasion, Jews fled by the hundreds of thousands to the east, to Uzbekistan, Kazakhstan, Tajikistan, but scarcely any moved on to Birobidzhan. They also did not want to go there after the war, although their homes in Russia, Ukraine, Belarus, and Poland had been torched and their relatives slain. Then, along with other words and people, Birobidzhan ceased to be mentioned in public. Except that in 1945 Kalinin did assert, to a New York reporter, that the Soviet government would, in accordance with the Constitution, turn the Autonomous Territory into a Jewish Republic as soon as it contained 100,000 Jews. To the journalist's question about why there were not already that many Jews there, the president of the Presidium of the Supreme Soviet answered that the numbers were only a little short. The journalist, of course, knew that at that time in Birobidzhan there were, at least, ten thousand, or even twenty thousand fewer people than before the war. That many people had died off or dispersed. In the subsequent years the Autonomous Jewish Territory became a zone of ethnically neutral, standard deportations, a great concentration camp following the vision of Lavrentii Pavlovitch Beria. After Stalin's death, and Beria's liquidation, Malenkov again trotted out the idea of the judaization of Birobidzhan. True enough, the Yiddish-language paper, the *Birobidzhaner Stern*, had already been shut down, there were no data about the schools, and the national composition of the population was kept under wraps. The newspaper Pravda in Moscow, at the beginning of 1954, stated that in the imminent elections the Autonomous Jewish Territory would be selecting five deputies, and the *Birobibidzhanskaya Zvezda* gleefully foretold the arrival of new Jews from Ukraine, Russia, Belarus…

(Available handbooks shed no light on the mystery. The *Encyclopedia* of the Leksikografski Zavod of the Federal People's Republic of Yugoslavia from 1955 states only that Birobidzhan was a city of 38,000 inhabitants along the Trans-Siberian railway, and that the population lived by processing wood and meat and the production of bricks. *The Jewish Encyclopedia* from 1955-56 estimated the Jewish population at 100,000 souls, comprising half the population of the Territory. Yiddish, at one time recognized as the official language, was pushed aside by Russian; the Yiddish-language theater had been closed. Of the sixty-four state farms, eighteen were Jewish. The *Great Soviet Encyclopedia* of 1970 specified that the city of Birobidzhan, founded in 1928 on the site of the flag-stop called Tikhonkaya, the center of eponymous oblast of the Khabarovsk district of the RSFSR, that it had 56,000 residents, plants for the production of knit fabrics, clothing, and shoes, two theaters, one Russian and one Jewish, and two Territory-wide papers: the *Birobidzhaner Stern*, which came out three times a week in Yiddish and had a circulation of 12,000, and the *Birobidzhanskaya Zvezda* in Russian, five times a week, with a print run of 15,000. According to the *Encyclopedia Britannica* from 1987, the city of Birobidzhan had 75,000 inhabitants, and the entire territory 200,000. The Region, it said, was predominantly flat, marshy, and dotted with boggy forests and pastureland that are now for the most part ideal for human use. In the north and northwest the valley is closed off by the Khingan Range and the Bureya Massif, covered with forests of spruce, pine, fir, and larch. The winters are dry and very harsh, the summers hot and humid. The population lived mostly along the Trans-Siberian Railroad line and the Amur River. They grew wheat, rye, oats, soybeans, sunflowers, and vegetables; in the

Amur they caught fish, mostly salmon. Along with building materials, shoes and textiles, they produced trailers for use with tractors.)

The connection of the Rot family in Novi Sad with Birobidzhan was of a mythical nature, as was the case of the Baron's. Such was, at any rate, also the mutual connection of the Rots and the Rothschilds, embodied in the shared first syllable of their last names. In the years between the two world wars, when they themselves had become reasonably well-to-do, the Rots began following the paths and undertakings of the Rothschilds with a familial interest and indulgence: the power of the Rothschilds somehow resided in the second syllable of their family name, in the "*schild*," the coat of arms, red of course, which had adorned the family house in Frankfurt-am-Main for four centuries now, while the folks from Novi Sad had no memories of any such real estate, which meant that the monosyllabic color in their last name was something they had to had to transmit through time only in their veins, leaving weathered red tracks on the cobblestones and dust. The lacuna in their genealogy the Rots filled with a story about the Bavarian city of Rothenburg, which, people claimed, got its name from the blood of Jews shed there at the time of the infamous Rintfleisch Massacre, and later pogroms in times of plague. One distant forefather of the Rots supposedly managed to dodge the mobs by concealing his origins and covering his tracks; he took a German last name from the city that took from him everything, and with this tailless syllable slung over his shoulder he shoved off into the wide world of peddlers. In a one-syllable world, the Rots and the Rothschilds could have been brothers: all Jews emerged from one kit. As chance would have it, yet another member of the broader family, the American Zionist leader Morris Rothenberg, was to be included in this story about Birobidzhan. Through his articles, an American Rot, the paternal uncle Leopold, happened onto, in the 1920s, the ideas of legitimate Zionism, and then with Birobidzhan, which was like a heresy, similar to the false socialist Messianism at that time sweeping through some circles in American and European Judaism. In that way, the imaginary journey of the Rots to Birobidzhan began via America.

Leopold Rot was a man with a restless heart, high but volatile ideals, forceful planning with weak follow-through, and he, with a multiplicity of changing residences and jobs to his name, ultimately found the solution to all of his problems in the idea that the promised land did not necessarily have to be in Palestine, or in gleaming Manhattan, but rather could be in some third location, equally distant from both past and present and accessible in equal measure to the successful and unsuccessful — especially to those who were not. As a Jewish semi-proleterian in America, he'd been preoccupied with survival as much as with socialist ideas, especially regarding the dying away of the state. The state is not forever, he wrote to his brother Emil in Novi Sad, whom he had not seen since he, without even a high-school diploma, had cast off for America. The society of the future was going to use the capitalist apparatus to liquidate everything that was old and played out, authority would be shifting to the people, and the state was simply going to disappear.

"This isn't visible yet from your corner grocery, but from the apex of this infernal Empire State Building it is clear that the future will know no borders. The Birobidzhan about which I have already written you will not be a state of the type the Zionists dream of, but rather the focus of Jewish revolution that will change the world. I am planning, as soon as my business takes off, to make a major financial contribution to Birobidzhan, and later to go there myself, although Barbara is against it. I would like for that to happen this coming spring. I've heard that a group is already preparing for the trip. I am quite sure that the Zionists are wrong. Jews do not need to be dreaming about a return, but instead about how they can go farther. In any case, I'll keep you informed about how things stand and my further preparations. Perhaps my next letter will even arrive with a stamp from Birobidzhan! How are Valika and the children? My best regards to everyone, and a hug for you, Leo."

Spring came, and then summer, and they heard nothing from Leopold from New Jersey, where he'd been living for the past two years, or from Birobidzhan. Emil's worried letters did not even get a response from Barbara, Leo's wife, or God forbid, widow, in the event that the unfortunate man had met with problems on the road to the chosen land, nor the landlord, if Barbara and the children had set out after him; the letters had also not bounced back to them as should happen if, by some chance, the landlords, Jews from Minsk, had set out for Birobidzhan or if their building in America had simply been torn down; there in that country without a foundation, that was a common occurrence. Three years passed, in ominous silence, and there wasn't a single syllable from any continent; this was enough for the notion of a poisoned apple of the "Birobidzhan" variety to ripen on the Novi Sad branch of the Rot family, an apple that was fatal to windbags and fantasts, who are hungry for everything built in the air. When finally, just before the end of the Great Depression, Leopold wrote from a new address in a new city in a different American state and referred briefly to his changed work and recent arrivals in the family, the Birobidzhan blister popped and released a great quantity of suppressed fear, gall, humor, and febrile hope. Birobidzhan became a metaphor for fever; it permeated sayings and proverbs, both humorous and bitter, found its way into curses and exclamations, lessons to children and free spirits, an Asian name spoken with a Hungarian accent, domesticated itself like a stray dog with a master it had selected itself. The merchant Emil Rot would say to his son: "I'll buy you a car — when I hold up a bank in Birobidzhan." To his oldest daughter: "You can get married — when the governor of Birobidzhan asks for your hand." The yellow, six-pointed Star of David became in his usage the Star of Birobidzhan, and before the deportations of 1944, he would say goodbye to his friend Sava Jakšić with the words: "Well, see you in Birobidzhan." After the sudden death of the American relative with whom all of this started, Birobidzhan as his inheritance was divided between the members of the family, and then it remained in their lexicon for two generations. Emil's son Stevan, a dentist from top to bottom, as sturdy as a filling, resistant to any kind of sentimentality, couldn't resist whispering, before the end of his wedding night, when he was very emotional, some comments to his chosen one about the moon that was setting and the sun that was being born in distant Birobidzhan. For his young wife Olga, that exotic geographical concept remained for a long time the apotheosis of Stevan's first and, unfortunately, last fit of lyricism. She endeavored to brighten her marriage with that ray of that sensitivity. She didn't accept the explanation that Birobidzhan was nothing but a swamp, inhabited by few people but many mosquitoes. She believed that, as in every credible story, beyond the illusion of swampy transpirations and moldy huts was hidden some shining guardian of love, a Birobidzhani Taj Mahal.

One could say that Olga, although born a Kraus, was the only person really to continue the Birobidzhan streak in the Rot family. Her first youthful turbulence had been keyed to Palestine, and, joining the *Hashomer Hatzair*, she made preparations to go there, after her exams and graduation, with a group of schoolmates, but the engagement with Stevan Rot postponed this plan indefinitely. After she returned from the concentration camp, she vowed that she would spend the rest of her life in her kitchen and dining room, and by the time of Israel's first call she was ready to pack up her kitchen and dining room in a trunk and hit the road. The first *aliyah* passed, and the second and third; everyone who intended to go, did so; at last Stevan let it be known that he did not plan on leaving his dental drill here, in order to smash rocks with a pickaxe there, and that he was definitely not going anywhere; and then shortly thereafter, in the fall of 1952, he collected his things and took his assistant and left, forever. Thus was a line drawn beneath Olga's losses: almost all of her nearest and dearest were dead, and her heart was laid waste. If we had only gone somewhere, even to that black Birobidzhan! She cried out when Stevan informed her that there was no longer anything to keep him there. If we had at least left for black Birobidzhan, she whimpered for a long time afterwards, stumbling around the room with a bandage across the front of her head where the migraines hit her, and her fourteen-year old son Nenad standing in the doorway like the guardian of the escape route to Birobidzhan seeing to it that his mother did not get past him by some chance. "To black Birobidzhan, to black Birobidzhan," she continued to wail for days, and every time her son would come unglued at the thought of these unhealthy passions that pierced the layers of nightgown, robe, and damask bindings around her head on their way out of the somber depths of her unhappiness.

In due time, Nenad Rot situated the family estate known as Birobidzhan on the prairies of the Wild West, and he populated it with Comanches, Shoshones, and Birobidzhanis. Boundless herds of cattle grazed on the tough, sharp-edged grass; packs of horses raced along the rim of a plateau and disappeared over the horizon. Forty years later, one evening, they bolted again into the life of Nenad Rot, who was then a middle-aged attorney in Novi Sad. A hint of danger, of general affliction, triggered and then debunked his boyhood daydreams. From far-off Birobidzhan a planetary shiver came howling, and it chilled his very backbone. The Birobidzhanski gallop echoed in his bones.

Some aspects of the Birobidzhan syndrome manifested themselves nearly simultaneously in Nenad's daughter from his first marriage, Dina Rot, and especially acutely and painfully in her husband, Miloš Bojić. They were going to transmit this malady to their children if they brought forth any, and all of their descendants and the descendants of their descendants would have their Birobidzhan, that enduring nidus and refuge that was hidden from the world, which was mentioned only inadvertently or in dreams. It was difficult to predict what Birobidzhan would mean in the future, but in the time of great convulsions, with whole worlds being ground into the past, nothing else existed. The European centers of London, Paris, Naples, Frankfurt, Vienna — were now just telegraph agencies, reference points: all roads led to Birobidzhan. Over the course of millennia, the center of the world had moved from place to place: Ur, Memphis, Babylon, Jerusalem, Athens, Alexandria, Rome, Constantinople, Mecca, Moscow, Berlin, New York, Tokyo: in the moment this story begins, the center of the global funnel, of earthly oblivion, is Birobidzhan. At the Belgrade airport, all flights have been canceled. One night on the monitor in the concourse a destination popped up that had never existed within the memory of any system: Birobidzhan. Through the electronic blinking of this solitary word, a metallic voice from the public address system told travelers to go to gate B-2.

"Birobidzhans *ad infinitum*! Hopeless!" said Miloš Bojić. He turned and walked out of the airport terminal.

CHAPTER TWO
THE EASTERN SIN OF NENAD MITROV

1

Nenad Mitrov got to know Marija Aleksandrovna at a reception in the home of Professor Gomirc in late 1925. It was there that was conceived, most certainly, that thing he would later, in a poem dedicated to Gomirc and his wife, call his eastern sin. The broader significance of this sin Mitrov could not have known at the time: describing, a few days later, to Madame Marija Aleksandrovna the murky depths of his soul, he, in fact, depicted a monstrous, as yet unnamed land that was in formation, perhaps just for him and his kin, in the east.

So Mitrov had just arrived. The first, thematic part of the evening, during which the guests were typically served up some musical numbers, a cycle of poems, or a literary-philosophical exposition, had been completed. The buds of the crystal chandelier above the piano, in the middle of the *salon*, suddenly withered, and the light, together with the human beings, backed into the corners where, filtered through the lampshades, braid, and glass canopies, it dripped into the liqueur and coffee, onto the pearl necklaces of the women and their husbands' hands that were busy with aromatic cigarettes and pipes, which in a number of mouths were suspiring zealously like miniature saxophones. They were the only things still hearkening to the man wearing a tuxedo, who continued to sit at the long black "Petrof" piano from Bohemia and flourish his hands with abandon. But the piano could no longer be heard: in spite of the desperate glissandos and chords, it didn't want to release any sounds, swallowing them, offended by the irreverent din; its sounds were like moans that do not dare to have any witnesses.

Actually, the conversation had heated up; everyone was shouting and trying like conductors to guide the general uproar by means of spry and rapturous movements, and they egged each other on and interrupted their interlocutors. The air, clothing, and words were impregnated with smoke. Three women of a certain age, beneath the dubious gaze of the portrait of someone's ancestors, extolled the cruel majesty of Dante's *Inferno* as opposed to the spareness and futility of his *Paradise*. A few steps farther on, at the end-table of rosewood, a professor from the *lycée* was solving the "Schopenhauer enigma," which a gaunt, pale young lady, a member until recently of the Parisian group associated with the famed Diaghilev, had propounded to him: does love of one's close relatives imply the ascetic abjuration of love of oneself? The mother of Madame Gomirc, a coquettish eighty-year old woman, was laboring to win over every young, clean-shaven male conversation partner for the cremation of people's earthly remains, which was much more suitable than the anachronistic placing of people into nasty holes and backfilling them; a young man in turn, was expounding a comparative history of the world based on arson and bonfires, while the small circle of guests standing by the glass doors to the terrace seized in the semi-darkness of the *salon* on parallels between the fall of the Roman, Ottoman, and Russian empires. "Do you mean to say that the rebels had a detailed plan?" gesticulated one meaty male hand. "They did not! The February Revolution was a spontaneous eruption of the masses!" A woman's hand ascended the seersucker sleeve, embraced the fleshy wrist, and gently brought it in for a landing. "Revolution is a mystery," said the owner of that hand, but a dour and fatigued tenor chimed in at the same time: "The Revolution devoured its secret. All the riddles are solved. The Sphinx is dead."

Nenad Mitrov and Madame Gomirc, who had scurried over to meet him, were still standing indecisively in the doorway of the *salon*, when out of the Dante circle floated over a melodious supplication: *"O, Satan, prends pitié de ma longe misère!"* to which the hostess, recalling at that moment the great passion of her guest for Baudelaire, led Mitrov with relief towards the corner from which the cry had originated. But they never arrived at their goal.

"Dear Marija Aleksandrovna!" exclaimed Madame Gomirc, halting in front of the piano. "You listen more devotedly than anyone to your husband!" The forgotten pianist, now convulsing like a netted insect, tried to pluck his limbs out of the ivory teeth of the black "Petrof"; the struggle with the inaudible Tchaikovsky ended up crushing him, and he would have definitely stood up at last, slammed the cover into place, and darted away, if just a step away from the instrument, curled around its oval flank there had not been sitting a woman with a lovely, motionless face and waiting for the outcome of the clash. "Spouses carry the burden of all of all man's artistry on their back," added Madame Gomirc, but then her eyes fell on the hunchbacked man standing next to her, and she blanched, mumbled an excuse, and escaped to the kitchen.

Nenad Mitrov was in every moment of his waking life — and sleeping was something he could scarcely do — aware of his physical deformity. Only in his dreams, sometimes, did he see himself as a young man as tall and slender as a castle tower, but in times of wakefulness this tower, from earthquakes unleashed by the raising of his eyelids, broke up and collapsed into ruins. Now he, however, forgot his appearance. For a moment or two, no longer: but he forgot. That woman was so unfathomable, distant, and impersonal in her beauty, that everything personally in her vicinity was erased. All things human were, next to her, petty; and yet he, a tiny gnome, could, in front of her, be a man.

Later, during the following days and years, Mitrov tried unsuccessfully to reconstruct the moment of his meeting with Marija Aleksandrovna. He was no longer sure where she had been sitting, or how: was she in an armchair with a high back, regal and stiff, as he recalled at first, or relaxed, inclined a bit to one side, half-stretched out on a sweet *recamier*, or was he just seeing things? Sleek like silver angora or cold like a stone lioness? If she were sitting in the easy chair, were her legs, pressed together by stern shantung, firmly planted on the floor or were they, barely touching the carpet with the tips of her shoes, floating and bending on the air currents like fins? And besides, was Madame Marija Aleksandrovna a sphinx, a siren, or a bird of paradise? Couldn't he remember how the conversation started, or whether there had even been a conversation at all? Professor Gomirc disembarked near them on his proprietary cruise around the salon, and he exclaimed: "The gale of bloody events hauled our Marija Aleksandrovna away from the shores of the Black Sea and cast her onto the open waters of history. I will ask the poet," and here he looked meaningfully at Mitrov, "I will ask the poet what poetry can do now? Will it be the sail on the raft of the shipwrecked, or the banner in the hands of the conqueror?"

Nenad Mitrov did not know what to say in that instant about the function of poetry. He had seen the bloody wave wash over the rock face of the Caucasus and pull Marija Aleksandrovna into the depths, and he, wretch that he was, did not have the courage or strength to leap after her and oppose the elemental catastrophe. "And my poems are like a drowning man, floundering in the throes of death," he uttered, as he himself struggled for air, and when the lady, alive and well, compassionately lowered her gaze onto him, he resigned himself and his poetry to the maelstrom. "My verse is devoid of inspiration and of the vital influence of a central, radiating vision," he began, only to choke up immediately, "but I grow intoxicated; I turn myself deaf and blind with just images and epithets, rhymes, and dazzling words. With their help I anesthetize the pain of the void and the dread that is depression. The ecstatic mysteries of poetry evade me — those magical charms of beauty to which Baudelaire ascends! If I could sing, I would have to dissemble, to mask that ultra-black woe that rends my heart. Without it my songs would be but screams and moans, simply horror and chaos!" Professor Gomirc waved his hand impatiently. Mitrov heard his own squeaky voice afflict the very air in front of Marija Aleksandrovna's face, commanding himself to silence, and then went on speaking, afraid that, if he were to shut his mouth even for a moment, Marija Aleksandrovna herself would speak up and with two words, like with two fingers, cast him out of her presence. The woman did actually lift her hand from her lap. She extended it towards Mitrov as if to push him away, but at the last moment she smiled and with an overpowering Russian accent said: "I see that your soul has depth, that it is passionately seeking and loving that which is beautiful." And waiting for the homunculus to grasp that he was being permitted to touch with his quivering lips that back of the proffered hand, she explained: "With one glance I know how to penetrate the spirit of an interlocutor and bring our souls into a delicate shared fluttering. You will be persuaded that I am telling the truth."

In the coming days, Mitrov went to his office, to the library, bringing home Sophocles again, a massive folio in a leather binding, and sat intently for hours above the tiny Greek cursive, went outside, walked towards the Danube, strolled with the affable Jakšić, who was Đura's nephew, and he complained to him about the problems with his publishers, and listened to similar woes from Jakšić, and even went to a party put on by the technical services department, something he would have avoided earlier. It was like life had gone on, but time had stood still; it had lagged there in front of Marija Aleksandrovna, in the semi-darkness of the Gomirc salon, where it was waiting for her to rise from her seat, move towards Nenad Mitrov and, not pausing at the border between the two beings, sink into him. Madame Marija Aleksandrovna did not, however, stand up. She remained seated in the spot where he had first seen her, but that's why Mitrov himself, every time stood up from his desk, went to his mother's room or into the kitchen, read to Madame Rozencvajg passages from *Oedipus Rex* and *Antigone* in Greek, translating them immediately, and she would stealthily wipe away her tears and stuff her damp handkerchief back up her sleeve. Then her son, in order to lift her spirits, would take out a little poppyseed croissant from the credenza, take a bite, smack his lips with relish, and artfully touching his mother's breakfast, say with his mouth full: "I see, Madame Rozencvajg, that your soul has depth, that it passionately seeks and loves the beautiful!" The elderly lady would turn her head to the side swiftly, so that her son couldn't see the approach of new tears that with her were always faster than words; she abandoned her needlework or her book, and with tiny aggrieved steps ran into her son's room, brought out an ashtray filled with cigarette butts, and consigned them to the garbage, saying: "What a soul! She's not a good woman. Forget her." Her son would chew up a morsel or two, return to his room, light up another cigarette, pick up from his desk the umpteenth outline of a letter to Marija Aleksandrovna, crumple it into a ball with one movement of his hand, take a drag on his cigarette, place a new sheet of paper before him, and begin staring at it.

"There is profundity in atmospheric, full resplendence, in blooms and fragrances, a profundity through which wafts purity's zephyr," was written in the version that, after many days, he finally sent to Marija Aleksandrovna, "but there is also a profundity in things that are degrading, full of darkness, mold, and sludge, depths in which revel the grim wraiths of depression, sorrow and ennui, depths that infect and demoralize every crumb of beauty and every scrap of idealism that wanders their way, freeze and numb them, deaden and smother, dissolve and evaporate them in the sulfurous smoke of the gloom and in the sealed fog of languor, depths filled with fly ash and sand, with all kinds of residue and rubbish, everywhere obstructed by impenetrable thickets of doubt and unforgettable particles of terror..." Mitrov, without getting up from his desk, filled fifteen or more pages of square-formatted paper with the countless terrors of his soul, fencing in by means of a tall, thorny manuscript a wild country at the end of the world, an "endless empire of nonsense," his homeland. The lady would still understand: she, having escaped from hell, and he, imprisoned in a different one, his own internal hell, would exchange, at least for a moment, their homelands: she would descend into his darkness, and he would climb up her wind-whipped cliff, if only in order to, from there, from a height worthy of a man, leap into the void. He folded the pieces of paper, stuck them in a large envelope, and gave the packet, along with a tip that was too big, to the concierge with the request that he take it to the address indicated and deliver it straight into the hands of the lady.

Marija Aleksandrovna received the letter, but she did not respond to it. She also never showed up again at the Gomirc residence. She was spotted twice in the theater, once at the hotel "Srpski Kralj," and then there were only rumors that she was still in the city, until it finally came to light that in the summer of 1927, with her husband the pianist, she had moved to Rijeka, and from there on to the west, settling down in some town in the south of France. That same year, in the fall, Nenad Mitrov, in combination with the poetry collection *Two Souls*, which had been brought out by the Novi Sad publishing house Slavija, also printed this letter, and five years later, on the Feast of St. George in 1932, he gave a copy of the little book, with the dedication poem enclosed, to the Gomirces.

"A tragic confession about my 'Eastern sin,'" read Madame Gomirc in an equivocal half-whisper that immediately attracted the other guests' attention. "Eastern sin?" She threw a random glance towards the balcony, above which at that moment all the compass points of the world were blending together in a timeless downpour. "There's no such thing."

"But there is punishment," Nenad Mitrov countered, watching the mud filter out of his shoes onto carpet. He pressed himself more deeply into the easy chair in which — in exactly that one, in every one — on that distant evening the unforgettable Marija Aleksandrovna had sat.

2

The words with which a poet paints his or her soul are often the same ones a traveler employs to describe an actual landscape. Every human soul has in a landscape its twin sibling. The deeper and murkier the soul, the more remote the countryside that's reflected in it.

The swampy land that the unhappy Nenad Mitrov saw in his soul was revealed in its geographical dimension and described by a young and, up to her untimely death, happy woman by the name of Larisa Reisner. She, it was true, had never heard of the little-known poet Nenad Mitrov, or the murky depths of his soul, nor had Mitrov had the opportunity to read a single one of her sentences, although the article in a Viennese newspaper about the Afghan and wartime reporting of Larisa Reisner did not leave him indifferent. But even if by some chance occurrence these two people had met and read each other, it would not have been their lot to recognize their mutual, tactile landscape. For Larisa Reisner was unable to publish this last report of hers in any Soviet or foreign newspaper; in fact, no one had any inkling that she had written it; she dictated it, while feverishly ill with typhus, already scarcely able to talk, to a sailor from the Volga, who had earlier been her comrade-in-arms and who found himself at her deathbed and conveyed the gist of this article to Larisa's husband, his wartime commandant, and later, after his escape from Soviet Russia, also to Marija Aleksandrova to whom some of his compatriots had directed him. And now the sailor, standing in the entry-way at Marija Aleksandrovna's, as the snowflakes that he had brought in on his hair and beard collapsed into bulging, leaden drops, saw to it that he delivered his message as fast as possible, but wanted it to take as long as possible, so that Madame Marija Aleksandrovna could invite him to come in, offer him tea, allow him to tell her about Larisa, and then when her husband returned, for them to put their heads together about a possibility for the newly arrived fellow countryman, find for him a mattress or something on which he could sleep in a kitchen or there in the foyer a night or two. He, Miška Ribakov, had stood there by the bed of the moribund woman as he was now standing before Madame Marija Aleksandrovna, placed his hand on her hot forehead, passed her a mug of water, and she eagerly gulped it down and talked, digressed and returned, moved her mouth and then shut it tight, as if what she was saying was some kind of secret that she had to conceal from death itself. The truth was supposed to be entrusted only to friends; to death one should lie. Now he wanted to confide this truth, Larisa's truth about the terrifying world she had seen, to someone who had been, as people had told him, a friend to her and who would not fail her.

Marija Aleksandrovna didn't take her hand off of the handle of the outer door, nor did she close the door all the way: the uninvited guest mentioned Siberia, snowstorms, rain, oozing wastelands, rocked from foot to foot as if he were traipsing through the mud he was talking about, and with every stride in place the floods and torrents approached, the quagmires and freshets, gloom and mold spread, along with lees and rubbish; underbrush grew rampantly and coppices full of frights, strewn with flyash and grit, clogged up with sulfurous smoke; she was presented with a world that was poisoned and overcast, in which illness flourished, time rotted, and the mind broke apart and went under. A world about which the man, even here, in the safety of the lady's foyer, shrank from speaking of. The sailor thawed onto Marija Aleksandrovna's doormat; through his mouth, overgrown with bristles, the voice of Larisa Reisner came forth, a kind of current of the soul, the last aquifer of that great water the secret of which, before her death, she was trying to entrust to him.

"I understand," said Marija Aleksandrovna. She opened the door leading to the steps and added: "That is very sad.. Who knows what all this exceptional woman must have seen and experienced in our unhappy Russia. But I, unfortunately, did not have the good fortune of knowing her personally. And as for the rest of it, my husband will definitely be at home tomorrow in the forenoon. He will be happy to recommend you to Mr. Kaluđerski. He's our son-in-law, a Russian and a successful man. A miracle of enterprise."

The sailor raised his collar and hunched his shoulders, tucked in his chin and resolutely, the way people do when they do not know where to go, stepped out onto the stairs. Then, hearing the howl of the hinges behind him, he turned around, leaned back towards the door into which Marija Aleksandrovna had vanished, and whispered: "Her coffin was carried by the highest functionaries of the Soviet state. They say that she was buried next to Lenin." Marija Aleksandrovna turned the key twice in the lock behind him, ran into her bedroom, threw herself down onto the couch, plunged her face into the peacock tail stitched into a silken pillow and sobbed with all her might. She had loved Larisa. Oh, how she had loved her!

Pillows were invented so that we could cry on them: the feathers absorb tears, and the images that run out of the eyes with the tears alternate on the pillowcase like on the screen in a cinema, blending with the patterns of the needlework, if the pillow has any, or just gleaming on the cushion itself: and people can see the source or cause of their tears, appreciate their meaning, and they feel relieved. And thus did the afternoon pass in Marija Aleksandrovna's little apartment. The poorly tended fire in the stove went out, her purple pillow grew damp and cold, darkened considerably, and was now capable of reflecting the faintest memory, let alone the striking image of the bright, spacious, abruptly cleaned-out apartment in the Petrograd of her youth, the Reisners' apartment, with a draft blowing through it and people milling about, both porters and their superiors; the first ones were carrying out things that were no longer even in the apartment, mirrors in which one saw mirrors that had already been removed; an abundance of music leaked from the horn of an already expropriated gramophone; and others were waving pieces of paper, and in exchange for objects they gave their names: one table, dining; one armoire, with three wings; one cabinet, for books, glass; some went out, others came in, they rang at open doors, scraped the parquet floor with their hobnail boots, pulling things they could easily carry, and in the center of the tempest stood Larisa, the seventeen-year old commander of her own house, which was going under, and she was giving orders to the people giving orders, hurrying along the executors and finishing up their minor tasks, disposing of a heap of old newspapers that was in the way; she carried a broken table leg, the handle from a dresser, signed papers, wrapped a woolen blanket around her father who was wandering about the icy apartment in a panic, wearing just a shirt, as if he were looking for the misplaced key to his life, opened up the miniature drawers on the secretary that is already sailing towards the cascades of the roaring stairwell… and then Larisa, composed, satisfied with the effect of the operation by means of which beneath the shroud and the layer of polish, naked life was breaking free, turned to Marija Aleksandrovna, squatting in a corner of the kitchen, opened the notebook, which she had not let go of the whole time, and while silence returned with the force of the tide into the apartment, read on and on to her friend from her first work for the stage. The drama was called *Atlantida*. Marija had a headache from the draft, from the big sell-off, from the anxiety and vexation, and she strained to follow the text and make out what was happening, but she could not help but hear the warning in Larisa's voice. She listened intently to how it vibrated under the high ceiling, pealed in the in the emptied niches, and emitted muffled crackles under the parquet, fragments in the corners, while the hero of the story, a young scientist, gave his life to save the continent. He stood on the square in front of the temple to Poseidon, surrounded by the concentric watery rings that defended the heart of Atlantis from external danger. It was the morning of the last day of the world, the sun was surfacing out of the ocean in the east, and with it came Poseidon out of the waves; the earth trembled beneath the hooves of his horses. The young scientist sallied forth to meet him, determined to stand up to the omnipotent god of the seas, for opposition is the most valuable sacrifice that a mortal can offer to an immortal. "O Poseidon, receive my rebellion!" cried the scholar and jumped into the gigantic wave that was breaking apart on the defensive rings and walls, and Marija Aleksandrovna stared at the girlish face of the youthful Alantidian, and for a moment she stuck out her hand to prevent his suicidal leap, but Larisa had already stood up from her chair and her words met the crest of the wave. All that was left for Marija to do was to hurl herself after them, to encircle her friend's waist with both hands, pull her towards her and lower her cheek and lips to her side. But it was too late. The young Atlantidian had already touched the bottom of the sea, which in vengeful rage then reared up, tipping over the world.

"Well, fine," Nenad Mitrov would say. "But who is that woman?" And Larisa Reisner, whose fate had intersected with his, in whose unverifiable experience one was being forced to seek confirmation of his somber fixations? Larisa Reisner died of typhoid in 1926, at the same time that Nenad Mitrov submitted his manuscript of *Two Souls* to the publisher. If he had known this, he would not have asked himself: to whom does this other soul in fact belong? To the unattainable Marija Aleksandrovna, to whom he was tied by exactly one salon encounter and the magic of inaccessibility itself, or to Larisa Reisner, with whom he, in a brace of poetry and death, was linked by the pitiless caprice of destiny.

The authors of commemorative articles published in the most important Soviet organs and given as speeches at formal gatherings on the occasion of Larisa Reisner's death did not find, in her biography, any black marks or bad omens. On the contrary. Hers was, by general assessment, a short and straightforward life, dedicated to the idea and practice of revolution, her truth. Even as a little girl, in that turbulent prerevolutionary epoch, Larisa Reisner absorbed progressive ideas from her family, according to Moscow's *Pravda*. The ideological and moral transformation of her father, Professor Reisner, from Tsarist academic to socialist, gave to new Soviet journalism one of its greatest, bravest, and sharpest reporter's pens of the day, equal to that of John Reed, who shared with Reisner an identical fame and, unfortunately, an identical death, added the newspaper *Iskra* from Leningrad. Maxim Gorki, in a statement to the Rome correspondent of TASS, warmly recalled Larisa's work with his magazine *Novaya Zhizn*, her finely turned poems, the biting, satirical glosses, and, above all, her sketches set in workers' clubs. The Irkutsk newspaper *Sovyetskaya Molodezh* pointed out her courage in skirmishes with the Czech Legion in 1917, and then, subsequently, in the battles of the Volga flotilla in Kazan, Sarapul, Astrakhan, and Baku. The military commander of the flotilla, who was Reisner's husband, a man named Raskolnikov, at a commemoration in the social club of the Soviet fleet referred proudly to the way Larisa succeeded, after the victory, as a commissar on the general staff, in winning the cooperation of the former officers of the Tsarist navy, Admirals Altvater and Berens. The *Kyrgyz Regional Reporter* carried parts of Larisa Reisner's travelogue *In the Land of the Amanullahs*, praising in an accompanying note the lyrical beauty of her style, while *Economic Life* underscored the analytic value of her notes from Germany, especially the importance of her reports in *Hamburg at the Barricades*, and designated them the extraordinary contribution of Larisa Reisner to the work of the Commission for Research on Methods for Improving the Quality of Goods. The Ukrainian literary almanac *Donbas* carried the memories of a handful of miners from the basins of the Don and Ural Rivers about Larisa Reisner's stay in their regions. Thus, this unique woman, concluded the paper, traveling by train for weeks on end, and by horse and cart, in the saddle and on foot, went down into mine-shafts, lodged with workers' families, not shrinking from the suffocating darkness and dampness at the bottom of the pits, wanted with her own eyes to see and examine the valuable yields and the death-traps of the bowels of the earth: she was putting together her book entitled *Coal, Iron, Living People*...

Marija Aleksandrovna did not read the Soviet press, and she was unfamiliar with these particulars, all of these works and meritorious accomplishments. The last time she had seen Larisa was shortly after the events of October had pulled them apart and placed them on opposite sides: Marija emigrated, to the West, and Larisa went on a diplomatic mission to Afghanistan. In the one letter to her old friend from that trip, and the last one, actually, that she ever sent to her, Larisa wrote: "Great stars shoot across the sky, and some of them descend to the trees that are as black as night, and they are lost in the somnolent leaves like in combed-out hair. It is wildly!" Marija read the letter several times, then tore it up and scattered the tiny pieces across her table and the carpet. They lay there like confetti after New Year's Eve, and there they remained on that morning, not so far off, when she and her husband abandoned the apartment in Rostov in a hurry. Madness is the crest of a lethal wave by means of which an excess of heavenly beauty overflows onto the earth, she thought; she picked up a shred of the paper and placed it on her tongue and swallowed it. Now, half a decade later, in a one-room rented apartment in Novi Sad, adjusting her moist eyes to a lamp just lit, Marija Aleksandrovna saw Larisa standing in that forest, as beautiful as night, amazed at the drift of the stars, on the slippery edge of the firmament and looking down onto the unnamed stage of a country that some tiny nobody, thousands of *versts* away, in his unhappiness gifted with planetary sensibility, recognized at the bottom of his own soul.

3

"More deeply than any woman before her, Madame Marija Aleksandrovna dove into my soul, but she did not flinch," said Nenad Mitrov, lowering his voice conspiratorially. Madame Gomirc was turning over in her hands the book she had received as a gift a few moments before. She nodded her head and sighed as if she knew that nothing about this was going to change. And truly, neither the woman, nor the man, nor a child, as the available literature shows, no one was going to dare to take a step further into Mitrov's soul, and no one would even repeat the effort of that improvident Russian. It will not be done by the women whose rightful, descriptive names we find in published, and, even more so, unpublished poems and diaries: "neither she whom he hates, nor she whom he idolizes," nor the "sisterly fellow-sufferer," nor "the madame aux cheveux d'or," nor Mademoiselle R.M., before whom "he cast down the banner of his longing," nor Mademoiselle Kupčević, in whose memory he would remain, he suspected, "like a dark blemish," and not even a certain Elinor under whose code name he filled a year-long journal and an entire notebook of poetry. No one would descend deeper into Mitrov's soul than Marija Aleksandrovna, neither his friends, few and far between, from whom he did not conceal his pain, nor the aforementioned Mileta Jakšić, who, for Mitrov's sake, sometimes sacrificed his predilection for solitary walks, and did not balk at taking a promenade in the center of the city in the company of a gnome; and not Žarko Vasiljević, to whom he was closes of all, nor Žarko's wife Tonka, Nenad's protector; not young Leskovac who would, later, pass the last evening of his life with Mitrov, no one from the "famous trio…on the rickety raft of reality and life," not one of the "Four Argonauts, the eccentric pilots in search of the wondrous and golden hand of poetry." Not his mother, Madame Rozencvajg. Not his brother, Hugo. He would do it, at last, a full fifteen years after Marija Aleksandrovna, in 1941, for a person to whom grubbing around in the human soul was the métier, a ruthless tracker of ultimate purposes and final mysteries, for a functionary of the occupiers' police forces, a doctor iuris utriusque, who would with the end of his rubber truncheon hit that which no one before him had, the very bottom and end of Mitrov's life.

But there was still a lot of time until then. By Đurđevdan, the Feast of St. George, in 1932, Mitrov was still sitting in the Gomirc's salon, for the first time after a long absence, remembering Marija Aleksandrovna, on to whose cheek, cleaving to the glass door to the garden, descended in that unforgettable dawn the first drop of light; and he listened to the maudlin complaints of Madame Matić about the awful weather, about the rain that was spoiling her reveille again, and she watched Professor Gomirc who, in the meantime, over these several years when they had not been in contact, had gone being the great navigator of his salon to a retired officer of a brown-water flotilla, who himself now gets carried away by the conversation about rain and water levels, breathlessly casts off into this topic, sailing now on the Danube, now on the Sava, or the Drina, Morava, or Tisza, runs aground on stumps and branches deposited by the torrent, and by the skin of his teeth, with his remaining pilot's reflexes, fought his way across the waves that float harvests across the Danube banovina, carrying livestock and barns, honeycombing roads, pushing into cellars and undermining them, and entrance-ways, stairwells, spreading floating islands of garbage and excrement, infiltrating even the most solid shoes by Bata, and staining with mood the trouser legs of tailored English fabric. Madame Gomirc, as always, looked on the bright side of everything, shifted the conversation from ordinary to medicinal mud and brought up the thermal baths at Rusanda, to which she had recently taken her mother. The topic of spas, which, as might be expected, was picked up wholeheartedly by Mr. Matić, for whom balneology was a passion of long standing: he praised Lake Rusanda, blushing with an ambiguous smile as if praising the beauty of the woman who suffers from some delicate affliction, and immediately, with undiminished enthusiasm, tossed into the story the figure of the swineherd from Melenci, who, in the 1860s, bathing next to their hogs in the sty, first discovered the medicinal properties of mud. First of all one Ranisavljev, nicknamed "the lame," cured his tuberculosis of the bone, and then he took the crutches, without which he been unable to stand before then, and split them up for kindling, and then there was the priest from Melenci, Nika Bibić, who for just one summer used that swamp to cure people of eczema that no one had previously ever been able to treat in any spa. Madame Matić, very self-conscious on account of the episode involving the pig farmer, as well as the clerical eczema that most definitely offended the sensibility of this salon, tried to return the conversation to the framework of the permissible. She noted that with the rising cost of living, spa treatments were becoming a luxury even for the best paid government officials, especially since the supplements for price increases had been reduced, and in the uppermost categories even done away with, which, of course, applied to her husband who by night was a balneologist but by day was an official of the highest grade, and to Dr. Margan, one of the head figures in the banovina administration; and then the conversation turned to the unselfish concern of Madame Matić for the lower strata of officialdom who are poor specimens, more miserable than everyone; and one of them was sitting right there across from her, crumpled up in an armchair like a discarded artist's model. Dr. Margan, who recently reached the highest civil service category, from a somewhat lower position in the police, was grateful for the opportunity to pass along, in this agreeable company, his fresh realizations about the enviable functioning of the German administration and the unbelievable efficiency of the Association of German officials, which was successful in defending the interests of its million-strong membership. "Administration is the nervous system of every state," he said, entering medical territory with his argument. "And so, on the health of that system clearly depends the health and well-being of the whole community." The strong, impassioned voice of Dr. Margan, from which over the years had burst all the capillaries on his nose and cheeks, rose up like some healthy nerve plexus, and above those present it spread its protective afternoon shade. "Unfortunately, the educational level of our administrative officials, clerks, and jurists is alarming, and it threatens the future of our people!" Elated with the sound of its own voice, Margan's heavy body got to its feet. "The highly regarded Max von Gruber warned us: without contemporary science, sociology, population policies, racial hygiene, and eugenics, there is no modern state, and no future. To the students in my seminar I repeat frequently the golden words of the great Auguste Forel: "There is duty to oneself, there is duty to one's family and kin, duty to the state and humanity, but the greatest and most illustrious is duty to future humanity, to the future!" Concluding on a high vocal pitch, the speaker lowered his head before the grandeur of the what he had uttered, before himself; and then in the shabby present he saw nothing in front of him other than the squashed figure of the low-ranking Alfred Rozencvajg. "And the future," he added, "is worth any sacrifice."

"Aha!" With that, Madame Gomirc snapped out of her reverie, into which she'd been pulled by all of this rain, these floods, and talk of medicinal baths and government administration. "Monsieur Mitrov, read us something from your book. It's been a long while since a word of poetry was heard between these four walls." Dr. Margan and Nenad Mitrov then looked at the same moment at Madame Gomirc. She was paging through the book, tenderly and and distractedly, as if she were caressing a paper dove. Margan extended his arms resentfully, and Mitrov shook his head, and then his hands, as if fending off a phantom: these brisk movements stirred the air, the middle pages of the open book stood on end, the hard covers of the book flapped and hit Madame Gomirc's thighs two or three times, until finally the book peeled off, was projected out of her grasp, and trembling uncertainly with every one of its letters, rose up above the table with the refreshments, made several circles above the small company, touched, dolefully, the crystal chandelier and directed its bluish beak towards the partially opened door to the balcony. Where is it going? Is it to the place where Marija Aleksandrovna, had already absconded, taking along in her little handbag of snakeskin a long, morbid letter that, along with her passport, birth certificate, and several inconsequential papers, were supposed to confirm her ever-disputed, uncertain, and unreal identity? Was it the road to Moscow where, beneath the walls of the Kremlin, Larisa Reisner lay buried? Or even further, towards the magical homeland? Or, with the involvement of Dr. Margan, did it intend to relocate only as far as the office of Monsieur Čukić, Margan's former assistant, so that in the future, one June morning in 1941, dusty and stiff, it would fly its last few hundred meters and drop onto the desk of the aforementioned occupying official, József Kenyeki, whose window, always open to possible cases like this, gave onto the rustling treetops and the park by the Danube?

4.

"In critical periods, poetic figures should be read literally, and then history will reveal itself to you, spread out like in a game of solitaire," Dr. Margan said to Dragovan Čukić, reprising to him, over their morning coffee, the successful appearance he had made at the Gomirces' salon. Dr. Margan loved more than anything reading newspapers and books over other people's shoulders, and to him a metaphor spotted in that way made itself all the more alluring to him. "When a person named Alfred Rozencvajg confesses his eastern sin, you can justifiably take it to be an allusion to politics and draw the corresponding conclusion."

Young Čukić envied his former teacher for his connections to cultural circles and marveled at the perspicacity and charm with which he developed and varied the themes he picked up there. Therefore he was a grateful and patient listener, even when Margan lapsed into verbosity and strayed into a fog of digressions, which happened a lot. And so Čukić came to agree with Dr. Margan and followed him onto the path on which it would be shown how even the self-reproach of a lovesick gnome leads to an aggravation of the eastern question, the fateful question of the day. Namely, the emigree named Marija Aleksandrovna, a fabulous particle of dirt around which the aforementioned Rozencvajg sobbed out an entire book of fake pearls, in her day kept in contact with some important actors in the Bolshevik subversion and regime, namely with the famous "red journalist" Larisa Reisner who, after her death, still veiled by clouds of smoke, left behind not only lyrical descriptions of the mountains and valleys of Afghanistan, but also traces of a bizarre and by no means harmless engagement. Analysts of Soviet affairs have known for quite a while that the founding of the so-called Jewish Autonomous Oblast (JAO) in the southeastern part of Siberia was far from being a phenomenon of marginal significance. Quite the contrary! There are many reasons to believe that this administrative creation, this ill-starred JAO Birobidzhan, was nothing but a fig leaf behind which would mature the most dangerous thing yet produced by Bolshevism, referred to in some sources as "the seed of Zion." The Soviets cultivated this hybrid in a thoroughly remote nursery on the edge of the continent, with the intention of using it, at the decisive moment, if everything else was going downhill for them, to lull the democratic world to sleep, and then they would throw it into the face of their opponents, and tie the hands of Europe and America in order to semitize the race and culture of the West and finally — to usurp everything! That is the meaning of the so-called new world order with which Stalin threatens us. Therefore the career of Larisa Reisner, and her unexplained death, show that this woman must have been included in the previously mentioned project and had certain important assignments in it. But which ones? Here Dr. Margan reminded his assistant of the importance of a well-formulated question in the policing profession. And the question is: who gave Larisa Reisner her orders — that is, for whom did she work? Was it, for example for the Russians, who intended to frighten the world with the Jewish menace and then dominate it, or maybe for the Jews themselves who were calculating, on their side, that the world, blinded by the Bolshevik conflagration, would not be able to protect itself in time from the inundation of Jewish elements, the source of which seemed so distant, so unmenacing, lost in the realm of fiction. Or did she work for both sides? Two Souls, good sir! Little Rozencvajg knew this. "That woman had two souls and two masters. Unfortunately, this is the case with many women." There was not, however, an unambiguous answer to that question, and it is understandable that individual elements in Larisa Reisner's biography, like, for example, her long-ago diplomatic sojourn in Kabul and her numerous eastern contacts, should have remained the object of scrutiny in some European capitals, including Belgrade, even after her death. There are questions that still need to be answered: did Larisa Reisner, other than those necessitated by protocol, have close, confidential contacts with Emir Amanullah Khan and his powerful mother, Seradshul? How many times did she meet with members of the British embassy? What was the nature of her ties to the semi-official representative, Mr. Furmiye, and his wife? What was the subject of the negotiations with a certain Mirza Abdullah Muhammad, the publisher of a liberal newspaper in Egypt, and an educator of dubious provenance? What kind of support was she seeking from the Marxist-inclined Turkish envoy Abdulah Manbey, and what promises and how much financial assistance did she receive from that builder of Asian railroads and disreputable entrepreneur and millionaire Vanderlip, who started to cover the triumphant paths of Alexander the Great and the Great Moghuls with railroad lines and shoddy consumer goods, and who commandeered the Asian market from the English? No less problematic was this woman's later sojourn in Germany, in 1923, and her contacts with the world of high finance and, simultaneously, her encounters at the barricades with the rabble of Hamburg, Dresden, and Berlin! What was the subject of her conversation with the official and unofficial representatives of the Ullstein newspaper trust, the Junker airplane factory, and Krupps artillery industry? And, finally, what was it that she said on her death bed, in the delirium triggered by some unknown flash? A final admission or political pettifoggery? A confidential message or another poetic lie?

5.

Nenad Mitrov was brought in to the police station for the first time on June 26, 1941. The gendarme who was under orders to come get him was a big, strapping lad with red cheeks, whose behavior made it clear to passers-by that he did not consider the detention of such a piece of shit to be an honor at all, and Mitrov did not dare ask him the question that the gendarme would also not have been able to answer: why was he being hauled in? On the short route between his apartment and the building at the corner of Dunavska and Balatonska Streets, Mitrov came to the conclusion that this must be in connection with forced labor, and he, walking into the spacious office on the second floor, with excitement that erupted in him together with the sweat beneath his tight bowtie. He started explaining that he, in spite of physical impediments, really was not refusing to comply with the obligations all to which he was subject, but already four commissions had had a look at him, and each of them requested that he take off his clothes, all of his clothes, and they examined his deformities in detail, which, of course, was not pleasant, especially considering the comments of the members of the commission, more jocular than professional; and so he, you see, was asking the esteemed inspector to decide things once and for all, and if at all possible to waive further examinations by such commissions. The man at the desk leaned forward a little from the high backrest of his chair and said:

"Sir, I summoned you as a poet, and not as a recruit. Your physical condition does not number among my preoccupations."

The man behind the desk was, to be sure, neither Dr. Margan nor his erstwhile assistant Čukić, but an advisor to the occupying police, the consultant for the auditing of foreigners, Dr. József Kenyeki. One might get the impression that the police, both domestic and foreign, were interested more than anything else in poetry and poets — for Kenyeki went on:

"You are a poet, Mr. Rozencvajg, and you understand intimations better than crude, direct declarations. Do you see my meaning?"

The desk between the two of them, made of dark oak, did not permit Mitrov to understand completely. Every courtesy uttered from the other side of the table — any official who's been fired knows this well — can in a second reveal itself to be an accusation. The window at Kenyeki's back was open just enough for the gentle current of spring air to disperse a bit of the tobacco smoke, and the bustle of pedestrians outside imparted to this conversation a more or less realistic backdrop.

"Every lawyer is, in his heart of hearts, an unfulfilled poet. Doubtless you are familiar with the phenomenon," he continued. "While he gives you a lecture on the law, his imagination is strolling through the clouds, while he is trapping you in his transgressions, his soul skips through time, and while he is imposing a punishment on you, his heart is celebrating ancestral sin! And like every poet, he derives strength from his own feeling of guilt. "*Poena potest demi,*" as Ovid says, "*culpa perenis erit!*" It's the unconscious desire of every lawyer to see a world in chaos. The destructive ecstasy of a Petőfi is nothing compared to the anarchistic dreams of a man of the law. The right of the poet is to transfer death from his soul into language, and my humble duty is to conduct death from word into deed. Didn't you translate Petőfi?"

The sweat on his neck cooled, the fear at the base of his spine tingled and clutched his vertebrae, and Mitrov smiled bitterly at the effort that even a shudder needed to invest in worming its way through his defensive hump. He understood the language and the intentions of Dr. Kenyeki. He welcomed the ironic elegance, as well as the ominous insinuations with which he seasoned his style. Mitrov, besides, was less afraid of death than vulgarity, obscene insults. For a long time now he'd wanted only one thing: a death that would not humiliate him, that would be better than his life, stronger than his poetry.

"I, unfortunately, have not read your poems," said the specialist on foreigners, "for I do not yet know your language well enough, but people whose taste I trust consider you a master of rhyme and epithet, a poet of stormy emotions."

Mitrov shook his head, and a moist lock of hair whipped around on his forehead.

"Images and epithets, unusual rhymes and dazzling vocabulary! Those for me are the narcotics I used to intoxicate myself, to deafen and blind myself, with the help of which I sedate the pain of emptiness and the mortal terror of depression. If I could sing, I would have to pretend, to mask this blackest of misery that breaks my heart like a ghoulish spider. Without it, my songs would be just shrieks and howls, horror itself, chaos."

Yes, the police station is a place where one can only repeat the words already spoken in other places. Nenad Mitrov knew that everything that was happening had already taken place, that everything he was going to say he had already said once, but that there was nothing else: there exists only that which repeats, and the human being repeats itself in order to survive, to preserve its life.

"Terror and chaos?" asked Dr. Kenyeki reproachfully. Then he pushed back his glasses, which had slid down his nose, and concluded: "I see that your soul has depths, that it passionately seeks and loves all that is beautiful. Am I right, Mr. Rozencvajg?"

Mitrov now sees his entire life, more clearly than ever. As long as he had been aware of himself, he had dreamt of the meeting of two creatures whose souls would love each other, with no concern for corporeal impediments. A few women had perhaps tried to focus in on the refined and beautiful center of his being, but a woman's attentiveness would rapidly wear thin, her eyes start to wander, jumping from his words to his eyes, from his eyes to his movements, from his movements to his traitorous and hostile physiognomy! No, the soul summoned to love does not succeed in forgetting the bad; in fact, they work together. Only hatred can overlook the body, only it can pounce directly on the soul and connect with it in a fatal clinch.

"You are right," Mitrov admitted, extending his arm towards Dr. Kenyeki as if he were offering some material evidence, but at that moment a door opened in the side wall, concealed by cabinets and shelves, and in rushed a clerk with papers protruding from under his bicep. With an agitated gasp, he said: "Pardon me, doctor, but the colonel is pleased to request the dossier, and I had to…" He didn't manage to get out his whole thought because Kenyeki slammed his hand down on the table, with so much force, with so much rage, that they all burst instantaneously out of Mitrov's dream, and he collapsed like an empty sack into a mutual reality crushed by morning light and voices. The detained poet realized that he was standing, immobile, in front of a man with a blurry, puffy face and that since he had entered the room neither of them had uttered a single word.

6.

Nenad Mitrov killed himself in the night between July 6 and 7, 1941, most likely just before dawn, just a few hours before an interrogation, the fourth in as many days, which was scheduled for 8 a.m. On the previous day, a Sunday, he'd had lunch with relatives, and the afternoon, as Mladen Leskovac noted in his *Remembering Nenad Mitrov*, he spent in his apartment. "He didn't go out to see anyone and he didn't let anyone in to see him." In the course of the night, he wrote three letters: one to the police, the second to his relatives, and the third to Tonka Vasiljević. He read, or tried to read: on the table was found, propped open, a book of Kosztolányi's novellas; he picked through his books, sorted out manuscripts and arranged writing utensils, which he always kept in order anyway, and smoked. In a porcelain fruit bowl, which served as his ashtray, grew an entire branching reef of crushed cigarette butts, matches, and ashes that night, beneath a sea of smoke. It was probably around three in the morning when he changed into his pyjamas and pulled the big easy chair, which he had bought several months earlier when his mother passed away, into the bathroom. He put it in front of the small gas stove. Then he attached the rubber tube to the steel port on the pilot light, licked it, and inhaled. The air in his small apartment was so saturated with carbon monoxide that even the firemen, during the afternoon, didn't dare enter without gas masks.

Why did Nenad Mitrov kill himself?

Mladen Leskovac, recalling his final meeting with him, said: "Regarding the reasons for his visits to the Hungarian police station, he barely ever gave even two words of vague explanation; perhaps he was not able to say more; but from the outset it seemed like he had grasped everything immediately, and tragically so, and likewise he repeated that he was not going to be able to get out of this alive: a Hungarian policeman, a Hungarian *doctor iuris utriusquae* with a rubber baton, menaced him, and struck him, and Nenad was ashamed to admit that he had suffered humiliation and a beating. Therefore it looked like Mitrov still did not know, even before his fourth interrogation, why he was being summoned; the police were persistently obscuring their grounds and intentions. They were looking for something from Mitrov: they expected him to admit something. But what?

Leskovac, in putting down his memories after the war, hypothesized that the interrogation of his friend must have been connected to the fact that Pavelić's police, and in tandem with them, Horthy's police, were searching for Mitrov's nephew, a chemistry student and poet in Zagreb named Viktor Rozencvajg whom they soon apprehended and shot. It appears that Mitrov knew nothing about his relative's illegal activities, but that the police definitely didn't believe that he didn't know, and so it was all a fatal "tangle of misunderstandings."

Bogdan Čiplić, too, in his *Memoir of Nenad Mitrov*, published a decade after Leskovac's, saw the main reason for the suicide in the treatment of Mitrov by the occupying police. His point is that the Department for the Control of Foreigners, or so-called "Counter-Espionage Office," demanded from Mitrov a list of Novi Sad intellectuals, of people of an anti-regime disposition, and this demand was accompanied by the usual extreme threats, calculating that Mitrov as a vulnerable, unhappy man would not have the strength to stand firm. Mitrov, according to Čiplić's testimony, made the decision to kill himself after the very first interrogation, but he hesitated regarding the means. When he failed to obtain the "potent drug" he had requested from his friend, Dr. Poštić, he opted for gas.

Mitrov's letter to the police, written just prior to his death, has not been preserved. It disappeared, along with the entire police archive from the period of the war: or it was destroyed by the Horthy authorities lighting out after the Germans, or by the German authorities fleeing the liberation forces, or by the secret police, the OZNA, as it erased unwanted tracks. Also not preserved, or at least inaccessible to the public, were Nenad's two remaining letters from his final night, which Čiplić mentions as "voluminous, peaceful, valedictory," nor any other sources that would buttress or challenge the stated assumptions. At the trial of Dr. József Kenyeki, in October, 1945, this case was not highlighted. Dr. Kenyeki was sentenced to death and hanged, so he was also unable to comment later on what it was that the police were seeking from Alfred Rozencvajg.

The postwar poet and functionary S.R. was of the opinion that Nenad Mitrov would have killed himself even without the help of the occupying police; his many poetic laments point to that. In S.R.'s assessment, too much has been made of the episode with the police. This was done in order to ascribe to Mitrov merits that he didn't have, and thus his defeatism had been admitted through the back door into contemporary literature.

Another poet, a female poet actually, whom Mitrov mentions in his verse as a "sisterly fellow-sufferer," was convinced that his suicide proceeded more from his clash with himself than with the police. Nenad did not grasp what was happening to him, what they wanted from him, but he, as always, suspected that he was guilty. He ran through his memories, looking for names, physiognomies, words for which he was responsible, which could have been the cause of this disorder; he tried to recall whether in despair he had ever made a pronouncement against anything or anyone other than against himself. Or had he found himself in trouble because of words he suppressed, because of his conspiratorial desire for beautiful women and beautiful souls, because of the grievous offense of self-delusion or false hope? Before his eyes passed the women with whom he had been smitten in the course of his barren life, to whom he had dedicated his verses and his sighs, women he was close to and women he did not know, female acquaintances and passers-by, initials-women, cryptonym-women, cipher-women, women as metaphors, women as allusions, and women as illusions, and above all Marija Aleksandrovna, that Russian *femme fatale*, who was the first to ignite in him the ungodly belief that a union of souls was possible inhabiting incommensurate bodies, that love at a distance is feasible, love unconsummated, unprecedented, unexperienced.

The concierge who took, a few decades-and-change ago, Mitrov's letter to Mme Marija Aleksandrovna, and then on several occasions during the occupation informed on Rozencvajg to the authorities, and on some other tenants and visitors of the building at #9 on the Danube embankment, also had some observations on the occasion of the suicide that he considered worthy of the attention of appropriate persons. No, what Rozencvajg's friends asserted was not completely accurate — that he spent the night in question alone in his apartment. On the contrary. An arrival was noted: a figure who surely must have had a connection to his decision to end his life, and perhaps this person even helped him do it. The custodian heard steps in the stairwell, but by the time he got to the door of his apartment, the individual had already moved on, and even if he or she hadn't, in the complete darkness it would have been difficult to make out anything; in the entrance-way there was not a single lightbulb; they had all been — yet again! — stolen. However, the custodian had been utterly certain that it hadn't been anyone he was familiar with in the least: no one from among Rozencvajg's Novi Sad relatives and acquaintances, who visited him occasionally after the death of old Mrs. Rozencvajg; neither Monsieur nor Madame Gomirc who were once pleased to host him; none of the writers, and especially not any of the esteemed officials whom he met there, least of all Messieurs Margan and Matić; no one, even, from the police station where, to be sure, Rozencvajg had of late been checking in, nor

Monsieur Paroši nor Dr. Kenyeki, nor any other civil servants, councilors, or gendarmes. It could not have been Rozencvajg's cousin from Zagreb, who was known to the authorities, whom he might have expected, nor other relatives from there whom he no doubt no longer expected to see; it wasn't a prostitute — truth be told, he never brought any of those to his place — but also none of the many ladies for whom he composed his verses. The kind of steps he heard were not the kind that brought anything good. He, an experienced caretaker who "had a degree in wastrels," who knew how a petty thief breathes, and a dangerous hustler, too — he could not with certainty assess what kind of visitor Rozencvajg had had. He had hidden, but he'd also taken pains to announce his arrival; he was burning with fever, but he spread his icy breath. That's what this person was like; such a woman — for it was a woman! — came to the pathetic Rozencvajg to whisper her dark secret to him and — shove the gas pipe down his throat.

The concierge's wife, with whom her husband shared his surmises, as he did with the competent authorities, at first cursed his drunken imagination, but then she agreed with him nonetheless: yes, it was a woman. A lady! She reflected for a moment and added: "If I'm not mistaken, she was speaking Russian. A Russian woman! The concierge admitted that no one speaking Russian had stuck out to him, but that he had heard Rozencvajg crying. But perhaps it really had been a Russian. The other residents were uncertain about whether they had heard a woman's voice, but they remembered with confidence that someone in Rozencvajg's apartment was walking back and forth, up and down, like a wild beast in a cage. These footsteps really were somehow animal, female, circumspect but angry, and not bumbling and wooden, like Rozencvajg's. Then the purposeful strides ceased, but right away someone started typing. At first it wasn't clear who was typing what. In the muffled night the steely strokes stabbed the walls like spikes going into pine. What method was this!? The *hauzmajstor*'s wife struck the ceiling with a broom handle, and other tenants then followed her example, too: the typewriter enraged them more than the loudest of the nocturnal showdowns between the custodian and his wife, with all of their shouts and oaths, and in the bat of an eye Rozencvajg's apartment was beset on all sides by impatient hammering: with house-shoes, rolling pins, bare fists. Finally the typing stopped as well, but that didn't mean there was peace and quiet: when the typewriter fell silent, Rozencvajg himself began talking. Rozencvajg! The man who lowered his eyes when he met you at the newsstand around the corner, abruptly, in the middle of the night, he's giving a speech to the whole street? It was a hot July night, the windows were wide open, and it was easy to hear his declamation. At the start it was kind of a mumble, but the soon the orator broke free, hit full stride, and began tossing out horrifying words, blasphemous ones, as if the devil himself had typed them out for him. But he himself was the satan. The satanic niece who pounded poison into his soul and vented the gas into his throat. If the wretch had wanted to resist this demon, he wasn't able to; he only screamed into the night. He was a tremendous whiner, but his lungs were little, and his voice popped out as a squeal, as when a fledgling has fallen out of its nest. "Good God," howled the *hauzmajstor*'s wife. "My God, oh God!" The custodian and the neighbors roared that he had to be stopped, but it was too late. Everything went the way it shouldn't have. In front of the building a *fiaker* halted, and out of it, like out of a top-hat, leapt a motley crowd, and, while the coachman was adjusting the horses' bits, the people, kicking around flashes of gleaming, polished shoes, white bibs, and silk skirts, assembled rapidly beneath Mitrov's window and started shouting something up to him. A woman in a long evening gown pulled a muslin flower from the bouquet at her low neckline, and she gave the orator a wave with it. The *hauzmajstor* who, wrapping a short robe over his pyjamas, ran into the street to see what was going on; he caught sight of Rozencvajg standing in the window, stretching out his arms and flapping them as if he were going to fly off. The concierge feared that Rozencvajg would actually do something like that, and such a thing could, regardless of what else happened, bring additional unpleasantries. "All ye who are decrepit and twisted or bent of build," shouted the hunchback, "whose limbs are stunted, maimed, out of joint…" The custodian made up his mind to go back into the building and by whatever means possible get to Rozencvajg and stop this circus, but at that moment almost directly in front of the entrance stopped a second car, this time some kind of delivery team loaded with people and luggage. "Keep moving! Nothing to see here!" yelled the *hauzmajstor*, but the coachman, without looking at him, leapt from his seat and started untying the rope with which the cargo was secured. As he untied each knot, some of the big items would immediately begin to squirm. They extricated themselves from the freight and dismounted onto the asphalt, where they all commenced looking for their bags, their children, their old people. "All ye whose bodies are disfigured with ineffaceable defects, whose hearts bleed from untreatable wound…." Now the custodian was catching every word of this, and the others could make it out also, for people had started to gather from the surrounding buildings and streets, as well as some he didn't recognize at all. "All ye anonymous poor, pitiable and fragile, you grotesque and repellent pariahs, you steal about and waddle around and kneel down like demoralized bastards, ready to accept the death-dealing knife without resistance." Meanwhile three more teams and one additional automobile had pulled up. Most of the people, however, had come on foot. Many of them loaded down with backpacks, bindles, and bundles like day-trippers, or with their humps resembling luggage in the darkness. They mostly knew each other, and they shook hands or at least nodded to one another in passing and walked silently on, looking for a spot for their families or stuff. The concierge, truth be told, felt aggrieved that nobody had informed him of this gathering. He stood at the front door of his building, wrapped in a robe with a Turkish sash, in outsized slippers, unprepared and wondering whether this was some sort of uprising. Or only some sort of police check? If it's the former, then what was he to do? What was his custodial and patriotic task? Some of the people assembled also must have thought it was a rebellion, because they impatiently turned their faces to Rozencvajg's window, but he was no longer there; the window was closed and the light behind it extinguished. The crowd was buzzing. Some of them turned to each other and said: "Where to?" Others waved dismissively and turned out their hands to indicate that they didn't know, and yet others pointed up at Rozencvajg's place, and then at other windows, while a final group looked worriedly at the river, at some place down by the river, towards the bend below the public beach on the other side known as *Oficirski štrand*, from where the opaque, oozing morning was already dropping. Down below, by the water, or upon the water itself, someone was shouting: "There is no god for the poor man! We won't let them trample all the freaks! Every gnome shall have his home!" From here, on the embankment, voices shot back: "Where to? Where to?" and "Let's go!"

The *hauzmajstor* did not stir from his gate until the end; he was watching to make sure nobody unknown got from the street into the building, or vice-versa. However, the next day, when the firemen broke into Rozencvajg's apartment, they found only his body. The concierge nonetheless remained convinced that Rozencvajg had not committed suicide on his own.

"You are quite certain that it was a woman?" Dr. Kenyeki asked, when they finally brought him the custodian, who this time was stubbornly demanding to see His Excellency, the boss of the Department for the Control of Foreigners himself. Kenyeki's yellowish, short-sighted eyes danced beneath the thick lenses of his glasses, like two egg yolks at the bottom of an enamel bowl. "You know, without a doubt, that a bottle of the worst *rakija* can, if you embrace it wholeheartedly, turn into a true beauty in no time."

"I guarantee it, your grace," the *hauzmajstor* said, as if he were defending his favorite bottle. "It was a woman. She gave him the order, turned on the gas, and dissipated. Like all women do."

7.

In wars of national liberation, along with people the imagination of building superintendents also gets emancipated, and that of other guards and caretakers, and this concierge's tale might belong to the type of uncertain testimonies that, through the virtue of questionable written protocols, transform a hangover into history. But this history leaves in its wake indisputable tracks and marks, even if its sources are dubious. This would be the case whether or not the building at no. 9 on the Danube embankment had not had a custodian. One of those traces was to be found in the manuscript section at the famous cultural foundation, the *Matica srpska*, where Nenad Mitrov's papers are kept. The manuscripts were, after Mitrov's death, and with the authorization of his relatives and friends, collected and prepared for publication by Mladen Leskovac. He pedantically transcribed the poems, arranging them — by sticking with Mitrov's outline but also his own assessments — into five volumes, each of which he provided with indispensable comments. These notes, like the poems, he typed out, with the exception of one that, in contrast to the others, was unrelated to the editorial concept but instead reflected the editor's own feelings, and which, in green ink on a little piece of paper, he wrote out in cramped but legible handwritten letters and inserted into the collection bearing the title *Cheerless Ecstasies*: "I do not love this poetry. I do not; and if I had not personally known Nenad Mitrov, and loved him, I would not be writing about him, or I would write negative things. Nonetheless…" It was signed: "M.L." This note revealed a touching attempt to mitigate the conflict between artistic and humane arguments; maybe it was going to be one of the keys in the hands of Leskovac's future biographers, but at this moment the note's task was merely to present the reader with Leskovac's respectful fair copy to which, on the pages immediately following, was juxtaposed an entirely different one, sloppy or jittery, and in addition unidentified, which in some inexplicable way was located between the same covers…What was this about? Although Mitrov's friends, gathered at his bier, vowed that they would, as soon as the war ended, publish his poetry from his private papers, there is every likelihood that no one touched these sheaves of course office paper after Leskovac — and thus the paper remained preserved, its edges crisp — except for one hand that never introduced itself. It only lingered in one spot. It sought out the poem "To All the Cripples of the World," and with a lead pencil it crossed out the word "Cripples," scribbling above it, nervously, in haste or fear: "Birobidzhanians." In addition, here and there in the margins, the hand marked a number of verses. Here are those places:

> *all of you anonymous poor, pitiable, and fragile*
> *grotesque, repellent pariahs,*
>
> ---
>
> *one to another why not offer our hands in friendship*
> *and why do we not band together*
> *forming throngs, combine in a phalanx tight and tough*
>
> ---
>
> *why would they not establish*
> *on the far side of their lookouts*

a community for us, new Jerusalem,
a city of victims and villains

O, why not combine and forge
our innumerable crucifixions…

The reader who comes across these pages will definitely wonder who, when, and why changed the title of the poem and marked up a number of the verses. We know that it was not Leskovac, and it's quite unlikely that would have done this any of Mitrov's friends or surviving relatives. Certainly it was not done by his enemies. Dr. Kenyeki after July 7, 1941 lost interest in Alfred Rozencvajg; Dr. Margan, on various assignments, spent more time in Budapest and Berlin than in Novi Sad, and the postwar poet and functionary, when his time came, could have resorted to some obvious means for compromising the already perished Mitrov — if the need had presented itself. So, who did it then? Some deranged returnee from the Don or Siberia? An ambitious OZNA collaborator? A KGB informant? A literary historian, a biographer of Mitrov who was not meant to be? Someone associated with *The Jewish Almanac* or *A New History of the Jewish People*? The author of *The Lexicon of Global Utopias and Conspiracies*? Who knew what the consultant for the auditing of foreigners only sensed? Who could have known that the Birobidzhan bogeyman was afoot in Europe? That the Birobidzhan storm was raging beneath Belgrade? Who hid the key to the Birobidzhan code? Who was setting up an escape to Birobidzhan, and who designated "B-Day"? What all did this "Lady from Birobidzhan" know? Did Birobidzhan exist, or was it a dream? And, finally, perhaps the reader will also ask, what did the signatory of these lines plan to do when he accidentally found this malicious and cynical correction to Mitrov's title, other than to reach for an eraser and remove the stain from his poem and the shadow from the poet's name, and thus extricate himself from the conspiracy in which, reaching out for an eraser, the signer himself had straightaway gotten entangled.

CHAPTER THREE
THE LOST TRIBES

1

In the spring of 1939, Leopold Roth, dismayed by the weak prospects of world Jewish socialism, and with other bad presentiments, said to his youngest son Oskar:

"Every people has its mystery. The mystery of the Jewish people is the whereabouts of its ten lost tribes. Where are the tribes of our forefathers, the sons of Jacob? Every Jew is obliged to devote at least a bit of his or her life to the search for them."

His son was stunned by his father's testament, but he didn't have the heart to ignore him entirely. In a short amount of time he had, a little from books and a little from the stories of a passionate collector of Jewish curiosities, a retired apothecary from Antwerp, come to learn the following: the famous traveler Eldad ha-Dani had, as early as the 9th century, brought from North Africa the news that tribes, or at least four of the ten missing ones, Naftali, Gad, Asher, and Dan — from which he himself descended — were holed up somewhere in the Abyssinian highlands. David Reubeni, somewhat later, claimed to be himself the brother of one of the leaders of the Israelite tribes that dwelt in the southwestern regions of the Arabian peninsula, while Antonio de Montesinos discovered misplaced tribes in South America. Rabbi Benjamin of Tudela, who in the second half of the 12th century from his seven-year odyssey through Europe, the Mediterranean, and the Near, Middle, and Far East, brought home to Spain a hefty book of notes, and reported in it that he had followed the trail of the aforementioned tribes even to Central and East Asia. Another advisor to the sober Maimonides wrote of his encounter with that portion of the lost tribes that, as it says in the Midrash, ended up on the far side of the River Sambatyon, while the Portuguese, lured to the East by tales of the lands of gold, silver, and copper, in the fourth, leaden one, came across a solitary, decrepit tribe which, hiding from its neighbors, walked around and around in a circle, never finding its way out of dense forests and swamps. The glorious Christopher Columbus, in the apothecary's firm conviction a converted Jew, did not set out for India on account of spices, but to find the lost tribes, and in somewhat more contemporary times travelers have found evidence of them in Japan, on ten different islands, from Hokkaido in the northeast to Yaku in the extreme southeast. And also many Jewish merchants who over the centuries, on foot, horseback, camels, and ships traversed land and sea, all of these tireless, painstaking workers who transported silk, spices, and jewels between China and France, four centuries before Marco Polo reached Peking — they were searching above all for that people that, winding up in Assyrian slavery, disappeared from the face of the earth: did this people crumble and mix with the sand, or had it somehow avoid danger and somewhere, lying low at the ends of the earth, await the hour of a re-unification with the house of Israel?

"But where are these tribes of ancestors?" groaned Leopold three months later, when he was on his deathbed, surrounded by family. It was a muggy summer day; the air was full of electricity and the woodwork crackled ominously like before a natural disaster. "I beg of you to dedicate at least a little of your time to them."

Nearly the whole family unit found its way to the gathering in the sick man's bedroom. Leopold had announced that he had something important to convey to his nearest and dearest, and they were hoping that behind this notification might await some cash or papers.

"Where is the tribe of Ruben?" With difficulty he straightened out his crumpled thumb and aimed it at the ceiling. "Where is Simon's tribe?" And he pointed his index finger at the wall in front of him. "Where are Dan, Naftali, Gad?"...With every name one of his shaky fingers shot into the air to search: "Where? Where?" He hardly looked at his two oldest sons, although he had inquired every day about them for weeks. It was as if he didn't recognize his wife anymore, although until then he had nagged her at every turn; from his sister-in-law Dina, at whom he was known to leer uncontrollably, he turned his head in fear; he now looked at her fiancé Jonathan, whose bulky body he used to envy and jostle with regularly, as if through a fog. He had no thought for the two or three more distant relatives; he focused his gaze on his youngest son and waited for his answer. Oskar glanced around the room. In the eyes of the relatives, he read apathy and impatience, so he opened the door to the hallway, stuck his head out into the twilight of the stairwell, and in a cheerfully admonishing voice began calling out:

"Well then, where is that robust Ruben? Where is intrepid Simeon? Ungovernable Dan? And Greedy Naftali and Gaudy Gad? Asher the Gambler? Issachar the Daydreamer? Where are Zany Zebulun, Fabulous Benjamin, and Joseph, the most beautiful of them all? Where are you, old fellows?? Here is a good man, and a Jew too, who wants to bequeath to you all his possession, and his soul."

Steps could be heard on the stairs. "Hurry up, for God's sake," shouted Oscar. Dr. Jacobs, however, like so many times in his career, arrived too late.

2

Until the death of his father, Oskar Roth had stood firm against his father's fuzzy ideas and been, in contrast, preoccupied with the concrete, visible part of the world, particularly with means for improving its visibility, optical lenses, and devices. He'd been in the grip of that passion since boyhood: at age twelve he constructed a stroboscope with the figure of a miniature man who was walking, and at sixteen he paid with his own savings for a trip to Mt. Wilson to see the dome of the colossal observatory open up beneath the banks of stars, and the telescope's barrel, crammed full of lenses, took manly aim at its heavenly target. With this same level of excitement he put his eye two or three times to the eyepiece of the lab microscope into which his young aunt, his mother's sister Dina, peered for whole days at a time, counting, on dried smudges, red and white blood cells and the little monsters that gobbled them up. Oscar, for his part, was not as excited by heavenly bodies or earthly cells as by the realization that the world was not as it showed itself to the naked eye. That's why he, without a great deal of hesitation, dispensed with concern about school subjects such as physics and biology, and that's also why he, from the evening, when lights went on in the surrounding buildings, would pick up the old pair of binoculars that, as part of his preparations for an unrealized Asian excursion, his father Leopold had acquired. He would aim it into the neighboring windows and, hidden behind the curtains, by himself and unhindered, expose the truth beneath the illusion. Most of all, he watched women: they lived within reach of the windows, close to the street, in the first habitations, and the men lived deep in the rooms; the women moved about, came into view, displayed themselves, but the men, incognito, waited for them in a corner; the women had body and the men had only desire, which made them invisible. He watched them pass through the illuminated square of windows, stop, look back, pick up something, put something down, move objects and children, touch, return and avoid touches, stop, and again yield to motion. They all, evening after evening, lived their individual window moments and, simultaneously, their mutual pan-womanly life; he, with the binoculars at his eyes, was the one who connected them, who, by observing them, enabled them to live more, longer, and more intensely than their individual destinies would have allowed, and then, when the lights went out and the windows darkened, to belong not only to their husbands but also to him, and to melt in the light of table lamps and overhead fixtures into one big, hot, ecstatic, inimitable Aunt Dina.

In those days Oscar concerned himself also with a plan to construct a device that would optically undress his very desirable aunt, something similar to an x-ray machine, and he filled his school notebooks with relevant blueprints. His aunt was the first to realize the true nature of her nephew's research and, when they decided that his continued education would not be useful, she took him to an acquaintance who ran a little photography shop. Her acquaintance, actually a relative of the aunt's fiancé Jonathan, inspected his future assistant, pressed a bucket with water and sponge into his hands, and explained: "The clearest world view, my boy, is the view through a shop window. Therefore, it has to be cleaned regularly. So — get to work!"

At the moment his father passed along concern for the lost tribes with his last will and testament, Oscar had burst into his twenties; with Jonathan he now shared a properly outfitted store, which the two of them had purchased from relatives. His father's testament had not substantially disturbed Oscar's life, but it did seem like invisible tribes were shading his photographic eyes and little by little diverting him from his set life trajectory. No, he did not yield to vain imaginings, as happened to his disappointed father; it was simply that he allowed himself, in moments of respite, when he would, after seeing off a customer, find himself alone in the store, with his eyes shut, in his thoughts return to the lost tribes and follow their elusive, errant trail. True enough, he was happy that after America's entry into the war, he was not among the thousands of Marines who set out for the east to stop the massive Japanese advance on the Solomons or some other such islands, thereby avoiding the risky situation of having to continue there, on the spot, the search for the abode of stray ancestors and that, instead, he remained behind the glass counter, selling cameras and rolls of film to boys who wanted, on the eve of their departure, to stand in front of the lens and immortalize their uniforms and, even more, to record with their own hand their mothers, fiancées, wives, and children on the veranda in front of the family home, and then at the docks, from on board the steel leviathans that would, to the accompaniment of shouts, sobs, singing, and calls from the undulating mass of relatives, detach themselves from shore and drop over the horizon.

Oscar's passion for Dina also assumed a new character, in those years after Leopold's death. With the saddening certainty that he would never possess his aunt's body, or indeed ever be accepted in her bed the way he had been until he was six, he shifted his aunt, not without internal upheaval, into the realm of higher spiritual rather than corporeal facts, right to the very gates of the invisible. But here, in this new blank space, she was eventually going to meet up with Leopold's, and now Oscar's, lost tribes. For the twisted lust for his mother's sister was a spike of ice that, once driven into the boy's soul, made it unperishably immature, a refuge of all the empty, dodgy, and unrealizable plans and projects. The changes in Dina's looks and behavior also favored the conditional dematerialization of Oscar's passion. Time itself, along with the war, with worry about their relatives in Europe and about Jonathan on the home front, melted the effervescent excess weight that had adorned her twenties and thirties, and from out of that deflated foam surfaced a new Dina, drier, paler, intermittently transparent. In this condition she was ready for the role of Great Leader who would her conduct her nephew to the sought-after tribes, rescue them from eternal oblivion, and return them to history.

Dina did not know the nature of the mission entrusted to her, or where she might have already set forth on the byways of Oscar's mind. She believed to the contrary that, as earlier, by a combination of public transportation, which included two subway lines, several bus stops, and a bit of walking, she was going to the shop in order to consult with Oscar about some purchases, since Jonathan, throwing himself wholeheartedly into his jazz and his horn, was completely neglecting his duties and rights as a partner, and scarcely turned up once a week, if that, between rehearsals of his quartet or between beers. He barreled into the shop, signed the weekly accounts and filled his wallet; she kept thinking this also — gullible Dina! — afterwards, when the work was done and the mutual cursing at Jonathan the goldbricker, she sat, reclining on the chair behind the counter, flipping through the catalog from some manufacturer of camera equipment and supplies, her eyes and nerves that had been irritated by the day-long gawking into the microscopic daub of human blood and excretions resting up in foggy forests and sunny glades, near silver glaciers and golden watercourses, but, in reality, she was already on the road, from page to page, from picture to picture, pushing towards Oscar's goal.

"You can't imagine how Jonathan hates nature," she would sigh. "He just chokes on clean air. Oxygen makes him break out in a fever!" And, of course she would, looking at her watch, get to her feet and go home, if abruptly, already there, deep in some Asian wilderness — for the flight through someone else's imagination is always swifter than the cautious probing of one's own — a Bengal tiger hadn't leapt out of the lens of the latest Pentax camera and cut off her escape route. "Nasty advertisements!" she would say, turning the page; but it was too late: the tiger in a fraction of a second would fly through the fiery hoop of the lens, similar to a circus hoop through which with feigned obedience jumped wild beasts, instinctive haters of fire, would scorch Dina with its hypnotic gaze and command: "Buy this camera, move through its red-hot lens, enter the shadows and darkness of your starting point. Before you lies a boundless realm of adventure!"

"This cat looks like your wife," Dina said then, masking her discomposure. She shut the catalog, and then her eyes, and with a few practiced movements massaged her temples, arose, picked up her purse and a package of groceries, opened the door, and waved goodbye to her nephew. But then Oscar also looked at the clock, turned out the lights behind him, and eagerly lost in heedlessness, after yet another flat, colorless day, charged through the lens after her.

3.

But what, truly, is on the other side of the ring of fire? Wasn't there just another ring, one more fiery illusion, and so on, endlessly? But the goal slips away and little by little the circles tighten around the enthralled traveler.

One morning in May, 1953, Oscar got a phone call from the Antwerp apothecary who sometimes got inexpensive chemicals for the shop. He said: "My boy, you should know…" After the death of his friend Leopold Rot, he considered it his duty to supply Oscar not only with lousy developer and photographic fixer, but also accompanying information. "You should know that a Russian..." The apothecary abruptly lowered his voice, and a piece of zwieback with butter and pineapple jam had just crunched between Oscar's teeth, and the name of the Russian together with the snack crumbled, but subsequently Oscar still understood that this man had succeeded in capturing on a photographic plate, without the mediation of a camera, a light, invisible to the naked eye, that was emitted by living beings. The leaf of a beech tree photographed with this procedure came out bordered with an aura that remained unaltered for some time even after part of the leaf broke off and combusted. This, to be sure, also applied to the human body. The Soviets are said to possess a photograph on which can be seen the illuminated outline of a man's hand with five fingers, although, at the time the picture was taken, it had only four fingers, since the owner of the hands, a young butcher's assistant, had through inattentiveness or some other reason lopped off the fifth at some earlier date.

Oscar forgot to finish his breakfast, but at first he didn't want to admit even to himself how much this news excited him. That evening, however, he told his wife Cynthia what he had heard. "I think this would please my late father," he noted cautiously. I bet that his aura is still bright in his bed. It's just that we don't want to see it." Cynthia dismissed this. "There are also other bright things on this earth besides your late father, but your brain does not pick them up," she commented. Oscar made no attempt to convince her otherwise. His interior eyes, besides, were not on the deceased Leopold at that moment, but rather on the lost tribes that his father had entrusted to him, on their far-off, flickering trail. Over the following days he made inquiries among a handful of his steady customers, passionate amateur photographers, about this phenomenon, but no one had heard of anything similar.

"Kirlian. His name is Kirlian," said the pharmacist from Antwerp.

When Oscar invited him to the bar where Jonathan played, and where with your beer you could get, on the cheap, a heaping portion of goose sausage.

"Kir-li-kir-li-kir-liaaaan!" clucked Jonathan. To Oscar's great disappointment, a quintet was performing in this club that evening, and Jonathan remained sitting at the table, next to his wife, and with each fresh swallow of beer, he leaned, like a tower of empties, towards her more and more.

"Kirlian was an electrical engineer in a mental hospital in Krasnodar," the pharmacist continued. He had an appreciation for goose meat, even if it was in the form of sausage, just as he appreciated the other delicacies that he had not been able to afford for ages, and he hastened to oblige his host with some high-quality conversation. "In Krasnodar," he repeated, and looked significantly at his wife's host, Cynthia, that is, once a long time ago before he embarked on the obscure path to becoming an apothecary in Antwerp, he had scraped out a living in Donetsk serving up swill that was barely drinkable, but which with sufficient resourcefulness one could sell. Since then, he saw an accomplice in everybody who had even a great-grandmother born in Russia. "On one occasion, it so happened that Kirlian…" Here the pharmacist had to break off, because Jonathan decided to start telling the story of how, precisely seven years before, in honor of the Allied victory over the Axis, he had formally asked for Dina's hand after a long engagement. They got married immediately, and they spent their wedding night in the car with friends and then by a campfire in a stand of pine trees that, it turned out, was a park on the grounds of a lunatic asylum. Blowing into the trumpet that, of course, he had brought along — or was it a saxophone? — Jonathan stoked the fire, until out of it started to sprout lilies, irises, narcissus, and other flowers whose names he did not know, and he plucked them and tossed them into the arms of his somnolent bride, who squealed each time and then blew on her singed fingers, until the watchmen…

"Jonathan, please!" Dina said. At that he opened a new can of beer and clucked again: "Kirlian-kirlian-kirlian!" His former guitarist Frank Shade once said: "For the first six cans of beer, Jonathan turns everything he touches into beer foam. But with the seventh, he transforms it into music. And with the eighth — into light!" Something of that light then fell onto the apothecary and the subject of his story, and everybody at the table could see Kirlian in the operating room for electro-shock therapy, standing in for the absent orderly, observing a panicked patient on whose temples, in the place of contact with electrodes, there quivered little bluish-red flames, the man tied to the bed struggled, screamed that he didn't want to die, called out for his mother, dropped the name of some judge, but the doctor didn't interrupt the treatment. Kirlian believed that the apparatus was malfunctioning; he inspected it carefully but couldn't find the problem. The next day the shimmer appeared over the top of the head of a woman who, in contrast to the previous person, surrendered herself with passion to the doctor and asked to die. Kirlian wants to photograph that light, but they cut off his access to the patients. Then he at home, in his kitchen, constructed a simple apparatus on the same principle and, along with his wife, Valentina, launched into experiments. The procedure he tried out first of all on himself. Valentina fastened the electrodes of a high-frequency oscillator and a photographic plate to her husband's left hand and then turned on the power. The hand lit up, Semyon Davidovich cried out — with restraint, though, so the neighbors wouldn't be able to hear it through the thin wall — along his fingers red stamps emerged, broke out, but on the photographic plate, once it was developed, a profusely glittering corona showed up. The Kirlians improved their device and on the following nights took a huge number of photographs of their four arms and legs, and then the limbs of their relatives and friends, and eventually all sorts of vagabonds, drunks, and epileptics whom they, despite fear of the neighbors and the authorities, brought to their apartment. They concluded upon comparing the photos that healthy, cheerful people emit a stronger, bluish light, while sick, unfortunate, and narcoticized people smolder, flatly, with a reddish light.

"You are all going to burn to a crisp in hell," exclaimed Cynthia, who had recently become contaminated with politics. Jonathan, however, was interested only in the musical side of things. "Of course," he said, "a luminous hand is worth more than two real-body ones. That one-armed Wittgenstein guy performed Ravel's 'Concerto for Left

Hand' as if it were meant for four hands. And that little artilleryman at Stalingrad who lost his thumb, he played, after the war, a piano concerto by Tchaikovsky so well that not even the conductor noticed anything. Only the first violinist saw a little flame, a shining hammer zipping back and forth and striking the black and white keys. The Kirlians have discovered the secret of the phantom limb!" And then, as if for proof, Jonathan lifted his unusually thin, delicate hand, which hung like an antenna from his massive body, for eavesdropping on the music of the spheres. "Our luminous duplicates outlive us the way love outlives the power of the body. They can hurt, they can shine, they call for that which no longer exists. The universe is deafened by the sounds of instrument long ago scrapped!" And Jonathan raised his other hand, trying to envelop the gigantic bubble of beer emanating from his tenth and final can, after which he would sprawl out in an upholstered chair and plunge into heavy, soundless sleep. He embraced the entire universe, visible and invisible, and Oscar noted bitterly that Jonathan's hot, sweaty aura would rest on Helena even after his death, while a wedge would remain between him and his stunted, bony, Cynthia even in death, and each of them would take with them into that other world their patch of light — if they had any at all. Cynthia, sensing that someone was touching her in their thoughts, swallowed with difficulty the morsel she had been the whole time been shifting around in her mouth. "Tawdry illusionism, that's what this is!" she said. "This Kirlian of yours is a Bolshevik Dr. Frankenstein. Kirlian the murder — his name says as much. That's why the Russians are keeping his invention a secret. And besides," she added, "every Jew who works for the Russians is worse than the worst Russian there is, and that Semyon, or rather Shimon Davidovich, cannot be anything else, and as such, he serves what your Rosenbergs are ultimately going to get — a turn on the electric chair, to the universal shame of Jews."

"Cynthia!" It had been a long time since he'd seen his wife in such a murderous mood. He was about to say something in defense of the Kirlians and to explain that they didn't really have any connection to the Rosenbergs, and that her, Cynthia's mean streak was getting unbearable, but it didn't come to that because his wife erupted in bitter, resentful tears.

"Cynthia, sweetheart!" Dina offered her a handkerchief over the table. The pharmacist felt responsible for Mrs. Roth's tears; he wiped the goose fat from his mouth and said: "Believe me, electroshock is, whatever these folks or those folks say about it, still the sole effective method, and it's fairly safe, with a very small percentage of cases that end in death. And meanwhile," he went on as he looked up no longer in a position to hold back the rest of the sentence despite encountering Cynthia's ominous anticipation. "Meanwhile, it doesn't just mitigate attacks of schizophrenia, but it treats inferiority complexes, apathy, emaciation, and frigidity."

"Your Rosenbergs are going to fry," Cynthia said. She turned to her husband's aunt. Through her tears she saw Dina smiling, her teeth gleaming, out of her eyes and temples crawled isolated flickers, and then immediately after that a wreath began to pulsate above her forehead, of youthful blue, like a cornflower… She had noticed earlier the way Dina flaunted her fake fire, how in Oscar's presence her dormant skin suddenly revived and out of her fatigued shoulders sprouted flame-wings, quivering like wings on a day-old chicken. And she, Cynthia, was gloomier than ever, a being devoid of her own source of light, a woman without a radiance.

"By God, they're going to fry," she said. "You'll see."

4.

America soon found out about Kirlian, and, just like Cynthia, proved to be distrustful of, and hostile towards, his discovery. Even Jonathan's musicians, young fellows without prejudices, did not take seriously the claim of their boss that sounds, especially musical ones, also have an aura, which is visible in certain circumstances and that the sound of a trumpet flames yellow like Sulphur, a bass smokes like a damp crossbeam, and the drums cast sparks as black as pitch, and from a guitar drips white-hot glass. "And fire, too, when it burns freely, has a halo," Jonathan said. "It smolders even after the fire goes out, and it's resistant to water and foam from fire extinguishers, and even the strongest hose can't touch it."

The newspapers, for their part, covered the political implications of this affair. One influential Washington daily claimed that the Russians, with the help of Kirlian's invention, were attempting to ascertain the true numbers of total American losses in World War II, and the exact number of victims of the Allied bombardment of the Balkans, and also to "photograph" the most highly classified state military secrets, nuclear ones, of the United States, which some of their keepers had carried with them to the grave.

A reader of *Newsweek* put forth a similar idea in his letter to the editors: he was convinced, and ready to prove, that the Rosenbergs' trial, including its fatal conclusion, had been staged by the Russians, with the goal of "reading," *post mortem*, from the aura of these two sacrificed followers everything that they had not dared or desired to hand over during their lifetimes. The Catholic paper *Christian Daily* declared heretical the very idea of the existence of auras for normal mortals, for biological egalitarianism of that type would devalue the sacred radiance of those who are exceptional. Thus, little by little, the belief gained momentum — as Cynthia had said first — that between the discovery by Kirlian and the fate of the Rosenbergs there had to exist a firm causal connection. If it seemed that the death sentence for the American fellow travelers might somehow have been averted, before the appearance of information about the Russian invention — despite the fact that the U.S. Supreme Court confirmed the sentence, and Eisenhower rejected the clemency request — that is to say, if something were going to happen at the last moment, it would be like some higher power intervening in the fatal course of events so that the fellow travelers, like the pilots of a burning airplane, were catapulted out of the electric chairs; but after people learned of the dubious discovery made by some ailing electrician from the Black Sea, the fate of the Rosenbergs was sealed. Kirlian's aura cast its rays on the secret of America's atomic weapon; both guilts crossed and confirmed one another, and it was certain that between the two cases existed some connection, and not merely a causal but also a mystical one. The circuitry that was closing in on Julius and Ethel Rosenberg was fed with energy discovered and directed by the Kirlians. Once again it was shown how all electrical phenomena on the planet are linked, that lightning that flashes above the Caucasus can lash the fastest cowboy in the Wild West and, by the same token, the flipping of a switch in the electric chamber at Sing-Sing, in New York state, produces a wreath of sparks on the temples of schizophrenics or other apostates in some Soviet mental ward, and maybe for a whole tribe, lost in the search for itself. It was an unpleasant moment, full of uncertainty, and Oscar decided to suspend his quest temporarily. But the consequences of the ominous connection were already manifest...

First of all, Jonathan's drummer, at the beginning of June, was called before the House Un-American Activities Committee, and then, on two occasions, they summoned Jonathan himself. The quartet simply lost its sound. Jonathan sat around the whole day, totally deflated and not knowing what to do with himself. He wore on Oscar with his tedious, sober bellyaching and sighing. Oscar was certain that, as early as the next, a summons was also going to be delivered to him and that he would have to explain himself before some committee or commission. In those days his older brother Theo decided abruptly to let his beard and sideburns grow, put on a black caftan and white socks, shaved his wife head, and plunged into holy books and life in accordance with the Law. The second-oldest brother, Michael, who hid his business dealings from Oscar and whose closest partner and best friend was killed in a gangland shoot-out, sold everything he owned and with a gold nugget in his pocket, in the greatest secrecy, and in a roundabout way, sailed for Israel. When he left, he told

Oscar: "Don't waste your time on the lost tribes. When the time comes, they'll find you. Mine almost caught up with me. And besides, why don't you follow my lead for once? Pack up Cynthia and get on the boat. In *Eretz Yisrael* you will have all the tribes you want. Sooner or later, she'll find hers there too. Our homeland is a planetary asylum for the lost."

Michael was babbling, and grinning, but the hooked tip of his experienced nose twitched in warning. And indeed, shortly after he left, around the shop with photographic equipment at 28 Western Street, not far from Holy Apostles' Church, persons who were clearly different from Oscar's customers and ordinary passers-by started milling about. They gazed at the display cases as if they were seeing cameras and tripods for the first time, scornfully but provocatively, in an obvious wish to be noticed; they poked their heads into the shop, and then moved off, disappearing in the direction of nearby Chelsea Park; and they returned, only to hang around in front of the shop windows. It seemed that their attention was drawn, more than anything else, to some antiques displayed at Dina's suggestion to oppose to the superficial gleam of new technology something with a sentimental patina: the former Leopold's binoculars, a symbol of all of the family's desires, and one small camera for detective work (of unknown provenance, defective), built into the handle of an elegant man's cane of the type one sees now only in English films about Sherlock Holmes.

"Maybe they're Martians," Cynthia said icily when her husband confided his misgivings to her. "The same ones who started the War of the Worlds back when."

5.

During all the years he was in love with Dina, Oscar had never longed for her as much as he did in those June nights of 1953. Tormented by insomnia, he looked out the window of his bedroom for hours on end at the spinning advertising sign of Insurers' Mutual, which, in a slow rotation, fed a narrow starry stream into the effervescent surf of neon-and-gold coins. The electric tide stirred his blood, too. The anticipatory heat, which over the course of the day hid out in elevators, skylights, and community laundry rooms, was liberated at night, spread, got into apartments, crept into beds, inflamed people's neuroses and unhealthy passions. Oscar, drenched with sweat, wiped himself off with a bedsheet, giddily pulling towards him, together with the weightless Cynthia. When he felt her near to him, he ran into the bathroom and got under a cold shower. While the water descended over him, posting noisy bars around him, Oscar's heart started to skip and flail, and tingling, love beams, shot through his abdomen like a swarm of wild bees. "Dina, Dina, Dina!" He was burning up, and the ice-cold water steamed from his fire.

A few years later, a New York psychologist, in his study of great outbreaks of contagious love in history, noted that in the first half of June, 1953, before the execution of the Rosenbergs, across the entire eastern portion of the continent, and somewhat less on the west coast, a genuine execution fever raged; it manifested itself in several different ways: as a wave of irrational anger and violence, as a severe epidemic of a hitherto unknown variant of influenza, as a sudden demographic eddy, in which people disappeared by the thousands, without a trace and, lastly, in contrast to all of the above, as massive erotic exaltation. The psychologist dealt only with that final symptom. On the eve of great disasters, wars, crises, earthquakes, and executions, a real "love fever" shakes nations, he asserted. In that way the heart and skin try to understand what is dodging reason. People who are afraid of battlefields, and to whom other routes are closed, flee into the bedroom. The fatal outcome of a disease is preceded by a brief improvement, and then a violent death — a moment of supreme love.

This love-fever entrapped, of course, even the Rosenbergs themselves. "My dearest, if only I could strengthen and comfort you. I love you so much," Ethel wrote to her husband from the women's cell block to the men's a short time before the U.S. Supreme Court confirmed their sentence. "As soon as I take the pen in my hand, I pause at the question: what do I say to someone I love this much, when I have to face the inexorable fact that in eighteen days, on our fourteenth wedding anniversary, they are going to kill us?" rejoined Julius, and the newspapers, still damp with printer's ink and the tears of the typesetters, carried and sowed all across the world these sentences yanked from letters and stolen by unknown means. And the political slogans intended equally for party comrades and the prison executioner, along with moving passages about their sons, and daydreams about the little piece of sky and the morning birdsong of a random robin beneath the prison window, and the little treatises on the wall about — still! — a happy future for humanity — they all turned, when faced with death, into choking sobs of love. "We are victims of

American fascism!", Ethel wrote to her husband on the day they perished, but the proximity of death translated this political accusation to "I love you so much!"

At that hour, the whole continent trembled in amorous anticipation. Men and women whose libidos had long been extinct, shower each other with torrid words and embrace. "Electric orgasm!" Jonathan said, and blew into his horn so desperately that all his blood ran to his eyes, and the plastic glasses on the bar shuddered so much from impotent desire that they burst. All passions that were concealed, postponed, forbidden, and forgotten, abruptly raised their heads and flocked towards fulfillment. Old men, canes in their hands, drift around in search of their first loves, sons reach for their mothers, fathers for their daughters, all sinful and all fatal urges bolt towards eternal life. The great clock of love ticked loudly on the prison sky. Only a few hours remained until it was carried out: the defense attorney Bloch, carrying Ethel's personal plea for clemency, tried to convince the guards at the White House to admit him, to see the president, but they took the letter and removed him from the white threshold. The plea for her life went unread. Nor was Oscar able to wait any longer. He closed the shop in a tizzy and rushed to the subway station. At Smith's bookstore across the street they rapidly changed the lock on the entrance; at the corner, on the display case in Holitzscher's jewelry store, a massive black man who looked like a desperado aimed a welding torch at pearl-like beads of solder to weld in place new cast-iron bars. In the corridors of the subway system they were repairing pipes, firemen checked hydrants, newspaper boys called out the evening headlines, which were ordering these preparations.

In the train to Brooklyn a crazy Tibetan with a beggar's cup in his hand announced, as usual, the fall of Berlin and the suicide of Tibetan monks, the masters of Agartha, determined not to fall into Russian hands, and at the next station hammers again banged from all directions, and finishing touches were falling on wood and metal.

Nor could the pharmacist from Antwerp contain the quiver in his voice: "You should know that this whole search for lost tribes is a search for love," he said that morning on the telephone, and he did not stop the flow of his sentences until he had talked all about how the famous traveler known as the Knight of Mandeville in the 14th century had witnessed that the Amurru tribe, or the Amorite people, had moved to Mesopotamia not from the Armenian highlands, as once thought, but from the valley of the river in eastern Siberia called the Amur, as he could tell from the name alone, and that, since these Amurru had in common with Israelite tribes words and customs, and thus an origin, it was legitimate to conclude that the lost tribes were not lost, that they did not arrive in the Far East by unhappy circumstance, at the whim of fate, but rather impelled by a nostalgic desire for their ancient homeland, for this Amur, their love; the search for the tribes was nothing other than the great River of Love... And that's why Oscar was now rushing, not thinking of earthly obstacles, of Jonathan who, listless and worried in recent days, almost indifferent even to drink, could be returning home before his usual time of 2 am. A tryst with Dina would be a tryst with the lost — the found! — tribes, with their own ten lost souls. When he touched his aunt's body, the shroud would slide off of all secrets. Yes, if he was ever going to find the tribes, the map of her skin would reveal to him the peregrinations that for these centuries the tribes had made through foreign lands, and only on her skin with its sprinkled freckles the color of cinnamon would he recognize the places worthy of conquest, his future cities. And vice-versa: if he ever knew his aunt's body, he would get to know it guided by the conquering enthusiasm of awakened tribes! Oscar's chest swelled when he thought these mighty words, but they served only to conceal his embarrassed trepidation. Insecurity always shields itself with a metaphor. The lost tribes: they are nothing other than the slow convection of bedroom air, a row of small guiding lights towards Dina, a gently derisive and melancholy allusion to the late Leopold whom they had both loved, despite everything, and who was in love with Dina, his beautiful daughter-in-law, but not so much so that he would not leave to his youngest son something of that fascination, along with the tribes of his final testament. Entering Dina's building, passing the empty booth of the doorman, Oscar was already reconciled to the fact that the lost tribes were just a form of memory, a sparkling people of love helpers who circulate around chosen souls till they combust.

But, when after ringing a long time with no response he depressed the handle and opened the door a sliver, he saw that the tribes… (But: behind every door a man opens in great anticipation stands a "but." That which is behind the door even when nothing else is there. "'But' is the monster that devours all your allies and logical connections. What sight presented itself to Oscar? Reality, or illusion? Truth, or a lite? A solution or a puzzle?)

6.

A report, drawn up on June 19, 1953, around 7 in the evening, in the apartment of Jonathan and Dina Levine, 65 Winthrop Road, in Brooklyn, and signed by the Sergeant Patrick Houle, confirmed the following: 1) the lock on the front door was in working order, with no traces of forced entry; 2) in the apartment, above all in the bedroom, there was evidence of violence: the double bed was in disarray, the linens torn in several places, the mattress slit and its contents (seaweed) strewn across the floor; 3) on the white woodwork and glass surfaces, a large number of fingerprints are visible; and 4) on the bedclothes, the woman's underclothes, and bedside rug, traces of semen were found, as well as negligible amounts of blood. In addition, it was later established that the fingerprints belong to unknown perpetrators, that is, people who were not to be found in the files of either the local or the federal police, and that the blood, type B, on the other hand did not belong to the presumed victim, Mrs. Levine, but probably to one of the perpetrators, and is possible evidence that the victim offered resistance.

The witness statements were to a certain extent contradictory and did not help solve the case. Oscar Roth, who according to his own statement reached the Levine's apartment at around 5:30 pm, encountered these ten unknown men, but not his relative, his maternal aunt named Mrs. Dina Levine. The apartment was a mess. It was in that special kind of disorder, said Oscar Roth, that lost tribes leave behind. Nothing was broken, ruined, and he did not see any bullet holes but only a certain number of smaller and larger gaps between objects, and some ephemeral damage. The three-winged wardrobe, for instance, was unscathed, but the veneer lacked its earlier gleam; the mirror on the little table in the bathroom remained intact, but it reflected nothing. And the cup for water and thermometer and alarm clock on the nightstand were empty: this installation was supposed to convince her distracted spouse that Mrs. Levine had a fever, that is to say, that all of these male creatures in their bedroom were simply the products of her influenza.

Mr. Levine arrived at their apartment around 6:15 pm (for a reason he could not explain to himself or the police, he broke off his quartet's rehearsal and rushed home), found his nephew, Oscar Roth, there, but did not see the unknown man that Roth mentioned. "When I came in, he was standing in the door to the bedroom," said Mr. Levine. "He threw his arms around me and started to snivel: 'I am lost, Jonathan. I am lost.'"

Police Sgt. Patrick Houle and his partner, Frank Pistoia, arrived at the above address at 6:40 pm. There they found Jonathan Levine, who had called them, but not Oscar Roth. Levine was kneeling in the foyer, in front of an open cabinet, surrounded by shoes, with at least ten pairs of them scattered around. He grabbed one and saved it, saying: "Oscar, goddamn it, where did you vanish to?"

Mrs. Cynthia Roth, who, figuring out that her husband Oscar had gone to his aunt's apartment, started out after him and, taking a taxi, got there at approximately 7:20 pm; the told a family friend and guardian, the retired pharmacist Isaac Epstein, that there, at that Brooklyn apartment, neither Jonathan nor Oscar was to be found, nor the unknown man, but only the pair of policemen who, therefore, on who knows whose orders, had gone into the apartment and caused the ruckus. When they caught sight of her, they said to one another: "Screw this. Let's beat it!" The retired pharmacist made a dismissive gesture and, not without a feeling of guilt, said: "Since my dear friend Leopold died, the whole world is lost."

There was a fair amount of truth in this assertion. Since Leopold had announced the search for the lost tribes, a lot of things had been lost. First of all, Leopold himself departed, and shortly thereafter his wife Barbara, who always followed him with a greater or lesser degree of reluctance, and then his brother Thomas, who was an advertising specialist for a factory that made fans and who had gone west at the beginning of the war to try to identify, at Leopold's expense, at least one of the lost tribes among the Sioux and Mandan Indians. He never came back. And almost all of Leopold's European kinfolk vanished during the war, and now, in secret, hiding the unmistakable symptoms even from himself, the apothecary was preparing to depart also, although he did not himself believe in the stories he repeated, or at least tolerated, not even the one about the lost tribes. But before him, within just a few minutes actually, Julius and Ethel Rosenberg were going to disappear, and uncertain was also the fate of Semyon Davidovich Kirlian and his wife Valentina, and all of those people who knew anything about the lost tribes. Some intermediary witnesses also vanished: a heart attack took Leopold's former neighbor, the Russian immigrant Fyodor Pavlovich Blagoveshensky, who, although far from well-disposed towards the Semitic race, exclaimed after Stalin's death: "I am certain that the noble tribes of Judea deserve the end of this Georgian hangman. I pray that his red spawn will never get their hands on them!" And from the words of a Yugoslav asylum-seeker after the war, who brought Oscar and his brothers unexpected greetings from a surviving Rot in Novi Sad, it came out that the recent disappearances of a multitude of people even in the country of Leopold's closest progenitors could be linked to tribes that went missing long ago.

Completely ordinary people also discovered that they were in the red. They lost their nerves, their confidence, their appetites, and their sense of time. They lost money in business dealings, bets, and at cards. At the moment of the Rosenberg's death, a housewife in Memphis was deprived of the power of speech, and in a court in her home state of Tennessee she sued President Eisenhower and the Supreme Court, seeking compensation for the shock she had experienced. A large number of men abruptly lost their potency and eleven persons, mostly from around the town of Ossining, but also from other places in New York state, found themselves, in an inexplicable manner, by the intervention of some unknown force, suddenly hurled some two or three kilometers from their homes or wherever they had just been. Some very young people lost their memories, and adherents of a sect of "illuminated ones" admitted that the holy refulgence on their leader's palms and the soles of his feet went dark for a period of time. Mediums lost their connection with hypnotists, and a very few, rare individuals were endowed with an eighth sense — contact with the world of spirits. Certain apartments, especially right in New York City, were left without light, water, and sometimes even air. Valuables vanished from secret safes — so to speak instantaneously evaporating like a drop of water on hot asphalt, the most expensive and hardest diamonds and pearls; out of pillows and mattresses went missing, bundles of bank notes stacked like dovetail joints, and long-forgotten inheritances. Children and old left headed out the doors of their homes, and domestic animals, after years of blind devotion, abandoned their masters. It was exactly as the Antwerp pharmacist had said: a world was lost. Another one, called and invoked, came along out of nowhere.

CHAPTER FOUR
FRAGEMENTS FROM THE WORKING DIARY ABOUT BIROBIDZHAN

Female continent, or island?

Birobidzhan is the unknown, the compressed pith of the human personality (sub-consciousness?)...The embodiment, the territorialization, the nucleus of neurosis.

Birobidzhan is a land without killing. The dream of a man (woman) who, in fear, for no reason (?) killed the old Arab.

Birobidzhan is a lunatic asylum.

Birobidzhan is the FINAL SOLUTION (Hitler's secret plan for his attack on the USSR).

Birobidzhan as the ideal city (utopia)

Already covered:

B. as a homeland in reserve

B. as a swampy nursery for Jewish seed (New Zion?)

Birobidzhan — the last preserve (on earth) of active magical thinking and life.

The Jews maintained (and the Russians with them) a distant homeland of magic. See shamanism!

PLAN

Part I: Women from Europe seek salvation to the south. Exodus. *Hysteria* of exodus.

Part II: Motion, roaming (exodus) in place — *hysteria*. Flora chases Haim? In place, or for real? Miša — our relative — to Greece or elsewhere?

Part III: forty years later Olga takes the relay stick (the baton/cold torch) of HYSTERIA.

Where are all the women who escaped in hysteria and into hysteria (as a refuge)

the Finaly brothers

the XY sisters, etc., turn out to be hidden

When will appear all the girls and women who have ever been sold?

But simultaneously, Olga Rot is awaiting the return of the transport of women and children who disappeared in the war. Russo-German business — one waits for the return of the ones who were sold.

All roads to Birobidzhan are through prison, police stations, and the like.

(the secret plan for the Rosenbergs to be transferred to Birobidzhan!)

"We are victims of American fascism," Ethel wrote on the day of her execution. Ethel wrote the majority of the first letters. Anxiety, longing, permeate these letters. But in them, there is no glimpse or presentiment of the terrible temptations and even more terrible fate that will follow. Everyday questions, petty concerns taken from the outside world pervade everything in a manner so natural that it seems that the author cannot think about anything other than arrest, prison, the concatenation of fatal coincidences, which will soon be at an end and everything will be picked up where it had been dropped.

Bizakodok are those letters, *bizztantak*, and impart strength. Unlimited love, knowledge, human *meltosag* and worldly understanding suffuse these lines.

The writer loves life. Its small everyday joys and tasks. All in all the letters are terribly frank and do conceal not a feeling of injustice *felazitot*.

Condemned to die on 5 April 1951, after a three-week period of deliberation. The exhausting process enervated the married couple, but the letters reveal that it did not break them.

The letters guide us through their lives. We get to know a simple, unpretentious couple who loved each other to no end. Their love of life is shocking. "And thus, despite the scandalous imprisonment and the irreversible judgment" — writes Julius — "we can say that our life was beautiful and productive." Firmly, with nearly superhuman strength, they fought for their lives. They did not feel a whit of fear.

Poignant is the concern they show, throughout their time in prison, for their sons Robbie (3) and Michael (7), and for their fate. The spouses work out in detail how they will receive the children when they come to visit them in prison, what they will talk about. It's moving how they want to explain everything to them — as much as is indispensable right up to the communicating (explaining) to them the way in which the sentence will be carried out.

The letters are free, open.

"My best wishes for you in 1952," Julius wrote to Ethel at the end of 1951. "Love, happiness, freedom, peace!"

Improbably filled with strength and beauty, the letter that Ethel wrote on 26 February, tells of the *fellebbviteli* court had confirming their death sentence. "My heart bleeds for the children. Today they're big enough to get their own information about what's happening, and in vain I'm fighting with myself, my mind is aghast when I think of their terror. More than anything I'm worried on their account, and with great fear I await the news of how they took this turn of events."

"My dearest, if only I could strengthen and console you! I love you so much!" A few months later the Supreme Court confirmed the sentence. Their defense attorney lodged a request for clemency with the president of the US; Truman did not want to make a decision so he left it to Eisenhower. On 11 February 1953 Eisenhower rejected their request. Julius wrote to his wife that the American president had not read their plea or even glanced at the documents from the trial.

Death's approach let itself be seen in the couple's moods. But they did not *csugednek*. Julius wrote: "Once, long ago, I lived happily in a place with my dear wife and two wonderful children. But now it's all over. We are awaiting death. In the longing for the sweet kisses of a wife and the warm embraces of children can be felt the promise of a return to a better life. I know full well how happy we would be if the whole family could live together once more. The terrible power of that wish and the support of well-meaning people from around the world animate me to fight to victory, with extreme determination."

CHAPTER FIVE

THE JOURNEY OF BERTHA PAPPENHEIM

In the first part of 1911, sometime in March, Miss Bertha Pappenheim, the president of the Association of Jewish Women and the founder of the Fund for the Assistance of Wayward Girls, started out on a trip to Palestine and Egypt by way of Vienna and Budapest; she wished to see the Near East, and the Balkans as well, with her own eyes, to check on things directly, to examine the social conditions of threatened categories of the population to whose protection she had dedicated her life — or rather, how the protection functioned, if it did at all, above all for unwed mothers, orphans, prostitutes (and then old women) in the general but most of all in the Jewish population, to update her contacts with the authorities on the spot and appeal to them to combat the white slave trade. In her agile way of doing things, sparing neither her time nor her strength, nor her rather modest savings, she spoke, over the course of three months, first in Budapest, the antechamber to the Balkans, and then in Belgrade, Sofia, and at stops along the way — Plovdiv (Filipolis), Edirne, followed by Thessaloniki, Istanbul, Smyrna, Jerusalem, a few other cities in Palestine, Port Said, and eventually reaching Alexandria (Ramleh), with a multitude of competent and non-competent authorities, she visited dozens of hospitals, orphanages, and brothels, but by the end of the trip she had to admit, confiding to one of her colleagues in a letter, that she had not accomplished anything and that her trip there would produce no effect, except for her personally.

The events that followed hinted indirectly, and over time it became obvious, that the missionary journey of the enterprising, decisive, self-sacrificing, rational woman from Frankfurt, could be linked to a movement or a condition of spirit, to the mysterious female zeal of women that right then and there giving birth to and *showing the first forms of its existence*: a utopia of a great, global refuge for women, a Female Continent, a country of women and female messianism — a messiah-woman who in the very near future will arrive from somewhere, from Egypt, and lead their people into an unpromised but well-deserved land. These mostly simple uneducated women and girls announced and prophesied the arrival of the messiah this time, but among them were also heirs to women-utopians such as Suzanne Voilquin, and even a few men; they were prostitutes, unmarried and single mothers, women swollen with venereal disease and tuberculosis, women born out of wedlock, orphans, pregnant minors and, in general, women and children from the street, as well as women and children bought or sold for the needs of Balkan brothels or Turkish public houses and harems. Some of these persons, through whom the arrival of the Egyptian was announced, remembered the unusual German lady traveler — who descended on brothels and boarding houses, asked questions of the people there, and engaged in real conversations.

That woman had by her presence already stirred in her interlocutors' passions that in the *objective world*, in life, in history, would call forth, set in train, or speed up events, which at that time and in those places would otherwise not manifest themselves. Subsequently there were a few additional related circumstances. From the history of psychoanalysis it is well known that Freud's famous Ana O. — Bertha Pappenheim — dedicated herself, after she fled from the arena, to social work with fallen girls. The moment she entered menopause, the climacteric or the third age of woman, she set out on a journey through Galicia and the Balkans, and one could reason that her decision to embark on that trip seemed to set in motion a whole wave of women's movement in those European spaces.

The secret name or code of the continent, an unspecified destination, as remained noted in the files of the Belgrade police department was "Island A.N.A." or "I.A.N.A.", interpreted as meaning "Destination *Atlantida Noster*" in Serbian. Some thought that it was the District or Island of Ana, which was just about to be discovered. Christian women believed that behind this name hid the name of the Mother Mary, while observant Jews saw in these three letters the Greek form of the Hebrew abbreviation "Yahweh had mercy" and connected it with one of Elkana's wives who had long been infertile and then her prayer was heard and she conceived and gave birth — the way a deserted, barren island would — to the region that was promised to them and that they would populate one day, and which by dint of their merits and divine favor would be fecund and secure.

Ana O., in Dr. Freud's code, had her cover blown by the wives of Belgrade's police officers, and she turned into a cipher for the new Promised Land.

To Bertha Pappenheim it seemed that in Poland and Galicia the syllables *a-na* came up a great deal. As if women discovered them and called them out. The syllables were common in Polish words, and especially in Hungarian. Like an echo... In all of these languages, the Slavic ones and Hungarian, that "O, Ana!" sounded like an invitation, a cry, a call for help. To Bertha Pappenheim, it was as if these women were addressing their secret selves, with a password that not only she herself was supposed to understand but also her sub-consciousness, the repressed contents of her being. She felt disquiet and fear.

In Budapest, during the month of March, 1911, describing in a letter to her friend, Miss N., her visit to the Hospital of St. Rochus, Bertha Pappenheim wrote:

"A hospital is the image of the subconscious. (This is the way to collect material for a presentation at scholarly conferences — so Bertha thought). A hospital is a building of recognizable purpose but it's still harmonious, of a pleasing appearance. Surrounded by a courtyard with a few sycamore and chestnut trees (currently with bare, but nice, healthy branches) and stone benches. A fountain. The courtyard is girded by a wall of nice, healthy brick protected with trailing vines — as is the case with many schools and academies. It was reminiscent of all the educational and training institutions into which healthy, slightly dissolute young creatures enter with lots of desires and fears, but without any experience, and who know nothing of life, and who emerge as tempered, self-confident, cooled, slightly rigid creatures, ready for a worthy bourgeois life."

The presence of some inappropriately or oddly dressed young ladies might confuse someone who, calling for and expecting a female custodian — an unusual woman moving on legs that look like columns, as if she suffers from dropsy — to appear and open the iron door to the courtyard; you would find yourself in a heartbeat in a warren of dirty, abandoned, and damp rooms and corridors and other accompanying premises, bare and dark, which seemed to be bound by some underground connection, an artery, to the very navel of the city's netherworld. Then one could tell that the charming vines, which on this grayish, formless March morning imparted a certain intimacy and softness to the walls of the buildings, were clinging to bars on the windows, that is to say concealing them from the eyes of the outside world and that beneath the perpetually young ivy, of hearty green color, sheltered and preserved from the external world, cling, grow, and thicken the sturdy iron bars. And through this curtain of cast iron and ivy — when it parts — one enters by tumbling into the dark hospital cavity. The shadows, darkness, and damp, the filth and madness that merged here from the forlorn alleys of the city and its environs, are inflicted upon a variegated female world, thrown onto iron bedframes and left to suffocate there like discarded fish at the shore, opening their mouths in mute panic with pieces and little threads of sentences snapping off in a mixture of snickering and crying, curses, requests, and complaints.

Shreds of conversation, the exchange of stammers and croaks *that Bertha Pappenheim did not understand*.

"In that building, there are two fully equal hells: women's and men's. Two wings of the building, two hells."

Did Bertha Pappenheim *see* all of that? Those few words of hers from the letter, especially that one part, allow for, and indeed imply, a multiplicity of such scenes, details. Her subconscious saw it. Later, in the train, in a tunnel, something of those scenes came out and manifested itself in the purple trembling of the emergency light blinking above the compartment door. Instantaneously they flew out of it and remained for a moment or two in the air, right below the light bulb, actually on the window pane behind which the dim wall of the short tunnel zoomed past.

Worst of all, everyone in the compartment was looking at the window. Everyone saw what perhaps only Bertha Pappenheim was supposed to see — if anyone at all was supposed to see it — but she acted as though nothing had happened, as if it were all completely natural. The lady said something to her traveling companion and pulled up the fur that she had slid off of her shoulder. A man took out a resplendent little container, probably a snuff-box, and started tapping on its shiny lid; a girl pressed her face against the glass so that she wouldn't see the terrible images that were appearing from who knows where. As if a mutual sigh of relief passed through the compartment when the darkness began to dilute. But it did not thin out entirely. It seemed like they spent at least half an hour in the tunnel. The darkness was now on its other, southerly side considerably thicker, as if the tunnel were many kilometers long.

Why didn't everything, or at least part of everything, make it into the letter that Bertha penned to Miss N.? Because a true explosion, an activation of reality, ensues only after the recording of events. A letter induces events, occurrences, history. Until humanity began noting things down, history was much slower, and events great and small, and general and individual, took place much more slowly, and only occasionally, at great intervals. A letter, a recording, condenses events on paper or on papyrus — or even in stone — the same way it concentrates characters and letters. Besides that, it's in the nature of reality, of events, to want to fail, to get past, to trick the record, or the image of themselves: events strive to remain unrecorded, free, to sail about at liberty, to whirl and twist through time and space, able to be ascribed to first one thing and then another, here and there, yesterday and tomorrow.

In other words, after each of Bertha Pappenheim's letters, she was upset, she feared reality and started to produce unplanned, strange occurrences, to "write novels and stories." Perhaps this was because reality is not happy about being registered, and it craves added value, artistically or in some other way, being transposed, surpassed, or at least falsified, mystified. Otherwise it is not complete.

After she described this scene, she in the letter suddenly left the hospital chambers. A reader would say she fled from them and reported on a book that she read that evening and about which she had a few comments. From Bertha's letter one cannot tell that the female patients were more excited than usual, that over time tension was growing, while wretchedness slipped out and stole away; the women were jumping on their beds, and a Jewish woman with tuberculosis snapped the straps on her shirt and began waving it like a castaway from Medusa's raft, shouting — turned for show to a supposed crowd in the opposite corner — something that sounded like *ana* or *anja*. It seemed that everyone at that moment understood and sympathized with her pleas, or her request or invitation — her revelation.

"What does *ana/anja* mean?" Bertha asked Miss A.

"It's the eternal invocation of mother (mama, mama)," A. said succinctly, after at first appearing to have missed the question. "If I'm not mistaken," she added.

"From the other side of the ward the other patients answered her like an echo:

"A-Anja-ana-ana!"

Then Bertha Pappenheim was convinced that this cry, shout, voice, was directed at her, that it was summoning her, seeking help from her or, instead, rebuking her for running away, betraying the sickness, the great sisterhood of female illness and suffering.

CHAPTER SIX
THE FEMALE EDGE OF THE WORLD

"For two days now, Miss A. has been very devotedly engaged on my behalf. I had met her before, at some congresses and conferences dedicated to the white slave trade."

Bertha Pappenheim raised her fountain from the letter to Miss N. and stared at the blue patterns on the marble slab of the small hotel escritoire. The cold of the stone, infiltrating the woolen jersey of her sleeves, had long since pierced her bones, and it now manifested, recurred, like a sharp pain that was almost audible in the night-time silence. In the dampness of the March night the ink dried slowly. Miss Pappenheim reached for the blotting paper, but when she touched its rounded handle with the engraved monogram of the Hotel Hungaria, she pushed it away suddenly, sharply, bent forward, and blew onto the sheet of paper as if to disperse the inky little beetles of unwanted, inappropriate thoughts. But, seeing how they stood in front of her, deployed in dense lines, she relented and calmly put the tip of her pen back onto the paper.

"Yesterday I accompanied her to the St. Roch Hospital, which has, all told, 140 beds reserved for cases of venereal disease, that is, exclusively for prostitutes, who trudge through the rooms, barely clothed and with almost no care. One nurse for a ward with thirty beds, a solid and dutiful woman, but totally untrained. All in all it resembles an asylum for the mentally ill. In the courtyard, a girl in a coarse silk petticoat, her hair unkempt beneath the towel she was using as a turban, embraced her companion who was wearing a ripped shirt and a hospital gown and silver shoes and short socks (*bas a jour*). In the ward at a table another girl with a stunning hair-do, wearing nothing but a very low-cut shirt, was wearing only a shirt, writing a letter. And while Miss A. grinned at a beauty of twenty years of age, I noticed another woman in a blouse of yellow silk adorned with lace (she like the previous girl was stretched out on a bed), drenched in tears — tears of laughter. A Jewish woman with black hair, a consumptive appearance, argued with her shirt, which was constantly falling from her shoulder, etc. The picture of physical and moral decline of creatures between sixteen and thirty years of age, about whom no one took note or took care, except for the police — in their particular way. Jews made up a third of these girls. I believe, however, that I am the first of their co-nationals to set foot, for societal reasons, in this chamber of horrors. Madame Professor B., to whom I had mentioned my intention of visiting the hospital, was incapable of understanding why I... ."

Bertha usually wrote her longest letters at night, on the eve of a journey. The earlier she needed to wake up the following morning, and the longer, more strenuous, and uncertain the upcoming stage of her travels, the more time she spent on her letters. It was important for her to clean out everything from herself as she was about to depart, and wrap it up in an envelope so that nothing was left behind in the hotel room that could later take root and tie her to that random place more than she wanted. Her friend Martha Freud had said to her ten years ago, when they met in Vienna: "My husband writes to me from Paris and says that he doesn't want to return home to his *beloved prison*, that he's some kind of Antaeus who loses his strength when he touches his native soil, and he gains strength when he is at a distance. But in spite of this, he always comes back." In contrast to Freud, Bertha herself did not muster the strength to leave the Vienna of her birth for good, and Freud had an indirect role in making that happen. Thus a man can spend his whole life in flight from his birthplace, everyone from his own Vienna, and in order to preserve his strength he travels from city to city, from country to country, perhaps until he finds that promised land, the awarded one, to which he can transfer his strength, and which will bind him forever and ultimately subjugate him.

Bertha Pappenheim grew weary or her patience ran out or she was already approaching the end of the page, and then the letter was sealed and now and Miss N. was never going to find out how the situation developed further. She had broken off the description and added a few remarks about a book she was reading on her trip. Absent from the letter was any further sequence of images, any further unfolding of the choreography of the nauseating comedy represented in that gray building by a crude female disease. To the rhythm of music of nerves, inaudible to a healthy person's ear, these individual scenes or, to put it better, sequences, the trivial, confused, apparently normal or perverse activities of these women, gradually intertwined and focused on one object or direction of anticipation, aiming at a goal unclear to any observer. Out of the chaos of tragicomic details, something came into sight, was awakened, was created, something unifying and binding. Everything that had happened before that moment was revealed as preparation. A series of small, nauseating absurdities slowly advanced toward resolution, toward conceptualization. Still other movements, voices, positions of the body were marked by traces of sexuality, impudence, wantonness, cartoonish sexual spasms, but one sensed that this was only a form or a mask — beneath the thinned and cracked skin of sensuality (eroticization) had emerged a deeper urge, which like now in the dusky compartment of the express train came with the twilight, decanted through window and seeping from the ceiling. The scene began in such a way that first of all other people showed up between those erratic and colorful crackpots, by the beds like independent and unglued shadows but attached to them; they were dark, stricken and silenced by disease, marked, stamped with chancres on their lips and living scabs on their noses and ears, by true madness in their eyes, and they crept along the walls and around the beds, wrapping, entwining their nets around the first ones who had just caught the disease but are still lively; all of the bodies, the one for day and one for the night, swirled, merged, and diverged like a wave and its crest, and the beds squeaked and rocked on that perilous open sea. A small number of women sat upright in their beds; a gaunt one in an oversized nightgown stood there, swaying and rocking as if she were on a ship while around her pillows flew past like storm clouds. It all looked like spontaneous, general fury, but it was somehow set and pat, coordinated, like a customary evening ritual of rebellion, of night taking leave and taking over from day, or some ritual departure, detachment and exodus from illness, a short dash out of sickness or a dash out to meet it. If it lasted a moment or two, this race of creaking rafts really would reveal itself as a regular game, a small playful attack of hysteria, actually as a pause, a preparation for a big performance in which all of these costumes, the dissolute and silly behavior as segments, were supposed to fit together into a whole, into theater and take on meaning, but then, unexpectedly it seemed, in opposition to standard choreography, the consumptive Jewish woman apparently abruptly resolved her nightmarish conflict with her own shirt, slid it off of her shoulders, stripped it off of herself with one movement, ran with it (like a map or a flag) towards her fellow travelers/fellow sufferers, climbed atop their beds, and stuffed her shirt through the bars on the window, screaming. The two or three words of the final hopeless rebellion in which collide the hope of salvation and conciliation with calamity...

A female continent? Who said that? Marta, or someone else?

The silent horizontal of the Pannonian plain suited Bertha Pappenheim, as did the monotonous bouncing of the train into the dusk and the smoky curtain of swarms of incandescent soot that the wind flung against the compartment window; it all kept her at a certain distance from the landscape. She knew: on a journey the most important thing is to preserve oneself from the perils of history and geography. Except for the steeple in the distance, some farmstead squatting in the middle of cultivated fields, and telegraph poles next to the road — there was nothing anywhere. The countryside was covered in snowy drabness, as mute and taut as empty paper. This is why one should not relax too much. For, in places like this, all kinds of things happen when one surrenders to a nap or even sometimes when one is awake. For instance, behind the crossing gate on the earthen road, where carts laden with lumber or dry branches have sprouted up, or next to the tracks where there was a small station building, painted yellow, with two *fiakers* at the exit, a huge rock can suddenly rear up and through it might pass a wide river, and on it can return to the sea that drained away long ago, and to islands and reefs. On gray of this windswept emptiness, Romans, Huns, and Avars can appear unannounced; everything that history and geography are in a position to think up can occur. From out of nowhere the Female Continent can appear.

Female Continent?

What did that convey to her? Did Miss B. perhaps say it yesterday, when she took Bertha, rather reluctantly, to a meeting of Budapest feminists, *among the lionesses*, as she put it? Or the day before yesterday did the president of the Association for the Fight against the White Slave Trade mention something like that, when he spoke for an entire hour about the need for international control over shipping on the Danube? Or did that arrogant rabbi, Dr. H., drop the term when, upon interrupting Bertha's first sentence, he announced coldly that Jewish prostitution, whether it was increasing or decreasing, was of no interest to him, and that the corresponding trade was even less so. Or that childish doctor Vámos, a venerologist at St. Roch's (who presented his unusual department as a precious little arboretum of his own, or a menagerie of worn-out and broken toys that were still dear to him)? Or had the female continent surfaced in Bertha's agitated mind as a warning or omen before a perilous journey, as the code/designation of a long forgotten starting point or a vague, scarcely sensed goal?

Yet was she sure that she heard clearly the words female continent? Was it not women's contingent or even something else? When only a word or two protrudes out of the twilight, it's hard to tell whether it is a bank or little mound next to the tracks or a cloud, a mountain massif or an entire world/continent above the horizon, at the end of the world.

The two ladies who'd been riding in the compartment since Budapest were also uninterested in the landscape. They alternately slept and chatted in Hungarian, French, and German, and they smiled sweetly at Bertha, and in return they plied her with the chocolate contents of a silver box and amused themselves playing cards, and also some casual and entertaining game that had no winner or loser and folded up like a hurdy-gurdy when they stopped; it had elicited more lively conversation between them than was necessary, as if the game were freeing them from something. The boy, apparently a relative, made use of this freedom. He was captivated by their game frequently stuck his hand into the *bonbonnière*, until his short attention span was taxed and he devoted himself to counting out loud the poles that zipped past ever faster in front of the Pannonian countryside.

The face of the young woman who was seated across from Bertha, at a bit of an angle, betrayed no reaction. By the pure chance or because all human beings resemble the landscape in which they were born, her face was broad, flat, schooled not to express anything or at least not what it was feeling and thinking, or concealing underneath its slate exterior. A small lesion on the woman's face prevented her from expressing herself with mime. Her eyes were closed, but she was not asleep; at certain intervals, probably regular ones, she lifted the lid of the little woven basket that she held in her lap and bestowed on the child next to her, a girl of some four or five years of age, a piece of marzipan or nougat candy wrapped in a silk paper. It seemed that the woman was utterly focused on this bestowal, or the length and uniformity of the intervals, the merit, the direction and force of the nation, or the counting of chocolate marzipans and children's treats, persistent or careful chewing and suppressed chomping. True enough, it was not certain that the strained attentiveness that dominated her face was connected with this relentless distribution of sweets from her lap, but it did seem certain that it would, if anything were to happen, change on that route between the little basket in her lap and the child's mouth, if either the basket emptied or the child became satiated, or if a piece of marzipan fell from her hand and tumbled onto the floor beneath their seats — that on that flat blank face would reveal an expression that had been suppressed until then, a stifled urge, and that character would erupt the way disease breaks out with vehemence following a long period of incubation. Let personal history be manifested, and let destiny be fulfilled.

Miss Pappenheim changed her mind about addressing the woman; she was going to ask her, circumspectly, and with delicate but unfailing interest where she was traveling, or rather where the two of them were traveling, and in which language they should communicate. In German? But does the woman know German? Before she managed to do anything, something that seem destined to happen, happened: either the child dropped the marzipan, or made some other wrong move (stealthily, or inadvertently the child nudged the woman's hip or shin) or from an unexpected lurching of the train at some unexpected whistle-stop, or some poisoned morsel she swallowed at some unknown time — an unbearable look of worry, anger, or horror, flooded forth from its cramped hiding space — and then the woman's eyes popped all the way open and her entire face arched upward in a soundless scream. She covered her mouth with her hands to hold it in, but the dark cloudlet that had managed to fly out of her mouth and pupils had already filled the compartment, so that it took several minutes for Miss Pappenheim to notice that the seat next to the woman and her basket was empty, and the compartment door was open, and only a bit later while she turned her head towards the window, slowly and stiffly like on a seized-up axis, only then did Pappenheim notice there a woman completely different from the previous one, as if there among glowing particles or on the edge of the already murky eastern horizon she glimpsed in reality that which had revealed itself on the inside of her eyelids and was now announcing itself, or decisions were being made there concerning life and death. Finally the woman removed her hands from her face and mouth; from under her fingers slipped a frightened "Oooh!" and subsequently an expression of horror — or it was the surprise at an internal discovery? The woman stuck the index finger of her left hand into the glass and kept it there as around the tip of her finger moisture condensed and a spread, and down the pane slid slowly first one drop and then another.

Miss Pappenheim thought about how a disease travels faster than an express train, faster than sound, and maybe even with the speed of light, and it would take a new Einstein or somebody like him to calculate that velocity; did it hit that velocity by multiplication or division, or by addition or subtraction of the various other known quantities such as the depth of the patient's soul, the weight of his or her suffering, and the distance in human terms from one life to the nearest living being, the speed of a sick person's longings...

The woman seemed not to have noticed that the child had left the compartment. In an instant that had somehow eluded Miss Pappenheim, she had self-assuredly put the basket down next to her, on the child's seat.

"Die Kinder..." Bertha said. *"Enfant?"*

The woman turned her head, or maybe it was only her eyes, towards her fellow traveler, looked with surprise at Bertha as if she were just now seeing her for the first time (or had just suddenly recognized her!) and from surprise at that encounter, that juxtaposition, at any rate at the same instant that the locomotive's shrill whistle blew as it rolled into a tunnel, the woman let out a shriek, still stabbing her finger convulsively at the apparition in the window.

A few seconds later, the little girl appeared in the doorway, and immediately behind her the conductor. The child came into the compartment and took her seat. The conductor spoke a few sentences in Hungarian, but the woman paid no attention to him. It was like she neither heard nor saw him; she was looking at the rounded wall of the tunnel over which scudded violet light. The conductor, or was he a gendarme, tossed his head resentfully, and held that position for a moment; his mighty moustache trembled. And, not reconciled in this indifferent reception, he made eye contact with the older woman, Bertha, and, pointing at the darkness beyond the windowpane, said in German, with a heavy Danube Swabian accent:

"You see, *mademoiselle* — this is the beginning of the Balkans."

With the last glimmers of light, the brass button on his uniform also extinguished, as did the provocative gleam on the spikes of the conductor's moustache. The train huffed and puffed and so to speak scraped its way along the invisible black walls of the tunnel beneath Fruška Gora. The door to the compartment squeaked, groaned, and then the lock softly, pliantly clicked into place. It wasn't clear if the gendarme was standing inside or outside of the door, whether he had entered or exited.

"Yes, the Balkans," agreed Miss Pappenheim, facing the spot where the moustache might reappear. "This is undoubtedly a male continent."

But at that place on the gray background formed by the window, which emerged from the subterranean darkness, a violet glare, the silky internal container of an envelope, that soft invagination into which retreated the unsent text to her friend N., replaced the scene that she should have been seeing, according to the suggestion of the train attendant and things became clear to her, actually as if her attention were just then waking up, and had grown keen on some other thought, some idea to which she had not paid attention before now.

Characters from the screen in a movie house she scarcely recalled opened their mouths, spoke; sounds flowed from the mouths, words and entire tableaux of sentences, concealed to that point by an unintelligible language. Traveling through sentences, Bertha roamed St. Roch's Hospital, thinking over her reasons for staying silent about certain things in her letter to N. But all of a sudden she could not remember what she had withheld.

The train. The other woman traveling separated from her fellow travelers and wandered through the labyrinth of silenced speech. In the same way a womb wanders in a woman's body, so a woman wanders through life. Prevented from roaming around a central point, she made figures through her life like a bad ice-skater, like someone lost in a forest. A woman who roamed, traveled, and did not find anything; the womb that traveled within her body regularly discovered new continents. One only had to succeed in interpreting the unintelligible language in which the continent was addressing her.

Dr. Vámos spoke to Miss A. in a cultivated and pleasant Hungarian and asked her to translate for the esteemed guests that this hospital was among the first in the world to introduce "*Salvarsan* therapy," and that they were assiduously following other scientific discoveries.

"Miss Pappenheim is perhaps unaware that a few years ago, syphilis was successfully passed from a human to a monkey, and then to a rabbit, and soon we expect for it to be transmitted to other experimental animals. The twentieth century, my dear ladies, will be the century of victory over syphilis, over that unfortunate American plague that, as in the case of other poisonous ailments from the New Continent, such as cocaine and tobacco, wanted to knock beautiful Lady Europe off her feet.

Miss A. turned to Bertha Pappenheim and said:

"Dr. Vámos wishes to tell you how dedicated he is to his field. He hesitates to speak German in your presence, and he begs for your forgiveness. He very much appreciates German science."

Then Dr. Vámos said:

"Be so kind, Miss A., and translate for our esteemed guest that I am one of the few men in Budapest who is a member of the Association for the Interdiction of the White Slave Trade."

But Miss A. did not have the chance to fulfill this wish, for in that moment Dr. Zoltán turned towards the window and shouted:

"Now, now — where are you off to, Mrs. Feldvari? Where are you going, my dear? You are no longer a star of the stage!"

Bertha caught a glimpse of a woman with an enormous, meaty body and dark, oily skin. She was draped with a bedsheet over her overalls and was standing in the wide-open window and shaking a bar overgrown with ivy from the outside. Miss A. Wanted to inform Pappenheim that Dr. Zoltán Vámos had a quite highly regarded presentation a couple of years ago at a symposium in Berlin, but she was unable to make herself heard over the buzz of the women who had rushed over to pull away from the bars. The doctor's attention had already been drawn to a nurse who swooped in from the opposite corner where the door was located. She was yelling at a different patient:

"Mrs. Frank! Where are you going, love?"

"Now Bertha stared at the creature who, naked from the waist down, crawling down the hallway towards the door, pulling behind her, through a puddle of her own urine, a long silken glove like from a gala.

"Oda, oda!" Mrs. Frank said in Hungarian. "There, there!" She pointed her finger with suicidal self-confidence at an indeterminate spot where the wall and the ceiling intersected, as she raised her bony, blue buttocks into the air like a plucked chicken carcass.

"What is this travel fever that has seized you all of sudden, my dear ladies?" asked Dr. Vámos, quietly and tenderly. "Our guest is going to think that you don't like it here."

At the mention of her name, Bertha Pappenheim was overcome by panic: was the doctor going to turn to her at the last minute with this same ingratiating cooing and pull her into the cloying mire of the syphilitic community? He was a short, heavyset man, with the eyes of a child and the shoulders and hips of a woman; although he apparently did not like women, he adored their diseases. Disease was the mud in which he played and from which he formed his figures, his world, or more precisely, a colorful tittering foam.

"And these friends of ours have embarked on another grand voyage," he pointed out as he indicated a group of women who were hopping from bed to bed and wresting pillows and blankets away from each other. The beds groaned underfoot. They creaked and rocked like a raft that was breaking apart in the waves, and they grew tired and frightened, settled down next to each other, and combined into a soft heap of bodies and limbs, stared mutely at the two ladies as if encountering them on the open sea. One of them even waved to them from the water and was relieved to find out that they were not ghosts, like the doctor and nurses, and retreated under the covers.

"And you, Miss Klajn, aren't you going anywhere today? Dr. Vámos was knowingly, kindly addressing the consumptive dark-haired woman, whom Bertha had noticed right when she came in. She was the most beautiful Jewish woman that Bertha had seen in her life. She would mention her later in a letter to Miss N., the girl — do we remember? — was still stretching and twisting her shirt, which kept stubbornly sliding off of her shoulder. The quarrel with her shirt — with her shoulder? — was still in process when the guests entered the patient's room, but in the meantime it had accelerated and become invested with an almost seductive momentum. In any case her shoulder was scrawny, and the shirt, which had no buttons — did they fall off? Get torn off? — was too big. Miss Klajn had already completely lost her patience, and she fretted with her shirt, tugging at it more and more sharply, and unloading onto the ruffles sewn onto the collar a torrent of curses. The shirt, now in desperate condition, completely lost, bounced suicidally and flopped from her high, angular shoulder, and the girl finally ripped the off the ruffles with disgust, as if she were pulling a dead leech off of herself, and threw it to the ground.

Then she unhurriedly took off her shirt, folded her arms across her chest like after a job well done, and, dressed now only in a dirty pink corset in which her gaunt breasts floated like an ice cube in a glass, stared victoriously, serenely, and inquisitively at Bertha Pappenheim, who was stunned by this scene and gawked back at her. On the woman's upper lip could be seen a large red chancre like a glowing coal, which Bertha had not noticed at first. Sickness is like rage; it had in the meantime accumulated and accelerated fatally. The girl's black eyes were burning, and her cheekbones seemed to combust all at once, too, because the remaining color of her face and her neck had piled up there and, via syphilitic blister heated up and smothered her thin, depleted breathing.

The tuberculosis in her was like a ray of romanticism, of nobility in the general vulgarity. Her disease was beautiful; it bestowed on her the flush on her cheeks and the fiery darkness in her eyes. Beautiful death as a sign of reward. Even her silk shirt, too large for her and without any buttons, was beautiful in a romantic, treacherous, and rebellious way, and the bluish shadows, the rash on her neck above her collarbone cast a shadow over the proud, mysterious beauty of her face.

How was Bertha able to take this all in and describe it in her letter to Miss N.? If she wanted to see it, it would be difficult to describe it successfully in a letter. Now the wheels of the train unwound the entire story. The hysterical fit of the woman in the train was a continuation of the one at St. Roch's Hospital. All women were closely linked through the sisterhood of unexpected attacks, like with a password. The woman here was watching the window, the wall, unhinged, with the same horror and passionate feeling as if she were seeing something on her horizon the way those women did behind the bars. The small group of them on the several beds were bound together like on a raft in the middle of an ocean painted black with pathos. The girl had already forgotten her clash with the shirt; she hated her shoulder more than the shirt; she hated her emaciated breasts below the both of them more than her shoulders; more than her breasts, her corroded lungs; and more than her lungs her hollowed-out soul, which Bertha Pappenheim was trying to penetrate.

"Put this on," the nurse ordered. She picked the shirt up off of the floor. "And sew the buttons back on."

Miss Klajn, however, did not move. She wasn't cold. The question was: at what moment would the cube of ice melt completely? Even her face was thawing and pouring down her neck drop by drop.

"She already left," the girl said, with the ridiculously tall and matted hair-do. "She is still waiting for her beloved, the one she's writing the letter to."

"She's waiting for her beloved," hummed Bertha Pappenheim. She turned back to the window in the train car and the whole purplish scene in the letter. Bertha recognized the great tension of the being that was simultaneously leaving and staying. She could comprehend the drama of a body that wants to leave and the shirt that wants to stay. She knows the inhibition of traveling in place, that terrible encompassing of all contradictions, that tapering of consciousness through which immeasurable expansiveness is reached, that spasm in which all of one's life is contained, the spasm-embryo… the substitution of the embryo.

The girl in the yellow silk blouse on the adjacent bed could hardly contain her laughter; it regenerated like a cough and brought tears to her eyes. She pointed her finger at Miss Frank, who was tugging on the leg of the bed. Miss Feldvari was removed from the window. The women on the raft expected the doctor and his entourage to close the door behind them; Bertha stepped forward to do that immediately, before the others, but she heard a cry behind her and, turning around, saw a consumptive, black-haired girl who sat as if paralyzed on the bed, pointing her finger at some place through the wall and without taking her eyes off of Bertha, yelled: "The female continent! The female continent! The female continent!"

Miss A. accosted Bertha in the corridor:

"Oh, how those wretched creatures babble about some world without men, about an island of women or some such, a new woman, the Great Mother, the female messiah, or she-messiah, who will come out of Egypt to lead them to a new, female Utopia. Someone must have infected them with these childish ideas in addition to syphilis. But where, Miss Pappenheim, did you ever see a bordello without men? The Jewish women are alarming the other girls with their messianic ideas. They also seduced poor Dr. Vámos — with the idea that the messiah will be a woman. They convinced the Christians that Christ was a woman or that Christ had a twin sister. What they are doing to us is driving wedges between our legs. I just wonder whether that lady from Egypt is going to come wearing a veil and a burka or in the chiton of some pharaonic dancer? Or in the garb of the Queen of Sheba? Or — "and the woman drew roguishly close to Bertha's ear — "in the outfit of her royal highness, our Queen Zita?"

"The good doctor is an excellent venerologist but a bad psychologist. They have definitely gotten into his head, driving him crazy with their ever-sicker fantasies. Once he confided to me that he had discovered that *Salvarsan* produces a side effect, psychological symptoms that are different form classic madness. He named this syndrome "syphilitic messianism" and is preparing to report on his discovery at a symposium this spring in Graz. The doctor is a passionate teller of little stories from the life of a doctor. Miss A. inquisitively looked at her interlocutor with a fake feeling of guilt — and I'm afraid that this hypothesis properly belongs in the realm of his leisure time."

Miss Pappenheim felt herself targeted by this remark; she nodded her head, although it was unclear to her what she was agreeing with. She could agree that to her this room resembled some horrific brothel at the end of the world, on the rim of hell or even in it, from which all men had fled, been eliminated, erased, and the women were flourishing monstrously, malignantly, in their thriving, mendacious, dirty profusion, with their ragged hair-dos, flounces and ruffles and lace, and even more so their real, bonafide filth, their festering pimples and sores, all their suffering and illness and born and unborn bastards.

At the station in Novi Sad, a young man, nicely dressed and handsome, got on the train; a smallish group of friends or relatives was seeing him off with cheerful shouts in an unintelligible language that was probably Serbian. He immediately directed, in Hungarian, to the women who were once again playing cards, a few good-natured words that made them smile, though more reservedly than at the action in their card game. But Bertha he addressed, after a brief examination of her clothes, in formulaic German, with a heavy local accent. And then he asked, immediately after they had come out of the tunnel, for permission to open the window. Upon seeing her pale face, he remarked, as if off-handedly,

"The lady is apparently afraid of the dark. Do I have your leave to open the window a bit? We'll be coming to a longer tunnel between here and Belgrade."

Bertha sensed the sting in his voice, but she ingenuously thanked him for the information.

"I've been looking forward to that moment ever since Budapest." Bertha Pappenheim surprised even herself with how much freedom and relief she felt after the excitement of the tunnel. As the afternoon advanced, she withdrew into herself more and more, like an inexperienced hunter as he draws near to wilderness, to thickets and brakes and woods. Now her breath came freely, and she talked coherently, clearly.

"The first time I heard about the Balkans was when I was eight years old. There was a king who was murdered at that time in Belgrade. I remember my father saying: "They flat-out butchered him: several bullets and seventeen stab wounds!"

"Why did they need to do all that?" my mother asked, and then she herself uttered a word that sounded to me so terrible that I never dared ask anyone what it meant: "Balkan." I thought it was some blasphemous curse in Yiddish that I was not supposed to understand. I was her size" — and she pointed at the little girl.

She spoke calmly, with relief; to someone, however, who might have been in a position to track the tiny, unconscious changes in the expression on Miss Pappenheim's face, there might have been noticeable a certain look of severity and suspiciousness — perhaps fear and anxiety — in the glance with which she grazed — or lashed? — the man every time he, with his outstretched arm tactlessly cutting off Bertha's line of sight, pointed his finger at some point beyond the window pane and began explaining to the little girl, who was all of a sudden interested, stimulated, something in her maternal language. The look of suspicion would sharpen into something almost openly hostile, whenever the Budapest ladies would raise their eyes from their cards and direct their own gazes to the grayish horizon and innocently, drowsily, laugh at their inability to see what the child recognized easily and facilitate the connection between the little girl and the unknown man.

"In Turkish, the word *balkan* means 'steep mountain,' and the nature of people who live in the mountains is sterner and more vicious than in the plains."

These words caused her interlocutor's well-groomed mustache to stick its thin ends up like curlicues, while beneath them flashed, provocatively and seductively, a golden tooth.

"Your Bismarck said that Serbia is a small country, but when a person approaches it, like a curled hedgehog it spreads its quills in all directions."

At the moment they were crossing a broad, olive-colored river, which the man said was the Danube, darkness descended abruptly and the little girl gave a quiet shriek. Bertha realized that they had entered a new tunnel and she grabbed the child by the arm. The man, probably nonplussed at finding himself alone with the ladies in the dark, and fearful that he might be accused of something that happened in the dark, carefully cleared his throat and in good German said to Bertha Pappenheim: "This is how the Balkans start."

The tunnel was scarcely a hundred meters long, but after exiting it, the dusk on its southern end was denser than when they had ridden into it. Even as the train was on its way in, and the locomotive whistled, the Jewish woman with tuberculosis yelled something unintelligible. Bertha thought: "Yet again I could not make it out. An attack of hysteria. For a long time now she had not allowed attacks of this sort to overpower her completely, but she was sufficiently honest towards herself and she knew herself well enough — knew her whole life, her unflagging industriousness, agility, altruism idealism, exactness, her sense of strain, her comportment, her plans, her desires, she grasped, understood it as a unique condition of constant, but controlled, mitigated, diluted, sluggish but irremovable, incurable, indecipherable hysteria. And she grew accustomed to, almost accepted, this condition. But now it was as if the world were vomiting up, disgorging in front of her all of its tortuous, sick, and terrible knowledge. As if everything that destiny had come to know, in various ways, and it knew a great deal and, concealing itself also behind foreign languages — it hid from her, removed from her path. To Bertha's advantage or disadvantage.

At that moment, all signs pointed to a rebellion; it seemed that the patients were going to fall upon the visitors and Dr. Vámos, like actors charging from the stage into the orchestra pit and the seats, and crush, trample, and vanquish, the few remaining and most stubborn spectators, and swallow them, ingest them like a gigantic octopus run amok. Miss A. seemed to think nothing of this storm, as if she knew it was only a performance, and she continued chatting placidly with the orderly. Dr. Vámos was already whispering in German, liberated, into Bertha's ear about the successes of modern science; he mentioned Wassermann and some other figures, lab animals, a monkey, rabbits, and humming like a refrain, the way the wheels of a train intone, "*Salvarsan, Salvarsan.*" The black-haired Jewish woman with tuberculosis had by now removed her shirt entirely and, standing on the bed in a dirty corset that was dancing around her, she flapped it, as if to attract Bertha's attention.

Bertha feared the woman would hurl herself to the ground, while Dr. Vámos was just concluding a sentence, which she had not heard, with the words: "continent des femmes" or something to that effect.

"Do you know, Miss Pappenheim, I would say that messianism has taken root in this ward. I would call it syphilitic messianism. Prostitutes, especially ones with syphilis, believe that they are called upon to save the world. Or at least women's part of the world. You know, the circumstance that one does not have to die immediately, in the nastiest way, that for a certain amount of time one can delay death and avoid the nastiest variant of it, has utterly confused these unfortunates. As you might suppose, their savior is supposed to come from Egypt in the form of the Great Mother. Someone has planted in their heads the ideas of that childish Saint-Simonian named Enfantin. There are worse people, more destructive people...But these are revolutionary enough, and harmful. If I were not a writer myself, albeit just in a small portion of my free time —" And here he looked with anticipation at Bertha Pappenheim — " I would see to it that I somehow curbed that additional source of disquiet among the women."

Because he had apparently heard, wrongly, from Miss A. that the visitor was not merely a social activist and the manager of the Society for Returning Wayward Girls to Life, Girls but also a fairly distinguished German writer, he began to relate to her to the final little sketch drawn from his physician's practice.

Miss A. was close by and tried to come to her assistance:

"If the Messiah is a woman, then she would probably be here. If a man came, he would only bring them syphilis, children out of wedlock, misery, and death. The women here are saying that you have come from Egypt and that you're going to lead them away from this place," Dr. Vámos said. "If I understood correctly, they will not readily allow you to leave."

Then Miss A. concluded her conversation with the nurse and shut her little notebook in which she had been entering data for her report at the upcoming congress.

The nurse-janitor, a gigantic sexless, mentally disabled woman, in a white apron resembling that of a butcher, closed the outer door behind them. As she left the courtyard, Bertha Pappenheim turned around to confirm her impression: now, as upon arrival, if one looked beyond the presence of two or three unusual circumstances, the building standing in the depths of the courtyard partially covered in ivy, peaceful, almost dreamy, resembled, an educational institution during vacation, or at worst some kind of municipal hospital, or a boarding school or a seminary dormitory. But behind the creeping vines and the bars that covered up and adorned such buildings were the grim maws of darkness and filth and madness that flowed here from all the alleys of the city and its peripheries, delivering these miserable and monstrous female creatures and hurling them onto iron beds and bars and leaving them there so that like fish in a net they slowly suffocate, dying in the torrid vapors of their own fantasies.

"I really am afraid of the dark," she said calmly to the new arrival who found herself unprepared for this continuation of the conversation in this place. "You're quite right. But before now I've never been scared of the dark."

The man had just pulled out his stopwatch to check the punctuality of the arriving train. He seemed to have tired of chatting with the women; he stood up and helped them get down their packages from the netting before the train approached Zemun. Before Belgrade, coming out of the tunnel, the train passed the tentacles of a wall overgrown with remnants of last year's grass and tatters of soot-covered snow. Embarrassed by her own reaction, she wanted to say something kind, mollifying, in praise of the Balkans. She was surprised by the exaltation that hung above the river at the entrance to Europe like a dried udder, a contorted male member. Her fellow traveler no longer remembered his comment at the expense of the German lady and merely smiled affably, but he apparently remembered Bertha's remark about the Balkans as a male continent.

"Now, Miss, you'll see Bismarck's hedgehog at close quarters — but since this building was designed by a Viennese architect" — and he pointed his finger at the window, behind which the lights of the Belgrade train station glided and slowly came to a stop — "there's no reason for you not to feel at home here."

The ladies from Budapest had already buttoned up their garments and were looking nervously through the window for porters as the train pulled into the station. The man, whose name Bertha did not recall and perhaps had not heard uttered, touched the back of her hand while helping her get up from the seat. She shuddered and got goosebumps; she was cold. In the poorly lit station the train dispatcher gave a signal with his raised token, confirming that the tracks were clear for the express train going from Budapest to Sofia and Istanbul.

"Yes," Bertha said, "the Balkans are a male continent." A wave of heat passed over her, from somewhere in the small of her back and along her spine; in the cloud of steam from the locomotive, this signaled an attack of hysteria. "But I, dear sir, never feel in Vienna the way I do at home."

"Will you be spending a lot of time in Belgrade?" the man asked with great courtesy.

"I'm traveling on," Bertha Pappenheim said. But when she saw that her young fellow traveler was no longer interested (his eyes were tracking down his satchel and gloves, his newspaper) and gave no sign of being interested in where the middle-waged woman was going, she added:

"To the female continent."

The young man failed to seek any further information. His thoughts had already moved beyond the tracks and platform. Nevertheless, he was considerate enough to assist Ms. Pappenheim with the formalities of passport control and customs, and to help the lady into a fiaker in front of the station, which in turn bore her to the Hotel Paris, where, as she had hoped, a reserved room awaited.

CHAPTER SEVEN
THE WOMEN OF GALICIA

Mrs. Helena Gutman was waiting for the opportunity to bring the guest up to date on institutions for the protection of women and the schooling of children. The guest, Bertha Pappenheim, as if she interpreted Helena's anxiety at problematic news as curiosity and a request, was talking, forgetting about the food on her plate and the fork, paused in the air, within reach of her mouth:

"A whole band of territory from Wrocław and Łódź and Warsaw and Vilnius eastwards to St. Petersburg and Moscow, to the south over Lemberg, Brody, Tarnopol, Ivano-Frankivsk, Kolomea, and Czernowitz all the way to Budapest, is being despoiled by the white slave trade, prostitution, and syphilis," Miss Pappenheim stated (and she exhaled cigarette smoke along with that final word). "In Warsaw children and young girls vanish every day, and the general belief is that it's the Jews who are doing the luring, buying and selling them, and these accusations, unfortunately, are not completely unfounded. Mrs. Henrietta Arnt, who came from Wrocław to hold a few conferences and lectures, bought two children for three marks apiece. It's astonishing that not a single community, not a single organization or institution anywhere between Konigsberg, Hamburg, Breslau, and Berlin can be found to take them in and put them up. But that's why stillbirth is a daily occurrence! Along with infanticide. The noble fruit is suffocated or thrown in the garbage. The family rejects children born out of wedlock, Jewish orphanages won't take any more newborn bastards, *and all that remains is to get baptized or die*. Meanwhile, the figure that our unfortunate co-nationals cut is depressing. Even little girls exhibit a proclivity for perversion. Their desire for pleasure, sloppiness in dress are almost comical. Dissolute. It's no wonder, considering there are no schools or education for them. There is one elementary school with 1200 pupils, half boys and half girls, and at age twelve the children are finished with their education and they have to find work or hang out in the streets. The local physician, a Dr. T., holds that there are very few registered prostitutes, but many hundreds, and maybe even a thousand, surreptitious ones. The opinion is that they are not being recruited as 'girls in the feathers' in the brothels, but rather as Jewish servants. There are not many brothels, but there are hotels and other dens of prostitution that recruit young girls. The women dress tastelessly and conspicuously; the sight of fashionable, tight skirts on Jewish women in Galicia makes one nauseous. They live above their means, and according to the principle of 'filth in the house, rouge on the face.' Face powder and perfume they buy like oil and salt."

"Furthermore venereal diseases are raging and tuberculosis is very widespread among Jews. Working with silk, bristles, and feathers contributes considerably to this. The basic processing is done here: the carding, binding, the mixing. Of great importance is the fabrication of mouthpieces for cigarettes and cigars and of toothpicks. The heating of the raw materials on special slabs over containers of alcohol and molten coal releases harmful vapors. But breathing the air that is released when silk and feathers are sorted and scraped, that is catastrophic. The bottom line is that feathers and silk are an epidemic, aside from tuberculosis.

In Tarnopolje, I heard various unbelievable things about corruption among Jews. It was so widespread that they had to cancel the autonomy of the Jewish community, and a man seventy-four years of age was named by the authorities to take care of the most pressing business. There's a struggle going on between Hasidim, Zionists, and liberal Jews."

Practically all tea-houses, kiosks, and soda stands are little more than markets for white slavery. And, as if there weren't enough of them in Poland, day and night from Russia pour in rivers of impoverished girls, right into the hands of pimps and merchants. In the district of Podolia, she had a conversation with the mayor and concluded that the League would be useless there, because everything was happening at the train station. Therefore: an assembly point at the station. This would be impossible to organize with volunteers. The merchants and procurers can be pursed in the night trains, but there are also the forty daylight trains to consider. According to a police official, the girls cross the border under some type of pretense, whether in the daytime or at night, but they do not get out in Maksimov or any of the other small stations. Instead they ride on to Tarnopol, where there are agencies for steamship journeys and the like. She thinks that a collection center at the station would be less effective than a woman stationed in Volocka, someone who would have to be suggested by the Russians so that they didn't consider her an Austrian spy. Basically what's needed is to get to know the situation on the spot, if one truly wants to achieve something. She tried to obtain an appointment for Volocka, through the mediation of St. Petersburg, or, more precisely, that of the princess of Saxe-Altenburg. In matters such as these the Central Committee in London or the local one in Berlin would have to lend their support... Of course, the person would have to be supported by the police; without that, it's all a farce. She hopes that her engagement will not be frustrated. The merchants and the girls shift for themselves in a hundred different ways; their channels are in place and difficult to ferret out; trains are their hunting grounds; one might say that the rail network of Eastern Europe exists first and foremost in order to deliver these wights to brothels and public houses, transporting them to the cobblestones of Thessaloniki and Istanbul.

The little spoon of *ajvar* in Mrs. Gutman's hand pulsated, veered from the accustomed direction and rendered its contents onto the white damask tablecloth.

"Oh, God," groaned Mrs. Gutman, and with the tip of a knife hurriedly removed the dollop, but a stain remained as a warning. Hundreds of thousands of unfortunates will be here, so to speak in front of their very eyes, transported south and to the Orient and abandoned, consigned to their implacable fates.

"The small amount of social work being done is fragmented, split between Jews and Christians, without any real effect, poisoned by frictions and disagreements."

"European cities are like festering boils," observed Haim Azriel (the French language in his mouth crumbled into guttural clumps and Dr. Savić was simply not able to translate for Josef and Helena Gutman). More and more new niduses burgeon forth, and new tentacles of female frenzy, vice, filth, and sickness spread in stealth. Not much more water will flow down the Sava and the Danube, and especially the Vistula and the Dniepr, before all of the streetwalkers infected with syphilis (like the woman who washed up by the walls of the Kalemegdan, at the Old National Bank building), or with hysteria and all sorts of nebulous cravings, will swarm in packs like dazed eels to their secret gathering places; they abandon fathers, brothers, sons, and leave in their wake nothing but a sinister infectious trail. Where are they heading? What is the objective of this deranged exodus? Why do they keep their destination a secret, that promised depot to which they will deliver their misery and their bastard children? I don't believe they even know the answer themselves, but they flock relentlessly towards this mysterious goal, and I think we should meet them halfway and help them in every way. Women have earned the right to have their own special hell/purgatory."

Haim hesitated briefly, as if he saw for a moment that this "proof" could be a joke, a little trick or and lure, and then he surrendered to the wave that was ultimately going to tear him away anyway. Haim spoke briskly, with an almost female feverishness, fervidly, passionately (with a passion the likes of which had never been on his face in Flora's presence). Haim's attractive masculine face abruptly took on an unnatural, feminine softness, and an incomprehensible rage or enraged impotence came over his face—and Flora's enemy or rival was trying to emerge, vying painfully to break out.

Miss Pappenheim sat rigidly upright in her chair. Dr. Savić, who had stopped his simultaneous translation when the strange outpouring had begun, observed Haim Azriel with curiosity, and then said with an ambiguous smile:

"There are hints of agitation and general excitement in the female population. Plato the ancient believed that hysteria originates when the womb, stricken by distemper, began to travel through a woman's body. And when the womb grows tired and stops, then the woman herself sets forth and continues moving."

"The specter of hysteria is haunting Europe," said Misa Gutman.

Grandfather Gutman said that in Galicia, Budapest, Thessaloniki, and Istanbul all the sick and old brothel women are isolated and then shipped to some distant country in the East, where they can ail and die in peace. Or the women themselves, when they feel death drawing near, scarper away from the brothels and streets. They pay the merchants and the brokers and flee to somewhere in Alaska, Siberia, or some country founded expressly for them.

"If a religion wants to become big and important, it has to sacrifice women," Misa said.

"Europe is sensing the need to cleans itself of women," added Haim. He took a snuffbox out of the inner pocket of his suit. "Women feel this themselves. There exists an act of self-cleansing. Women who're sick, contagious, instinctively get out of the way, in the same way that women among primitive peoples remove themselves from the community when they menstruate. Women clean a house with filth in it, and by disease they get rid of themselves, too. It's the new method. Absolute. A method for the ideal housewife. Like a bee that, pricking an intruder, turns completely into a sting, and thereby concludes its life, so the absolute housewife cleans her home and ends up purging herself as well."

Mrs. Gutman picked the tableware as if she were counting it.

Bertha Pappenheim laboriously raised her eyes and lifted her fork from the walnut cake, which like a tall sedimented wall doused with sweet rain, a heavenly sherbet, rose up impregnable in her dessert plate. She gave Haim Azriel a tired look.

"Why were there no women on Columbus' ship? So they could sail faster. They had to step on it. Invading territory, opening up new worlds, is just like the conquest of women," Haim went on. He looked mockingly at Bertha again.

Flora wanted something more from life beyond being discovered and conquered. But she shrank now into her chair. The awareness and knowledge of syphilis was for her like a nightmare through which she had to pass in order to comprehend the world, to earn the right to think about freedom. As syphilis was slowly being defeated, so its replacement spread — the fear of syphilis, which was actually the panicked fear of free love, of the spirit of these new times, the fear of liberation from fear. Syphilis as a burden balanced by freedom and progress, and syphilis as the price of progress, of the journey. She believed she had emotional syphilis. She wanted to say something about this movement, this journey, and about how women even when they sit immobile at the dining room table with their eyes locked on their plates and when they bustle back and forth between the kitchen and the dining room, are in fact *traveling*, circulating; their legs carry them towards a goal which is unknown even to them, they run, distance themselves from all humiliation and disillusionment, but they cannot escape their distress, only circle around it and postpone (and wish for) the moment when the door to hysteria opens, and they close their eyes and abandon themselves to the river of women and children who are fleeing, delivered over to their own legs, their journey and the trackless wilderness on the way to their nonexistent, submerged destination... (to a new self?).

Flora believes that Bertha Pappenheim is the woman who is traveling to the Land of Women.

CHAPTER EIGHT
THE BIRTH OF HYSTERIA

It was after three a.m. and Bertha Pappenheim was seated at the escritoire in her room at the Hotel Hungaria. Actually, Bertha had just stood up from the table, organized the papers, pasted shut a letter to Miss N., and deposited it into her handbag; she went into the bathroom and came back out with her teeth brushed and her face washed. She hesitated for a moment and then pulled her silk robe closer around her. Shaking from cold, she sat back down at the writing table.

Raising the mirror on the top of the secretary revealed all of the small compartments, drawers, boxes and cassettes with keys and without, little niches. The secretary almost opened up on its own, turned inside out, offered its soul with relief, revealed its female nature. Beneath fake marble panels, in the bright interior lined with cherry wood, lay exposed, beneath the now transformed scene, the meager contents of a woman's *nécessaire*: the cobalt blue of a powder box, like a dusty little lake, on which floated a big pink powder puff, two porcelain jars with pomade and *eau de cologne*, and on the back of the lid there was, of course, a mirror in a shiny, thin frame adorned with a delicate garland, lighter in color and a little smaller than the decoration on the exterior of the secretary. Everything was finely crafted down to the smallest detail. The planned and faceted world of male imagination, language, and needs (and habits), retreated before the simplicity represented by the mirror, confronted by a face — any face — of a woman. And now when the true, inner nature of a hotel writing desk became self-evident, the defects of the table also became explainable, that is, of the object that is, in its function, male: its insufficient depth and height, the clutter of its drawers, the coldness of its marble plates and a few other incongruities that were hard to detect but not pleasant for the user and not conducive to writing. It was obvious that this was not a writing desk at which one could compose serious, scholarly, or business letters, articles, reports, but was made expressly for short journal entries, travel notes, brief messages to friends, and above all for postcards, which were to be found in one of the drawers of the desk, with drawings and reproductions of a Budapest panorama on the front, along with scenes of *csikosok*, cowboys, from the Hungarian *puszta* on the back.

It's already 3:15. "I have to get in touch with Miss N.," she said out loud, and those were the first words spoken in this room for two weeks, not counting the porter's "Thank you." In her voice all of a sudden: panic, worry! After she'd put the letter to Miss N. in an envelope, there remained in the air something that did not dare remain there. Bertha picked up the pink powder ball. In that moment she felt like a schoolgirl, at the chalkboard with a sponge in her hand. Looking into the mirror before her, she plunged the ball into the powder and then it became obvious that the letter she wanted to write at this hour of the night was not composed of words like the one already in her bag, but of light pink powder and rouge and lipstick. For only swirling pink powder could express the speed and unexpected twists and turns in the current that she felt in her hands, on her neck, and in her stomach; only thick eye-liner could convey the squall, the lightning-fast clouds that obscured the horizon and rolled along her nerves, and Bertha Pappenheim, yielding to that *internal storm*, subordinating herself to it, stunned by the pressure, takes her powder-box and with a swift, angry dancing motion pours out the pinkish powder over the frozen, stunned mirror and over herself, and then with the lipstick the color of raw meat, with a vigorous spiral plots on it the vortex that is her face. Tiny convulsive twitches spread across her shoulders, and her loose hair that until then was restrained, clenched by hairpins, combs, those thin yet cruel and unrelenting retainers, keepers of tension and intense strain — now, with them suddenly, recklessly pulled out, the hair, still a little rumpled, woolly, frees itself like a forest of springs, of tiny silver lightning bolts around her head, and the features of her face — her still beautiful face — the line of her eyebrows, the network of tiny wrinkles around her eyes and mouth, every hyphen rises up and straightens into an exclamation mark: Hysteria! Hysteria! Bertha's face as it is — still — shown by the mirror, her shoulders and body that can also partially be seen in the round mirror, give notice, and are preparing to overflow and pour out of her skin. Freedom for hysteria! All of Bertha's life in the past three decades, her activity, her social work, all of her specious freedom, her security! — they were based on the suppression, suffocation, restraint, and masking of hysteria. What had over the years (or forever) seemed to be abstinence from love, from emotion, pleasure, was in fact abstinence from hysteria. That ancient cure (or "cure") for hysteria — it actually stopped her life then. Everything stopped then. Oh, that perverse Greek! The one who realized that hysteria is the wandering of the womb through the female body! Her, Bertha's womb, in that distant year of 1882, just when she had matured and begun (in hysteria) to wander inquisitively, fitfully, insolently, flamboyantly, rebelliously, self-sufficiently — and aimlessly! — hysterically! — all of a sudden she was cunningly halted on the threshold of her great adventure, of her great life-journey. And there she stood, abandoned, forgotten, tethered, confused and secured with illusory health for a full three decades. But now there was a signal! The moment she ejected her last egg, on the verge of real (senescent) futility — it quivered, that old uterus, it unhooked itself and shoved off on its final hysterical journey.

Where? To the female continent? To the surmised continent that had just sprouted from the sea — the land of free hysteria! The continent that women discovered when they were guided by their wombs. A promised land, to which one arrived, for which one searches, not by faith, nor by atonement, but by insight or imagination, but rather by excess, through messianic hysterical sobbing, protest, and spasms, cries.

The mirror, Bertha's nightgown and peignoir, and the parquet floor polished to brilliance all around and the air above Bertha and her hair — everything was strewn with a hysterical pale pink powder. Hysteria shouted out the form and color, like the initiator of life and female existence.

Every journey is an attack of hysteria.

CHAPTER NINE
FEMINIA

That evening, on the third and final day of her stay in Belgrade, Bertha Pappenheim was a dinner guest in the family hone of the merchant Josef Gutman in Majka Jevrosima Street. The afternoon session of the congress of the Federation of Women's Associations of Belgrade had run long, and the guest from Frankfurt had not wanted to miss the opportunity to advocate energetically for the revocation of the shameful, pathetic, and stupid regulations that treated prostitutes in pensions and brothels like prisoners, with no right of free movement, and so it happened that roast goose was a bit more roasted than Mrs. Gutman had intended.

An hour of waiting seemed longer to the family members than it was, not because they were especially sensitive to issues of punctuality or other such European manners, but because in those times of sharp and unpleasant isolation from Austria-Hungary and Europe, and of baleful winter and muffled danger that blew up the Sava and Danube towards the Habsburg Empire, every contact with European Jews delivered to Serbian Jews a tiny bit of hope, of anticipation, at least for those who were Ashkenazi. It was encouragement that things were not going to go altogether wrong, at least not more than intra-Jewish relations required.

Thus the host Josef himself and his brother Solomon as well as their distant relative Haim Azriel expected, as successful merchants in leather and wax that, as members and shareholders of the Export Bank, where Haim served as a member of the board of directors, that this middle-aged woman, who had set out alone on this journey through the Balkan countries with the (purported) goal of tracking down and closing in on the white slave trade, had enough powerful patrons and financiers, that powerful Jewish community in Frankfurt and Vienna, and that her presence in Belgrade could be used to reconnect the ties cut during the customs crisis known as the Pig War.

"If that Viennese, Maximilian Kraus, invested in Serbian markets even during the crisis," asserted Josef, rotating a pocket watch in his hand like a compass, "there is no reason that new sources of Jewish capital won't open up for their Balkan co-nationals, now that the crisis has passed."

Josef's spouse on the other hand awaited Miss Pappenheim with wonder at her mission and her courage, since she was immersing herself in these risky peregrinations around the Balkans, but the hostess was also appalled to think that this worldly Jewish woman of dubious religiosity would deliver herself at the dining room table of a welter of stories about Jewish whore-houses and illegitimate children.

When the guest made her way in, at around 8:30 in the evening, in the company of Dr. Savić, moving energetically and with a lively demeanor that hid her fatigue, opening up immediately to the members of the family, Flora at once sensed that this was the kind of person whose presence always broke new ground, something that in turn encouraged motion, change, other events, calling upon matters to take shape, happen, show themselves in their true light and therefore often to be received with mistrust and unease, fear, repulsion, or frequently with expectations that are too high. Moreover, the current moment was such — stretched too tight — that even the presence of some lesser personage or some insignificant occurrence could part the curtain that concealed a real condition, real feelings.

"By the way, Belgrade is an exceptional city," said Bertha Pappenheim. "I feel exceptionally good here." And while she took jam and water for the third time — Mrs. Gutman explained the Serbian domestic custom to her — and brought to her lips big, translucent amber cherries from a little crystal bowl, she felt that this was the moment to gratify her hosts and praise their city. She was only on her third day in Belgrade and Serbia; the next day she was due to travel on to the south, to Sofia, but what she had seen had mostly been encouraging and she was going to do all she could to convince, at the very least, her collaborators and friends in Frankfurt, and possibly the broader German public as well, that these people whom Europe called "nose-cutters" were in fact an intelligent and liberal-minded society, very partial to Europe — even if in certain things a bit anachronistic — and future-oriented. Still, the cobblestones and sett were frightful and she could barely walk through the city. People in Vienna had warned her about this, but nonetheless she preferred walking to being jostled around mercilessly in a vehicle. At any rate, a person can't get to know a city without pounding the pavements. "Well, cobblestones are cobblestones."

"Fortunately, the crisis is over, and there is no reason why the paths of capital cannot converge on us again here in Belgrade," said Josef Gutman. "Besides, according to the new agreement, a passport is no longer even required."

"Oh, yes," noted Miss Pappenheim agreeably, as she set the little spoon back in the dish with water. "That will very much facilitate the human trafficking."

Actually the guest did not hide the fact that she sought out these events and fora. Otherwise she would not have packed such a large number of them into two or three days and their descriptions into ten minutes. For a short time before they sat down for supper, she, not wasting any words on the reasons and motivations of her journey — as if she were informing her well-versed colleagues — she told them where all she'd been and whom she had met in Belgrade — and with what results. Straightaway, on day one, she had visited the Austro-Hungarian consul who in his office had had since November a very important petition about the trade in women, and then she saw the German consul Dr. S —, who had to admit that he was considerably better educated and for heaven's sake more competent than his Viennese colleague. He directed her then to the Chief of Police (*Shef de suerte*), who had spent eight months studying in Frankfurt am Main and was now endeavoring to present the guest with specific figures about prostitution in Belgrade and Serbia. Beyond that, she had met with the exceptionally kind Dr. Savić — here Miss Pappenheim leaned amicably towards to her companion — and with a police official she visited the Jewish quarter next to the Danube and toured five public houses, which she had to say were newly constructed and appeared to be quite profitable properties. "It's interesting to note," she said, "That Hungarian women make up the majority of the residents of these boarding houses. And there are very few Jews. In

Budapest and Galicia, unfortunately, things are very different."

She gave her report to the Gutmans in a tone like she was speaking at a congress, as if about facts that they did not know. Regarding the number of prostitutes, however, there was no agreement. The chief of police maintained that there were about five hundred, while Dr. Savić put the figure at around three thousand.

She counted off visits to numerous prominent and influential ladies, especially the spouse of a respected colonel who took her on a tour of an attractive home for children, and she talked all about the women's association founded thirty-five years earlier by Queen Natalija, which had made available an asylum for elderly women as well as a women's newspaper. Miss Pappenheim had, to be sure, succeeded in meeting also some other people, had also made the acquaintance of a Christian family, the former mayor, a minister, and a professor whose last name she didn't remember, but all the more striking in her memory was the taste of the sweet rose petal jelly that they served her in that home. Of course she also visited a Sephardic family and learned many new things since, to her shame, she knew nothing of the Sephardic community and also had not imagined that in a city as pleasant as Belgrade there could be such sharp divisions between Sephardim and Ashkenazim, and indeed real animosity and quarrels about the new synagogue, an otherwise attractive and harmonious building. She briefly described her half-day excursion to Pančevo where, according to an earlier arrangement, a telegraphed message from the consul to the captain of the border police, she was given information about the question of human trafficking. Unfortunately she had not been able to meet with the captain himself, but his assistant did apprise her that of the three hundred girls who had come to Belgrade from Romania to look for work, through the frontier post at Torontálalmás, fifty to sixty had disappeared. All trace of them had been lost.

"In any case," she said, "the Association for Women's Safety (*Secour feminin*) from Frankfurt is supposed to get in touch with the authorities in Frankfurt, because that is a matter for the National Committe for Hungary, in whose prerogatives the Frankfurt association does not dare intervene."

On her way back Zemun, she managed to convince the accommodating official in the captaincy of the need for the harbor authorities to engage an agent for the detection of the trade in women. At three in the afternoon, she was already back in Belgrade, dead-tired it was true, but able to listen to a presentation at the women's conference, speaking up herself at the end and appealing indirectly to the responsible authorities in Serbia to renounce the outdated and silly regulation that called for the charges of the *pensions* to be treated as prisoners. "I talked about the case of one twenty-year old woman who had not seen the light of day for two years."

"Every conversation about women," Haim Azriel said in French, aware that in addition to the guest Flora understood that language, "should begin with a feeling of indebtedness, with an offering to the shade of one man, a tragic genius whose work was unconventional and without compromise and bleak in an irresistible way, stirred minds and spirits in Vienna and other European cities, and who killed himself in his twenty-fourth year (the age I will reach very shortly), because he had not seen a way to deal with the woman in himself, nor with the woman outside of him, and who was over and above that a baptized Jew who did not know what to do with the Jew in him and with Jews in general, not seeing any solution, or exit, from the 'Jewish question.' Miss Pappenheim might personally have known, but surely has read, her unhappy and ingenious fellow citizen and co-national Weininger, whose work was tireless and uncompromising, and gloomy in an irresistible way. Bearing in mind his trenchant and hotly contested judgements about women, Miss Pappenheim probably in her heart of hearts herself suspects that her labors with fallen women are in vain, and perhaps outright useless. He himself thought that perhaps merchants, whose work Miss Pappenheim wants to prevent them from doing, are in fact a doing a very useful task. When the English, several decades ago, in the desire to cleanse their country of convicts, transported them to Australia, they did not dream of setting up some new world. Perhaps every brothel or harem is the seed of a new continent."

"And that is how women disappear," said Miss Pappenheim with a smile.

Mrs. Gutman did not understand what young Azriel was saying. With her eyes, she asked Dr. Savić to translate for her. The doctor translated for his hosts, prudently and carefully, selectively, but the French word "*bordel*" had international currency and his hostess averted her gaze more and more. She knew, by dint of her suprapersonal female intuition, what her daughter had perhaps not sensed: that this sudden, inexplicable hatred, this intolerance and disdain on the part of her future son-in-law towards fallen women — about whom she herself had a very set opinion indeed — had other roots. She understood that this man, who was in fact not meant to be her son-in-law, was already packing his bags. That from his raspy words uttered through the smoke of a cigarette (which he had insolently lit before the end of the dinner), and through the silver cigarette holder and out of his little paunch, her daughter's world was crumbling. As was her own, too. Flora, although her French was poor, had no doubt that the cynicism and sudden hostility in Haim's behavior concerned her directly. At first it seemed that Haim was joking, that he only desired to embarrass the guest, to pit his exaggeration and ugliness against Bertha Pappenheim's own exaggeration and ardor and unrestrained activism and to needle Flora, who perhaps up to then had been reserved and bashful, and who had clearly not shown him well enough how much she cared for him despite everything, regardless of her parents' warning.

Dr. Savić would have liked to bring everything back into the realm of medical science and practice, but after half a day in the company of women activists, and two glasses of wine, he had neither the strength nor the will to do so. And he was sorry to cork back up Haim's vehement Brueghelian phantasmagoria; he regretted stopping, with one stroke of his blade, the excruciating outburst of Haim's hidden inclinations and obsessions, which were probably going to separate Flora and him definitively, and show her that nothing could be expected from this gloomy man, neither love nor respect, nothing save the vertiginous passion of complete opposites, explosive intolerance, and pangs of conscience. Therefore Dr. Savić had no choice but to add fuel to the fire, to provide everything that had streamed out as emotion, caprice, *idée fixe*, with scientific explanation and support, so that what was supposed to be the medical side of things turned into the continuation and support of Haim's fantasies. Considering his poetic nature in which he sought solace and aesthetic compensation for the emotional wasteland of a loner, and the loss of life and hideous scenes on which he choked every day, the doctor kept up the game without a single twinge of guilt. He was aided in this by his sense of humor and his long muted nature as a dreamer and poet who controlled his pragmatism and thereby made his work somehow bearable.

Did Haim Azriel, deferring the fork with a piece of goose, look at the guest, graze Flora also with his gaze, and announce: "All of the scum should be shipped off to some deserted island full of frogs"? Did Flora herself then, before the end of the gathering, disappointed and clearly aware that Haim had irredeemably distanced himself from her, drinking too quickly her glass of wine, verbalize the idea of the female continent, about women, and about a promised land in which they would find salvation from male cynicism and violence, and about a woman, a powerful and irresistible person aware of her mission, the female messiah, the she-messiah, who would summon her fellow-sufferers, as the story goes?

HAPTER TEN
FLORA'S VISION

Flora Gutman saw the approach of dawn on the still dark ceiling of her bedroom — her watch said it was just after three — but she was simultaneously in her room and in a boat, one of the boats that, carried more by the tide than its paddles, was drawing near to the shore. The vision compelled Flora to be outside the picture and in her bed, staring at the ceiling across which the gray morning is spreading, and simultaneously to be in one of the boats. She was tired, and she still needed to paddle to land, and then an urgent and weighty task stood before her; before the sun rose completely and the work of day commenced, she had to see to it that this vision stopped and solidified, so that a new country was explored, named, elaborated into a story, and the story into a plan, some purpose. She had to think fast. If she closed her eyes and abandoned herself to matinal faintheartedness, bitterness, and hopelessness, the new shores (a new continent) will float away like a life vest that was within reach but then was forced away by a current in the water, or by an unexpected wind. She needed to populate this vision swiftly, organize life inside it, transform it into a notion, a clear idea — and if necessary, into an *idée fixe*, a firm and enduring subject of reverie.

CHAPTER ELEVEN

THE SECRET LIFE OF BERTHA PAPPENHEIM

The hysterical circle

Over the course of her life, Bertha Pappenheim had often been afraid that ideas about hysteria might reveal themselves to be unreliable. What if the illness of her youth were now to come crashing down on her head again in her mature years?

Her life was not her property alone. Like a prisoner, a Mason, or laboratory animals. There was that segment of life that belonged more to someone else than to her. Her recollections were not entirely her own; they were more like documentation, part of a joint archive and the history of a global disease. She did not recall it all and did not feel it was obligatory that she remember that segment of her life; the fear that she had forgotten it did not gnaw at her. In her current life, she did not rely on it. It was not her experience alone, but it was a shared one, one for which she was not responsible. She didn't have to deal with lessons as consequences from that segment of her life. Let others do that, and let science do it, or art. It made no difference. Accordingly, Bertha Pappenheim had no obligations towards Ana O. (nor towards those to whom Ana O. was obligated and to whom she remained indebted). For all that, Bertha Pappenheim did consider herself to have duties to many other women.

She helped the doctors to remove, to extrude hysteria, her disease. But with the relief, the cure, also came an emptying, an impoverishment. A feeling of defeat, of being deceived. Exploited.

Later, for decades, she devoted herself to the struggle against social pathologies. She could be found everywhere women were in spiritual or physical pain, in places of female suffering and humiliation. These places had an irresistible draw for her. Like a perpetrator, a guilty party, she turned up at the scenes of all kinds of crimes against women, sites of humiliation and squalor. That's how it was, or at least it looked that way. But weren't things actually the opposite of this? Was she not, with her presence, her intercession, provoking distress? Did not her suppressed, apparently cured hysteria, unconsciously and in a concealed way, elicit hysteria, illness, and misery?

Everything: social pathology, the white slave trade, prostitution, abortions, infanticide, and the like, was the domain of hysteria, a manifestation of it. The hysteria of her youth had possessed a "pure," medically recognizable form. Through poverty, through prostitution, hysteria—medically recognizable — fanned out malignly from its usual channels and altered its characteristics, mimicked other things, concealing itself, taking the form of social pathology, and it relentlessly extended to the whole of the healthy world. A mass hysteria that grips individuals in isolation is an *invisible carrier* — THE VIRUS OF HYSTERIA.

Why had Ana O. appeared thirty years earlier? What did this part of her personality want? What did it mean to convey by means of hysteria? Why did Ana O. speak up? Breuer and Freud did not look into that. They accepted the therapeutic message that Bertha Pappenheim placed in their hands. Ana O. of course had her assignment, her mission even; otherwise she never would have been heard from, manifested herself. What did she intend to communicate? What did she want to create or destroy? To distract or attract the attention of science, and even of the broader public, from something, or to something? Breuer and Freud obscured the issues; everything was grist for their mill, and Ana — so it seemed to her — obeyed them for her own benefit, but she forgot her message, the message of her sickness.

Breuer and Freud probably caught hints of this. That's why they gave her the ordinary/mythical name Ana O. That O, the egg of a primordial beginning, contained in itself all diseases and all medicines, starting points and destinations; it was a target, ground zero, the first and final continent, it is the ocean and the Orient and an island in the ocean. Omega, *the last letter of creation* (the alphabet), omen-augury, premonition, doom or fortune, good or bad harbinger: O as in oxygen, without which there is no life; oasis (in the middle of a desert); lens (through which other people see the world); Odysseus-woman, the first woman-wanderer, an artful and elusive she-builder at whose suggestion the Trojan Horse was constructed, a cunning returnee who alone emerged alive from all temptations; occult; *oculus* (eye); the shape of a halo; orbit; orgasm…The name Ana O. is a synonym for the great global (universal) hysterical circle (from which there is no exit), the hysterical eddy, vortex, which pulls the world in and swallows it.

As in an individual, so also do large, mass hysterias circulate through time and space. Hysteria is not merely a small, individual maelstrom: large circular and spiral hysterias arrive from history like Haley's Comet, every few decades or centuries, and they rattle nations and states. It's a hysterical spiral path. A great global, cosmic paroxysm, during the course of which came to exist a country, a continent, as a symptom of some deep-seated neurosis. That is how America originated, and Australia, and that's how all lands of the sun originated, all utopias, holy lands, promised lands, countries of women, countries of children, all countries that are thought up, warm and cold ones, tropical and/or snowy ones.

Every one of them has its prophet and its messiah.

All of these lands are born of volcanic eruption in an act of geological hysteria. Human hysteria is the initiator and the foreshadowing of the global, geologic, and political hysteria that creates new countries, islands, of the sort that previously existed only in the darkness of human subconsciousness. These are not the mass hysterias noted by chroniclers, but rather a weird, puzzling chain of individual hysterias.

Bertha Pappenheim would sometimes, abandoning herself to linguistic hysteria, forget her German and speak only English, or read French and Italian texts out loud in fluent English. In addition to linguistic displacements, geographic ones happened to her as well. She mixed up places and spaces, even the countries of the world, and she didn't know where anything was. Through mystical ecstasy one arrives at knowledge; through hysterical ecstasy one reaches substantive, deep ignorance. At times she could not imagine any goal, or orient herself. A wandering Jew, whom the ground beneath her feet is dodging, and who, everywhere and nowhere, recognizes her goal. A goal that eludes and deceives her. A movable target, a mobile and fugitive homeland, a wandering promised land.

Hysteria as a wandering uterus. A uterus as an ornamental feather on a hunter's hat.

Where was she traveling? What is she dreaming about? A country of free hysteria? Is that the meaning of a female utopia, the utopia bound up with a woman's state? The place where illusion, woman, and hunger are all the same: *le fama, le femme, le faim.*

The discovery of actual continents is accompanied by the discovery of imaginary ones. Accompanied by "geoimaginates." In the world there must exist a balance between the real and the imaginary. Disturbing the balance results in disasters, above all wars, upheaval, and natural disasters. Is the female continent real or imaginary?

A country has a geographic, magnetic, and female/male pole. There are female and male regions of the earth. She was familiar with the "magnetic idea" of Madam Blavatsky and how it held that in certain parts of the world women were numerous, and in others men, and that gender magneticism was in operation. And sexual diseases, the spread of syphilis, corresponded with the sickness of the earth's poles, with the creation of a certain magnetic imbalance.

But if there exists a female region/pole on the earth, there also exists a female culmination of the world. As in the act of love, so in the life of the planet, the end of the world is not, does not, have to be everywhere and for everybody simultaneous.

Traveling around the world on ships, men discover worlds. With women, the womb can, if it is not destined to give birth, decouple from their insides wander unhappily around the world of the body. Instead of a fetus, a child, which has no clearly charted direction or route, which grows and sets out towards the exit, towards light — the barren, empty uterus, detaches itself in a dark hour, when it has gotten too old and its ties to the other viscera have dried out like petioles in the fall. Thus: the womb that *is afraid of fruit and flees from it*, roams about and upsets body and soul, the brain, sowing turmoil, rebellion, and fear.

That's how Bertha herself felt on this journey of hers: like a uterus that is wandering around a body. Hysteria was an evil, sick substitute for pregnancy, birth. Hysteria as alternative, unsuccessful exchange. During the attacks of hysteria that are great, collective, mass, continental, global — there are created, and they surface, false islands and continents, false oceans, false states, false cities.

Through the window of the train, just before Belgrade, Bertha caught sight of the full moon: "Women will return to the moon," she thought. Then she told the little girl who was watching her with great interest. "The moon is a female planet. Woman came to the earth from there," she said, remembering the film by Georges Méliès.

If women are not able to fight successfully for their rights and a full life here, then they need to *leave for some other place*. To found a new world, a state, in which they can set things up as they should have been from the very beginning.

Instead of a male CITY OF THE SUN, they will establish the CITY OF THE MOON, of the amazing moonlight of the Far East. That aquatic city, INSTEAD OF AN ISLAND IN THE WATER, will be the world OF WATER that rules the islands.

CHAPTER TWELVE
HYSTERIA IN THE HOTEL HUNGARIA

"If God is female," said the asthmatic Jewish woman, "or at the very least had a sister, a mother, or a wife, he would not allow this. This kind of nastiness. A bearded Messiah will not come. Neither true ones nor false ones will know what is going on with us. All that's important to them is preventing the Great Mother from coming out of Egypt and pulling us out of the shit. But she will come. All of my sisters know this, from Warsaw to Istanbul and Alexandria. She's going to lead us to the New Country."

"The New Country is already full of whores," answered one of her fellow travelers lying calmly on her bed. "There's no room."

A third: "Women are disgusting. One should drive them to the ends of the earth. All of us, including me."

A fourth: "They sell us to all comers, to brothels, so we don't group together and rebel, organize, raise the flag of revolution, set up a republic. Human traffickers and the police work together. All men are united in their fight against women, and the women fight amongst themselves. The police and the merchants, the thieves and the pimps are in cahoots. Whores and ladies of refinement — they are not. They fight amongst themselves to the bitter end; they come to blow over men."

A fifth: "Unmarried Jewish women kill their children as embryos to spare them a nefarious birth. Once they're born, there is nowhere they can run, nowhere to hide.

Women don't have a country for themselves. Every species has a hole for itself, a nest, a lair, where it can take refuge. Women are always on their way to someone, always in someone else's bed."

How is it that all of a sudden Bertha understood Hungarian?

Among the women a lively conversation was being carried out, quarrels, and the atmosphere was fiery, but Bertha was not able to understand what they were talking about. Occasionally Miss A. came over to her to pass along something of the contents. And later, when she was leaving, she told her that the women were complaining that they were going to be interned here forever, for the rest of their lives, so they were going to run away, etc. And that one was ranting about some woman, the Great Mother, who was going to come from Egypt and lead them, ultimately saving the female sex. It became clear to Bertha that she understood a great deal of this, a lot, almost everything, and that the asthmatic Jewish woman sometimes, through her coughing, spitting into a large napkin and concealing what she'd expelled, she repeated in Hungarian — the Female Continent — several times, and Bertha understood. She had memorized several superficial words during her stay in Budapest: good day, please, thank you very much, the menu, please, the check, please... And then these women suddenly tied together, invoked a string of words, dozens, hundreds of other words that of course she'd heard but had not tried to memorize. Or, she understood the conversation — not by means of language but despite language, because it was in all likelihood carried out in some un-language, or in a universal female language with no words, no dictionary, that was innately familiar to all members of that sex. In the way that there is a language of insects, there is also a language of women, a universal female language that is not aimed only at seduction, at sex and motherhood, but for social intercourse, agreement, the mutual understanding of women. The language of intuitive understanding by which, however, certain abstract concepts, ideas, can also be communicated, and not merely emotions and instinctive urges.

What happened in the hospital? Just now while writing a letter to Miss N., imprisoned in the solitude of a Budapest hotel, it seemed to Bertha that she grasped the meaning of what was happening, of this flow of events. In fact this was because she did not know the language. If she had known it, her attention would have been dispersed, and she would have tried to find her footing in the initial, surface stratum of conversation/events. But this way, with the distance of a lack of knowledge, she could encompass the whole scene with her powers of perception — and understand it. She grasped it right down to the level of every single word. The literal and the hidden and the figurative meaning of the words — all were simultaneously clear to her. It was a moment of revelation.

After three decades, she had a premonition that she was on the threshold of a discovery. This was not an attack but rather a vision, bursting open slowly like a soap bubble, typical views of the world, time. Not an explosion, an eruption, but an implosion, a retraction into itself, *an attack of hysteria on the world within her.* A hysterical fit as communication between women, a medium for the transmission of a message, of the most authentic realizations about the world and herself. Through hysteria the most important knowledge is carried. These are discoveries, emotions, like current between completely different women who are almost complete strangers to each other; it's the power of mutual *understanding* of the world. Bertha Pappenheim in her hotel, through an attack, saw *again* and *grasped* in its full significance the Jewish woman's attack of hysteria. Both reality and dream, and birth and death, childbirth, sexual intercourse, dying, are only forms of an attack of hysteria. The universe is hysterically bent, slumped over.

Bertha's entire life since her youthful attacks is a hysterical explosion in slow motion, a fission that has masked itself as something different — as an active, useful, enterprising life. Hysteria is the initiator of life, and a form of female existence.

The decay of radium is a slow-motion attack of hysteria for an atom. An atom of helium, or radium electrons and protons from itself in a fit of hysteria. Hysteria is a language in which women and nature converse and interact; it is the sole meaningful and comprehensible answer that women have to this male world. Every discovery made by a woman, as Madam Curie showed, is a mode of hysteria. Hysteria is not just a restriction but also an expansion of consciousness. *Only the hysterical characteristics of the world are given to a woman upon inquiry, upon discovery, and they are foundational.*

Why did God not send a single female messenger?

Abraham, Moses, Buddha, Zarathustra, Christ, Muhammad. In addition, there won't be any new male messiah coming, but if he does, he will bring pestilence, misfortune for women, disease and madness, syphilis and death. The she-messiah will come from Egypt. That's the place where the sun is born. She will come, clad in silk gown or looking like the Queen of Sheba.

Bertha had these realizations in the train. At the end of the tunnel she said: "The Balkans — they are a male continent." And from that sentence, through the entrance into light from darkness, an understanding appeared to her; it was the idea that had tormented her the previous night and all of that day, like unbearable physical pain.

At St. Roch's Hospital, in the conversation of the syphilitics and lunatics, Bertha gained most of her experience with the many types of female misery. The Budapest prostitutes in the fever of their self-discovery said or did everything that their fellow sufferers from Galicia, Łódź, Warsaw, Vilnius, Lvov, Minsk, St. Petersburg would say or do, but they did it in a less objectionable manner, with a dose of their own peculiar elegance, style, and even irony.

Of course, Bertha Pappenheim's presence not only activated but also arranged the whole process, gave it a kind of choreography. A repressed, secret segment in the persona of Bertha Pappenheim always drew forth, pushed to the surface repressed content found in other people. There exists a certain amount of collective unconscious in the human race. New material pushed into one's unconscious provokes — through a system of linked thinking/linked subconscious — the eruption from someone else.

With Bertha herself, an attack of hysteria went on and on (at low voltage), uninterrupted, like a secret world. Her body jerked as she lost the use of language. She was drenched in sweat, with a feeling of insecurity, and she was overcome by a more or less conspicuous crisis. But no one noticed how long the attack endured, just as no one recognized the inner sickness behind the luster of her eyes. In her spasms was transpiring not only a restriction, but also an expansion of her consciousness — other, different realizations.

She now felt a vague need to write a letter now that would be distinct from all of the others up to this point, the informative, clear, pithy ones that were exhaustive on important matters. She needed to write a letter — not a poem, not a narrative — but a letter, somehow different, female, written so to speak with red lipstick and the black eye-liner, with foundation: a letter that would write itself, which would, like scent and powder, fly forth and liberate itself from the little bottle, from her hands, her lips, from her lungs, from her head, which will swarm from all of these sources and hiding places and spill onto the table in front of the mirror, a letter that she could not stop and control, that will contain unpredictable words, voices, through which will burst in self-emancipation words had been hidden or suppressed in her, until now. Events will come to light, events of which she had not been aware, which she had forgotten, or which had not finished happening or had been prevented, held up before they found expression. A text, a letter, that will erupt uncontrollably, like a cry, a shout, a fit of hysteria.

Actually since she set out on her journey, she had been vexed by a feeling of pressure inside her, and she was preparing for an attack of hysteria. What else could this restlessness be, this cramp in the muscles of her neck and shoulders, this twitching, trembling, vibrating, in her stomach? After thirty years of self-control, sensibleness, goals: a crisis of the balance sheet, a reappraisal at the gates of old age. She comprehended that years and years had passed, that there was no going back. Not even in the spiritual sense. Even if her previous curiosity were re-channeled, and aimed in a specific direction. She was still pretty. Perhaps prettier than in her youth. The only thing to which she could return was her youthful hysteria. In fact, she understood that the unease, the unspecified, headlong longing for youth, was the longing for her youthful hysteria. The only open door in time leading to the ineluctably vanished youth. Her life had two beginnings: a "natural" one — birth — and a second one, after the appearance of the article by Breuer and Freud. That second life was since O., ab Ovo, etc. In that one word, that one name, her erotic life was used up, her fate rounded off. Or: with that O. commenced a life apart from her. A life without hysteria, without qualities. Life co-exists. It did not include, but rather excluded, the real content of her life, her personality. Until that event (and that book), her life proceeded inside of that circle, that egg. Since then the interior was abandoned, forgotten; life survived outside of the O.

Was it not a certain *envy*, a craving for repressed sexual desire, deformed and disguised, at the bottom of Bertha's fervid "struggle" against human trafficking? Didn't she secretly *yearn* to *be given*, sold, so that in a direct, sexually intense and harsh way, there would be a *repeat* of and a *conclusion* to what had started in childhood, that familial drive, and then the *driving duress* of the doctors, psychoanalysts, for sexual contact to be carried out in the crudest way manner way possible only to then, later, absent itself?

Her potential fight for the *freedom* of erotic life, replaced by the struggle against sexual enslavement, lack of freedom, but a lack of freedom through sex. Her unfreedom was *the unfreedom of sexual deprivation.*

St. Roch's Hospital from the outside looked like a colorful lunatic asylum, and the colorful foam of death, of a deeper, different, distinctive sickness as if they were "covering up" syphilis: tuberculosis, hysteria, astounding obesity or extreme exhaustion, ailing livers and kidneys, bloating and false pregnancies.

Miss A. says: "They have elaborate fantasies. Their brains are disintegrating. One says that somewhere at the end of the earth there exists an island or a peninsula on which only women live, and to which men have no access. These are the daughters of the Queen of Sheba who have no need of men, who are free of them. They are grown daughters who will never become mothers; every one of them is the last one on earth, or they admit men into their presence as slaves, so they can have children."

Starting then, when she was visiting the hospital, Bertha was afraid of having an attack of hysteria. She was experiencing all the same things as before: great strain, shaking, the need to scream — or numbness. But instead of her, the attack would start up in a Jewish woman or someone else.

That same evening in the Hotel Hungaria, she emancipated herself for the first time, and now she was going on without shame or aversion; she felt, after thirty years of self-discipline and sensible living, a call — or was she herself sending out the call? — from the magma of her subconscious, the chaos of the hysteria of her youth. "Up!" she shouted, pulling and plucking out her hair, forcing it to stand up despite gravity: "Up!" She expelled her anguish, the things that had been completely hidden for years, so it could burst forth and spill out in a luxurious, untethered fit of hysteria. Freedom for hysteria! All her activity, all the freedom for women — and her own (illusory) freedom — was based on repression, abstemiousness, suffocation, and the camouflaging of hysteria. What came across to her as abstention from love, from surrender to her emotions, or to pleasures, was in actuality the abstention from hysteria! That previous, long-ago "descent" into hysteria — it had in fact halted her life (all of a sudden now she'd become aware of this). Everything had stopped then. (Plato had known more about women than any woman did.) Her uterus, as soon as it had matured and begun to wander inquisitively, brazenly, and ungovernably — or aimlessly — was stopped.

And not only hers; once a close friend of hers had said: "Since the time Bertha emancipated herself from hysteria, the entire world has been shaking without interruption, in a fit of hysteria." Was this internal or external, a personal or a global hysteria? Or was it — not a journey and not an adventure of the uterus but simply its slow descent, stacking, repose, like settling soil deposits itself as sediment.

Behind her is a double bed; from the "male" side of that bed an emptiness watches her. The walls have aggressive, sarcastic masculine eyes/ears. Hysteria is the only adequate response of a woman to a man's world.

Bertha hunches over the secretary and is writing a *hysterical letter*, an invitation to a journey:

Miss Bertha Pappenheim has finished all of her business in Frankfurt. Did she do everything that she could have?

No.

In Frankfurt, Miss Bertha Pappenheim has been engaged for over thirty years with the Society for the Protection and Care of Wayward Girls and the Foundation for the Assistance to Fallen Women. Now, separating herself from these tasks, has she set out across Europe and the Balkan countries to make personal investigations?

No.

A long time ago, things that an outsider would call peace and order were introduced into the story. Along with the illusion that what was gone was gone forever, and that this applied to the past. As if Bertha Pappenheim had made a clean and formal break from the past — and Bertha Pappenhim sat at the small escritoire in a hotel room. She is anxious, and the night is slipping away?

Yes.

Bertha Pappenheim is a modern woman, but at this hour of the night she hates the present, and she is inclined to withdraw into times past. She senses the approach of an attack. The yearning for times past. A yearning for a fit of hysteria. Yearning is attacking on all sides. Is hysteria attacking her?

Yes.

What does she know about hysteria? Hysteria is a journey, a wandering inside the walls of her own body, the search for an exit.

No!

The fear of a fit of hysteria?

No!

The desire for an attack?

Yes, yes, yes!

Her one link to her youth. A substitute for life. The uteruses of all women are in collusion. They roam in order to connect women. Great movements are afoot, wanderings, the migrations of women, mass hysteria.

Bertha Pappenheim and Ana O.

Young Flora was beset by impatience that was even more pronounced than usual, but this impatience did not center so much on the arrival of the guest as on signs of favor that she expected, for which she hunted, in the words and eyes of young Haim Azriel, whom she silently called her fiancé. Haim's behavior had become so unpredictable, so moody and out of harmony with Flora's expectations. Haim had come into their home as the friend of Flora's older brother, Misa Gutman, and gradually inserted himself into the plans of Josef Gutman. Hope was born for a future partnership despite the reservations that Josef had about Sephardim.

Haim's interactions with Flora were those of a bashful boy, someone naïve and reserved, who has no idea what kinds of feelings and expectations he is awakening, but the eighteen-year old Flora, regardless of her genuine inexperience and reticence, was intuitively suspicious of his shyness; she had certain painful presentiments with regard to his truthfulness. The whole family, aside from her, considered things to be taking an apparently natural course, which would, after Haim completed his law studies in Budapest, have its resolution. The young woman was the only one who knew that there was no natural course of events, that the supposed signals for which she hunted on his face, in his actions and words, meant about as much as the moving, palpitation, and rustling of leaves on the nearly bare twigs and branches of the chestnut tree beneath her window. If the signs had not been there, would that absence have indicated security, the certainty of his affection, or would it have signaled the absence of feelings and intentions on his part? Perhaps the arrival of this energetic and unusual European woman as a guest would be a good sign, or a bad one — they would see about that. Maybe in her presence, for some reason unknown to Flora, the true significance of Haim's behavior would be revealed and in the presence of a witness who, as she expected, knew a great deal and understood everything, things would show their true colors, and she would judge the situation in her own heart — in all probability she would not have access to his. She had a feeling that this enterprising woman who would be sitting at their table naturally belonged to those who could influence the course of events, who speed up that course or slow it down, challenge it or stimulate it. Where else would she draw the strength and stubbornness for her ventures?

As for Haim Azriel himself, he was probably the only person in this slightly expanded family circle who was pleased that the guest was delayed, because he had just revealed to the hosts a few delicate particulars about her past, which he had picked up from reliable sources in Vienna: Miss Pappenheim, he hinted very discreetly, the woman they were expecting, was actually no other than the famous Ana O., whose early-onset hysteria was the foundation stone of those celebrated methods of psychoanalysis, that chimera that rests on seismically quite unreliable material such as female hysteria. But wasn't it just indicative of this so-called women's emancipation movement that was apparently advocated and practiced by women who were, for the most part, hysterical by nature?

In her youth this woman, when she was nineteen, so terrified, with her hysterical passion, the esteemed Dr. Breuer who had agreed to treat her, that he fled pell-mell, relinquishing even the entire field of psychoanalysis, the essential mechanisms of which he had foreseen, to his practical-minded collaborator, the spry Dr. Freud. Bertha Pappenheim was traveling in order to produce hysteria in herself once again, to produce just the feeling or a trace of youth, the running of moribund people and the projecting of the dead into life.

Anxious that the lady might turn up at any moment, Haim Azriel talked more quickly, more rapidly and hot-bloodedly than he had ever spoken before about his studies, about a single issue of the law, or even about one of the Alpine peaks he had conquered during his vacations — or about his feelings for Flora. He enjoyed his statements, his words, to such an extent that he abandoned himself to his own voice, and his irony and feminine feverishness indicated how enamored he was of the subject, but also of the object, the person about whom he was speaking: love and lascivious intimacy, affection and repulsion, an entire spectrum of — contradictory — feelings. He ran through an entire scale — as Flora did when she was practicing piano — and tried out, as he prepared each and every portentous declaration, the whole register of his voices and the emotions that had been concealed up to that point. It was the exaltation of his being. The things about him that had been beautiful and masculine abruptly acquired an unseemly female softness. His rage, his shadowy side, took on a feminine profile. Of the altered lines of his face, a woman broke out, an enemy and a rival; in front of Flora emerged a hostile and opposing figure.

Flora was scared to think that this face might foreshadow that of Bertha Pappenheim.

CHAPTER THIRTEEN
PSYCHODRAMA WITH HYSTERIA

The body of a woman is an island. The uterus is the one fixed point, the brace; everything else flows, is in motion. Her heart throbs to the left and to the right like the pendulum on a wall clock. Her lungs flap, almost imperceptibly, like the wings of a heron above a pond. The blood streams in her veins like ocean currents around a continent. Let the woman lie or run — that flight of the lungs over the ocean speeds up or slows down, but the situation is always precisely the same. Even when in a panic it ascends too high or collapses right down to the surface of the sea, the uterus stands, so to speak, untouched by the storms of the everyday in its mantle, shrouded in moonlight, like some internal island that has a different, parallel flow of time, another climate, its own destiny.

But when a thought gets stuck, her soul sticks to the ground, or her eyes shrink back and her gaze becomes fixed, her belly sags — then the uterus gets going, cuts loose, and starts wandering around her body. That's the way, since the time of Plato, that uteruses have roamed. An organ that wanders while thought is petrified. The woman remains stiff and silent, or she screams.

Miss Bertha Pappenheim knows, thinks she knows, why she has set out on this journey. In Frankfurt she achieved what she could, founded an association, and the circle of her protégées was gradually broadening. Now she was starting to check personally in the Balkans and the

Near East on the condition of women in peril and the operation of the organizations that were supposed to protect them. Her personal emphasis and special mission were the fight against the white slave trade and the sale of Jewish children.

But now it is already evening, and she is seated at the small escritoire in her room at the Hotel Hungaria in Budapest. On the marble slab the purplish patterns swirl beneath the shimmering table lamp; they become agitated, are stirred into waves. The letter to Mrs. N., just now completed, sways before her tired eyes like a rickety raft on the waves.

Her womb's journey will conclude somewhere else. She will not return home to Frankfurt, for in the life of an individual, a woman, a womb, there is no way back, just a greater remove from the beginning. On every journey her uterus has a destination of which her mind is unaware.

An empty womb in search of fulfillment.

CHAPTER FOURTEEN

AT THE GUTMANS'

Bertha Pappenheim said that, unfortunately, the Jews' enemies have concerned themselves a great deal with Jewish issues, and this most often entailed employing the methods of the Russian tsar and the Cossacks. She herself, regrettably, had also had painful experiences with both Jews and women, above all with Jewish women, in Eastern Europe, in Galicia — and this she had seen with her own eyes — in the Balkans and in the Ottoman Empire, in Thessaloniki and Istanbul — where Jews were dealing in Jewish women and acting as their procurers.

Miss Helena tried to bring the conversation back to noble actions: the Circle of Serbian Sisters, Queen Natalija, the Jewish Choral Society, various cultural topics involving women and Jews, but Grandfather Solomon chimed in on the first topic with a story, about his recent return from Jerusalem no less. There, with his own eyes, he'd witnessed a scene in which a drunken Jewish prostitute was distributing money to children while prophesying university calamity and the ruin of the children. "Miss Tea is inconsolable that such an unimaginable scene is possible in Jerusalem, but I say to her again that such a scene is, to me, equally painful in London, where it is imaginable." He himself founded an organization, a little *cercle*, which was collecting money for Jewish prostitutes to be transferred to some third location.

"Prostitution is not the only tribulation," said Bertha Pappenheim; "in one city on the border between Russia and Galicia, Jews are selling their own children with no compunction at all. Despite many departures from the rules of behavior before marriage, there are few Jewish children born out of wedlock. Old women, doctors, *medicins et les faiselises d'anges* — they're on hand to destroy life in embryo, and even newborns… The role of Jews is ignominious in the trafficking of children and women. I can confide this in you, since you belong to this people."

The conversation was conducted partly in German and partly in French, and it was translated from both languages for Helena into Serbian, Yiddish, or Ladino while she alternated between briskly offering the cold, creamy salad known as "*urnebes*," clearing away the bowl used for soup, and passing around the stuffed goose (already a bit overdone) and roulades of diced giblets topped with horseradish sauce, and for anyone who wanted it, the *ajvar* that she loved so dearly; but Haim lightly slid the plate with the sauce to the side and pulled towards him only the cold roulade that he liked so much, and, crossing his legs, blew smoke in Helena's direction. She in turn suggested they go into the salon. And he said, almost in a shout:

"Why hold back merchants from doing their work? Jews in Palestine buy land hoping to establish a state for themselves. Now I hear from you that they are selling their own women. Every Jew is a peddler. If there's nothing else, they sell their women and children."

Bertha Pappenheim acted as though she hadn't heard this.

"Last year the police in Egypt, hunting for minors in the official and semi-official brothels, uncovered seventy-one such cases. One child was four years old; others were between six and ten, and the majority were ages ten to sixteen. Last year also the police prevented the disembarkation of sixty-four underage Jewish women in Port Said. In the view of these authorities, such numbers should be multiplied by ten. The Zionists care nothing about this issue. It does not correspond to their program or number among their interests. Nobody worries about the fact that it might be more necessary to find a land of salvation for fallen Jewish women and for Jewish foundlings, bastards, superfluous children."

"The earth has two poles," Haim added with an ironic smile. "I'd let the ladies pick one. They already have their associations, alliances, policies, their law and their history, their philosophy and literature, and tomorrow they will have their science, their church, and their state."

"The idea of some far-off land is the subconscious desire *for problems to back away*," Bertha said measuredly. "For them to be recognized, named, and localized as the other. Distanced."

Dr. Savić said it was true that the world apparently was turning once more to its female side, something that he, in contrast to Haim, considered fortuitous. It seemed that theoretical sciences of the most contemporary kind were, as far as he could tell, dropping the aggressive, masculine principle of cognition of the nature of things, and striving more and more to avoid injury and endangerment and, especially, to avoid altering circumstances during the examination of the object at hand, the phenomenon under investigation. As he spoke, Dr. Savić looked at Flora Gutman, more with his soul than his eyes, fearing that his very gaze could change something fundamental in the perfection, purity, and harmoniousness of that being. Everything he'd seen in the hospital was diseased, morbid. He was scared that his "infected" glance would mar her innocence, taint this beautiful creature. He was a good Christian, sincere in his Orthodoxy, but ultimately was more fond of, devoted to, and partisan towards the Virgin Mary than to her son and the rest of the Trinity.

Grandfather Azriel said he'd heard that in Galicia, Budapest, Thessaloniki, and Istanbul all prostitutes and women in brothels who were sick or too old were culled and shipped to some distant country where they ail and die in peace. Or the women flee the brothel themselves, bribe merchants and sailors and flock to somewhere far away in the Far East or Alaska or some other country he couldn't name, in order to free themselves from the terror of men, merchants, and pimps and every other kind of abuse, at a great distance from brothel life. And, by the way, while they were talking about roaming, he would love it if the lady could use her influence over his son Miša, to get him to dispense with his psychoanalysis and other Jewish sciences and persuade him to be a good doctor, perhaps even a gynecologist, obstetrician, or surgeon.

Bertha, visibly upset, responded that she did not get mixed up in such things, that she took care of abandoned girls and orphans.

"A medicine with new features, *Salvarsan*," Dr. Savić noted placidly, "is going to be used to treat all women and men. But in the opinion of my colleague in Budapest, Dr. Zoltán Vámos, this new medicine also has side effects. There are indications in support of a hypothesis about a wide-ranging agitation and mobilization of women in this part of the globe. All of his wards and charges, and, according to him, many others across Europe, and even some well-educated young ladies, were feverishly awaiting their messiah, some sort of Great Mother, a she-messiah, a woman of great beauty and wisdom who would be coming for them, out of Egypt, rescuing them from the power of men and guiding them into the promised land of deliverance. The messiah-woman, this great physician from Egypt, by a simple touch of her hand will cure them of syphilis and thereby demonstrate her power. And then the healed women will leave with her for far-off Egypt or some other land in the East where no man will ever set foot. A female messiah, a sister of Moses. It is the right moment for a woman to come — after so many males, Messiahs in Judaism. Her name is not known, but every woman, at least a part of her, hopes that she herself will be the one."

"There's nothing new in this," Bertha said. "This female messianism derives from the Saint-Simonism of Enfantin and his theory that the fiascos of Jewish history are rooted in the unshakable male rule of the Hebrew God. If women cannot fight to achieve their rights and have full lives here, then is it not more natural for them to establish their world somewhere else, a state in which they can set up things as they should have been from the very outset? Instead of a male City of the Sun, they will found a Female City of the Moon. These ideas are being spread for the most part by educated and unhappy people."

"Not just by them," added Josef Gutman, who up to that point had been peacefully gnawing on a turkey leg. "There are persons who, without being aware of it, carry in themselves, in their veins and brains, the secret delight and fire of Jewish mysticism and the Kabbalah. Therefore, along with patent mysticism, there also exists latent mysticism. These are people from the middle class, merchants, bankers and brokers, plumbers and tailors, as well as doctors, and people rich and poor, the educated and the totally unschooled, adults and children, men and women (very frequently women), who transmit the germs of certain lore and ken like an infectious disease. Or it's more of an inclination, a weakness, susceptibility. They transmit it surreptitiously, the way a disease spreads, to their offspring, but also their neighbors, acquaintances, lovers, husbands and wives, the way tuberculosis is transmitted, and venereal diseases and catarrh. The custodian in our building, Bela Dajč, you all know her, half-idiot that she is, she preaches about a happy future, pandering for a pittance the poor girls from the countryside to whom she rents miserable little rooms. Supposedly her son came home with these ideas from Paris or somewhere. Over time these sick fantasies begin leading normal, everyday lives, in an irony of fate accepted also by intelligent people who make them happen."

"Syphilis is the disease of the modern era," said Haim. "America sent a message to us, in revenge, via Columbus' sailors: take it easy with the conquest of new continents! Move slowly with the conquests of the new era of tomorrow! Every new continent or part of the future is a festering chancre that will infect you. The future is invincible. The future always beats us to the draw; it feeds on illness."

"Syphilis is a disease of whores and conquerors and those who subjugate new worlds. It is the ticket to a new world," Miša Gutman said. "Syphilis is the basis of utopia, of messianic lust."

"I heard a Jew say he believed that syphilis arrived from America as a punishment for old Europe for all the pogroms, the bonfires on which they burned our ancestors," Josef said.

"The perturbation of prostitutes is like the perturbation of rats; it hints at bad times to come. Epidemics of women's diseases, of women's fear, hysteria, and madness, are always omens of a universal cataclysm or danger. Women have premonitions about wars, floods, and earthquakes. Women seek their own salvation, a way out of time. Wars are imminent. The human race will survive only if women find shelter in a safe place. That is the female continent," Bertha observed.

"I wonder only where that Egyptian lady will take all of the streetwalkers and their bastard children (probably only the girls?), all of the underaged pregnant girls, the wretches who've been bought and sold, all of the suffragettes infested with hysteria. All across the cities of Europe these new tentacles and this female pestilence sprouts, and they spread in secret like syphilis. Frankfurt, Nuremberg, Munich, Warsaw, Minsk, northwards to St. Petersburg, all the way south to Alexandria, women spray the blue continents, like festering chancres, with their sick desires. Streetwalkers and their packs of bastard children, like migratory birds or dazed eels, abandon their fathers and sons, husbands if they have them, and tear off to their promised hinterlands, leaving a contagious trail behind them. The Egyptian woman still has not communicated with them, betrayed the secret of where this New Australia will be, this disgusting warehouse where all of their illegitimate children, poverty, and woe will plunk down — yet the women are already careening towards this secret goal. From corner to corner, from square to square, from brothel to brothel and bed to bed — they are already whispering to each other the code-word, the enigmatic name of their she-messiah, and the name of their destination, their new island of Cythera, the country of love, *terra erotica*.

The presence of the guest from Frankfurt not only did not constrain the tantrum with Haim's mad imaginings, it actually encouraged it. At first Flora believed that this was some grim joke by means of which Haim, revolted by something else entirely, wanted to bewilder and overwhelm the guest, even more than he wanted to lash out at her, Flora herself, who had for too long been too reserved, bashful. Or was it that till now she had not shown him with sufficient clarity how much she cared for him? But as his speech wore on, the young woman felt that this grim joke — if it was a joke — was definitively driving them apart. Flora was dazed by this torrent of words, and panic seized her when she thought of Haim dragging down with him all of the women, members of the association, prostitutes, and those who'd been bought and sold, as he watched their guest with intense, sardonic delight. She could already foresee that moment when he, Haim, in his bitter fervor, and his hatred, or his illusionary hatred, would stand up from the table, race out of their apartment and their future life together, and at the first corner, in the first brothel, mingle with the women about whom he had been talking with such loathing, and whom he definitely desired more than her. And she could see this torrent of words sweeping

Haim away and casting him out among all of the suffragettes and prostitutes.

Miša Gutman, who had thus far uttered only a single sentence, now seemed roused by Haim's bilious address, and he raised his hand:

"Every Jew who declares himself the Messiah is in fact craving upheaval, conversion. Examples: Jacob Frank, Shabbatai Zvi. And every woman who awaits her she-messiah in fact wants to turn into a man. Or at least the prude wants to turn into a whore, and maybe vice-versa. The lack of courage, the indecisiveness, and the impossibility of achieving this results in hysteria. That's why women and Jews are hysterical, because they can't change their spots."

"Prostitution is a Jewish disease," he said, with a sharp glance at the fifty-year old guest. "The brothels and unlit streets of the Balkans and Levant are full of our co-nationals. And, sure, the procurers and human traffickers are of the same tribe. You're going to see this yourself, if you care to look. But you won't be able to explain this with social misery and similar materialistic reasons alone. The majority of human illnesses can, in my opinion, be reduced to one single cause, and that is hysteria. Even many infectious diseases such as syphilis are spread according to the principle of hysteria. And hysteria is, whatever Mr. Freud claimed, a female illness. Female and Jewish. This is a matter of disease, miss. And prostitution is, at bottom, a manifestation of hysteria. You know Plato's wise theory about the womb traveling around a woman's body, causing symptoms of hysteria. When women move from hand to hand, from bed to bed or city to city, what else are they other than hysterics?

Miss Pappenheim blanched.

"It seems that not even I am immune," the young man said on a more conciliatory note, "and that until recently I myself was perpetually on the road between Belgrade and Vienna. Anyway, what are all these mighty Jewish exoduses, if not expressions of this great unfortunate malady… All Jewish heroines have been hysterical. This has sometimes, as you know, brought momentary advantage to their people. Both Esther's hysterical revenge and Judith's risky hysterical heroism. And the wives of our progenitors in the Bible were hysterical. Was not the longstanding barrenness of Sarah, of Rachel, not of hysterical origin? And is not giving birth itself a type of hysterical fit? If you ever take a peek into a delivery room, you'll confirm that this is so."

Miša was speaking in a falsetto that at every moment was capable of springing up in his throat and spilling forth, stretching out and crumbling like a glacier. He was almost shouting and at any moment he might fragment, along with his voice. Josef Gutman arose from the table, holding aloft a piece of *kitnikes* on a little fork, as if he were about to hurl it at the impudent young man. Flora was crying, her face sunk in her hands. Her mother had already left the room and at that moment they could hear her shouting at the cook.

Dr. Savić, who had visited the Gutman residence before, listened with discomfort and simultaneously some degree of fascination to the young man with curly, dark hair who was looking up and then back down in strange convulsive movements, holding his head slightly askew like a violinist performing some Paganini with diabolical bravura. Dr. Savić did not dare disagree openly with the young man who was sleepwalking into raptures, for he was familiar with the habits of this house and the positions and roles of Miša and Haim within it. And had he dared, he would not have contradicted him, although he saw that the young woman sitting across from him was suffering, for him, in an odd, paradoxical way, as a man of practice and — why not say it? — of science, a man who despised and considered himself the moral enemy of old wives' tales and balms and salves and the corresponding paranoid phantasmagorias, was all at once entertained, intrigued, even suddenly unusually attracted to this strange outburst. This was a fantastical construction that abruptly, somehow, lifted up off of the earth, through the alchemy of lies, all of the abominations, the terrible concreteness, materiality, the horrors of the nasty disease with which he was confronted every day, that buried him in work, pressuring and polluting him. This alchemy involved a magical reversal, a mixture of paranoia, hysteria, conceit, obsession, and raw lies, that metamorphosed, transformed things into a myth, a vision, prophecy — in every sense something that belongs to the past or the future but least of all to the present. Thus, he did not rise up openly in defense of women's honor and common sense. Instead, turning to Miss Pappenheim, he said:

"In our Serbian language, the words 'infection' and 'conspiracy' sound rather similar. The treatment of syphilis is also the treatment of ideas. I think that the idea of a female continent has called forth a real explosion of prostitution and venereal disease. Investigations will bring to light what kind of causal connection exists. Because of this, I believe that my esteemed colleague Dr. Vámos is right when he says that *Salvarsan* has effects beyond its field of therapeutic effectiveness. It outstrips this therapy, and liberates a person not just from disease but also from the compulsion to prostitution, a more complicated malady. You said that there's still a law in force here that forbids girls in brothels from leaving the premises. A woman does not dream just of a female continent; she mastered her own meretricious dreams, the desire to flee from herself and her man, and she directly tackled her restlessness, fear, dependence. She isn't waiting for the Messiah, for he will not be anything different or go anywhere new. She only wants to get out of the darkness of her room and out of a bed hired for the hour. In a hospital, in the ward for venereal diseases, we still have not seen the end of the of atypical rebellions and female violence. And although they are all without exception homeless, they can no longer return either to the bordello or to the street. They sneak out, they escape with some trick or excuse, and they simply disappear — as if the earth swallows them up."

Young Haim Azriel was listening with galvanized attentiveness, not noticing the look of absence on the face of his future fiancée.

"So that's how women vanish," Miss Pappenheim commented with a smile.

Mrs. Gutman had long since stopped eating. She directed a hostile glare at the cholent on her plate and dashed every few minutes into the kitchen to help Roza, even though the walnut torte was already prepared, plated, and ready to be taken out to the table. But she began getting up less and less from the table because of the risk: without her there, something even more unpleasant might occur. She was powerless; she did not know how to fight back against this conversation, how to get involved in it and change its direction. But she sat there at the table protecting some customary arrangement of people, cutlery, dishes, and other things, like a gatekeeper, a guardian of her crumbling world and its morals. It suddenly seemed to her that Bertha Pappenheim was, by the end of this evening in a peaceful, middle-class home, amidst the bowls and little serving dishes with chicken in aspic, *ajvar* with cucumber topping, goose-liver pate, regurgitate all of her garbage, an entire heap of smutty inside information about Jewish whores and whore-houses in Pest and Galicia. Before her departure for the south, she was "airing her dirty laundry." Her husband was trying to head off this distasteful, unworthy subject with some information about politics or banks, trying somehow to put these wicked flights of fantasy back on the track of common sense, as if he still saw in Bertha the agent of some Frankfurt banking institution:

"I don't know how things stand in the lunatic asylums and brothels of Europe, but everything is fine here. Life has stabilized; it's more secure. Especially for Jews. We are climbing step by step; our people are winning others' trust, and there are more and more of them in profitable businesses. In domestic and foreign firms here, there are already around twenty Jews. In Belgrade you already have several banks in which there is strong Jewish influence and although this is profitable, at placcs where their money is maturing such as the Merkur Bank, they set aside something also for the poor. They take up collections, especially for marriageable girls."

Bertha Pappenheim listened vacantly — even though Gutman was shouting — to these notifications of Jewish banking activity and dividends, but she couldn't take her eyes off of the young man, that handsome Sephardi. He only talked, and he ate nothing, constantly waving his damask napkin with odd, desperate, high-strung movements that the guest thought she had seen before; they were nervous, and mesmerizing, and he would bring the napkin to his mouth and then, probably realizing that this action was pointless, superfluous, he frowned at that piece of noble fabric that until just a moment before had been snow-white and gleaming, so that Bertha saw before her once more the consumptive Jewish woman from St. Roch's as she, with her shirt already ripped off, flew towards the barred window and began to wave it as if a regiment were parading past out in the street. But — Bertha could hear it now, and she had just started to understand clearly — the woman wasn't shouting to any soldiers, nor to anyone else, for below the window is an empty courtyard; she's shouting to some place farther away, up into the air, towards the rooves and over the rooves, down the street, down the Danube, or in the direction the sharp north wind blows, as if she has seen a new continent out there.

"Usury is a pact with the devil," Haim said placidly. "Like a drug. Morphine. Use it right away, with payment deferred. But the devil always comes for what is his. And everything is his."

Miss Pappenheim, as if yanked away, whipped around, by that woman's voice (her cry, her summons?) shifted her eyes from Haim to her hosts' daughter and remarked unexpectedly:

"If everything goes more or less according to plan, I estimate that I will be, around the end of May, in Alexandria already. I have certain addresses and recommendations for Sofia, Edirne, Istanbul, Smyrna, and of course also for Palestine; I am counting on our diplomatic representations, but I do not know what all awaits. It's certainly going to be neither easy nor encouraging. You'll be hearing from me. It so happens that I am already writing to my friends and co-workers. It is not my hope to change anything, but perhaps my experiences can be of use to someone else besides just me."

But Flora no longer believed anyone. Not Haim, not Dr. Savić, not the guest with her pleasant, trustworthy face. She sensed — actually, she knew — that Bertha Pappenheim was not here by accident, that she was not just a self-sacrificing solitary woman, a hunter of human traffickers and an activist, but rather that person about whom her presumptive but star-crossed fiancé had been speaking, a woman who urged women on, gathered and led them, somewhere, to some country about which she herself probably knew nothing, a woman who really believed that she was traveling with clear and noble intentions and a plan of some kind, around these Balkan cities and the Near East, and that not even she herself was aware that she was traveling somewhere else and for the sake of something different from what she herself believed. And she realized that nothing in the world could be repaired, but she could only forsake, flee, retreat before the cynicism, coldness, villainy, and soullessness of the male world — run and hide her disappointment, her defeat.

CHAPTER FIFTEEN
EPILOGUE: FLORA'S VISION.
The Impression

As Bertha was finishing her last sentence about the cities through which she had obviously already journeyed in her thoughts, Flora said to herself in Hungarian: *the female continent*. As if she had already heard those words somewhere, for she did not know any more Hungarian that what their servant Rozi had taught her. Those two words, like her body, were floating in the malodorous air, like the last remains of a sentence, a thought, which, over the internal fire of disease, had also melted.

She felt like an attack of hysteria was near. A low-intensity attack, invisible on the outside, it resembled excitement, or even joy, or exaggerated health, promptness, tirelessness. Hysteria as cognition through intense tension. Hysteria as journey, and journey as hysteria. Traveling in place in hysterical reality. A Jewish woman who puts on the garb of a Sisyphus, gets ready for the trip, and then sits back down. Preparation for a trip that she will not see through. A cube of ice in a glass that liquefies. Even the dry gleam in her eyes has begun to dissolve, and eyes that had been dry until just a moment before melted, and tears started to run down her face.

Through the tears she saw the country to which every girl flees during her life. That land changes its name, and to some extent its appearance, its characteristics and function. A safe harbor for frightened girls, a hiding place for the injured, a country of atonement. A woman renews her strength here, runs, keeps out of sight, and awaits an enemy or a lover. Some of these countries are made up, some of them have a real topography, and some of them correspond only to some interior landscape.

This was a vision and, simultaneously, awareness of the meaning of the scene witnessed. Two naked women were sitting on the grass alongside clothed, composed men. In the west, the sun was going down and a few boats were drawing near to the horizon. This was not a monastic or ascetic vision, but one of happiness, abundance.

The world, she knew, cannot be definitively divided; women cannot everywhere and for long periods of time live without men, but let there exist a corner, a place of rest or cleansing, however one might imagine it, in which women — at least for a certain time — will live in their own way, free, dedicated to science, music and poetry, and health, theirs and that of their children... and to their emancipation. A country in which they will learn to live alone, to acquire the courage for an independent life — if that is their desire and their commitment.

A country where the great rehabilitation will commence, the healing of half of humanity. A long stay for one's studies (or quarantine), a great apprenticeship. Women, living in families, among and together with men, will only slowly or not at all prepare themselves for a life worthy of a human being in the 20th century. Therapy for dependence on men, the way one is treated for dependence on morphine. Therapy for venereal diseases, shame, moral and social misery.

This is an image of the world, reflected on the restless, rippling surface of water, a world washed in a lake at the hands of a billowy spring breeze. The bright spring vision which over the years will darken more and more as the reflection on the water turns into merely heavy and ever darker — water.

In this image seen through tears, the naked women are also dining on the grass and the ones in the boat hastening towards the exiting sun. The whole land of Impressions — a land of "easy" women, volatile and elusive beings, a land of the moment in which there is a constant flow of change, a land without weight — and thus a land of easy life, easier to bear. The crimson of the sun in the east, the bluish water and sky ("A landscape is only an impression, and only a momentary one.") in the middle of the blue-green water and haze and under an orange-yellow sky — two or three boats, as if the inhabitants of the country or the water are gaining their impressions individually; with every blink of the eye a boat seems to emerge from the mist or the whiteness encircling the picture, the map, the Impression-country.

Who are the residents of this Impression-country who arrive in this way, almost in stealth? They come just at dawn, under a veil of drizzle, in a brief moment when they can be noticed, perceived. Both of these images that Flora is familiar with from prints, exhibited at the *Salon des Refusés*, showed her that the Impression was — the land of the rejected. The country for one generation — each generation has its end of the world, like a color which is based on the intensity of light, which is inconstant, changeable, fluid, the way that country is fluid, a country of imagination, and yet — for an individual or a string of individuals — real.

Cythera/Arcadia/Utopia/The City of the Sun/The Impression. The Impression is a country in which things disappear, get lost, get erased — dark colors, distress, sorrows, problems, just like happiness and beauty. A land in which fluctuation is — medicine.

Twenty years after this conversation, the country will receive its name, but its purpose will have been changed.

The desire of woman remained. Some people claimed that it was a Jewish country; women maintained that it was the great, raw core of their republic. *La fama est le femme, est la faim…*

CHAPTER SIXTEEN

SUTINA

It was in those days, at first light on a gray morning, that a policeman arrested a woman in front of the old National Bank building. She had no identification and spoke no Serbian. She was dressed incongruously, skimpily, draped in a pelerine of fine soft fabric beneath which her dirty silk nightgown was visible. She looked rather like a backdrop, a picture, a poster set up on the street at the entrance to a brothel. Taken down to headquarters, since in her handbag the policeman found money, a few crowns, but no personal documents of any kind, she was right by the door to the chief's office when she spit blood onto the floor of the corridor, and they led her away to the hospital, where it was revealed that, in addition to tuberculosis, she had syphilis, and so they summoned Dr. Savić, who was barely able to find out anything more than the policeman, except that her name was Sutina or Sulina, and that she had in the battered little round hat box she carried some underclothes, a petticoat, a pillowcase and a towel stamped with the name of a hospital in Hungary; and then the Austro-Hungarian consul was called, in order to guarantee payment of her stay and to effect repatriation.

The medical condition of the unfortunate young lady deteriorated and Dr. Savić urged that the patient remain for several days. She was, in addition, very fretful, and whenever she saw Dr. Savić she asked him for the time and date. It was as if she were in a rush to get somewhere, and feared being late, but she was either unwilling or unable to explain to the doctor why she had left the hospital in Budapest, and where she was headed. There was a young nurse in the hospital who was from the Vojvodina; she was a genial and forbearing creature who endeavored sincerely to take care of the women patients, and took pity on them; she referred to each one of them as "my dear," and, most importantly, she also spoke passable Hungarian. She spoke it well enough, and so, although she was always busy, she found time to listen to her patient's complaints. The young woman lamented that she had been raped and robbed of her money in the train. She requested that the nurse return her little suitcase, for she, Sutina, had to continue her journey. "But how are you going to travel like this, my dear?" And she responded that she knew an address in Thessaloniki, and the name of someone, and that without fail she was going to travel on beyond that to glorious Constantinople, where she would learn more about what the future held. She knew that she was gravely sick, and that was why she was in a hurry, and she could not wait around for the other women who could not come until later.

The doctor introduced this story about Sutina into the Gutmans' house, and Flora was very much moved by it. Dr. Savić promised to take her, if her parents gave their permission, to visit the patient as soon as possible. Flora set aside some of her underclothes and warm socks for Savić's fallen girl. She did not wish to go too far with this philanthropy, in order to avoid appearing ostentatious, which she was not, but if she had acted in accordance with her feelings, she would have packaged up the best and most expensive things she possessed. But it was not yet time for that. The hapless girl's bodily organism, finding itself in a hospital bed, suddenly relaxed, yielded, and instead of composing itself and recuperating a little, strengthening, it very nearly surrendered. After quite a bit of time had passed, Flora went again to the Jewish Women's Association and informed the women there that one of their co-nationals lay in the municipal hospital, a girl from the margins, with no home and no means, and she asked if the Association could be persuaded to provide for her. The girl was severely ill, but Dr. Savić was saying that she would live. Let the association continue to concern itself with dowries for poor brides-to-be, but also allocate a little something for someone's survival.

Dr. Savić, by continuing to deny, postpone, Flora's access to the hospital, stimulated her lively curiosity with his unusual stories. One morning, he said, Sutina—who was all but mute, by the way — abruptly started speaking in a language that was a kind of broken German, in the beginning quite incomprehensible, with a significant admixture of Yiddish, but gradually, as she spoke, and her speech issued forth like a freshet, the German became less and less adulterated until after a while it more or less reached the level of refinement of the purest literary language. Polished and fluent, beautiful, it flowed out over her weak, decaying teeth.

CHAPTER SEVENTEEN
FLORA GUTMAN

Flora said: "It's a country where a woman can dance on the street, or walk, run, or sing, and no one will lock her up in a lunatic asylum or a brothel."

Madame Helena explained to Miss Pappenheim the relationship between Sephardic and Ashkenazi Jews. The Lutheran School on Vuk Karadžić St., in which the "German Jews" sent their children, had German as its language of instruction, and it was accredited, just like all the other primary schools. The Sephardim went to Serbian schools; but in the religious education classes, they studied history according to the Bible or read prayers from the missal, which they did not understand. She gave Pappenheim background on both groups, and then Flora talked about how the Ashkenazim and Sephardim have separate congregations, and how the building of a new synagogue created dissension among them, and it had gone on and on and lasted till King Petar Karađorđević himself formally dedicated the new building.

The Serbian-Jewish Choral Society there had a majority of Sephardim (of course), but also a few Ashkenazim. Helena still feared that Flora was going to fall in love with a Sephardic man — for there, at the rehearsals of the choir, originated many marriages, not only because people had the chance to get to know each other and meet regularly, but also because the choir often sang at well-to-do weddings ("First class!") in the synagogue, complete with the cantor. Rehearsals were held on Sundays and workdays, in the evenings. Flora sang extremely well. Helena prized her daughter's talent; she saw it as a counterweight to Flora's preoccupation with the matter she called "suffrage."

Berta Pappenheim looked at Flora with sympathetic interest, as she blushed slightly. Flora was lovely: slender in stature, with a sweet-tempered face, but her beauty, for her mother's taste, who was following Berta's eyes, was a bit boyish, too restrained — the features were maidenly but her expressions, the way she moved her head, her manner of talking, these were curt, serving to mask her female insecurity. Only she, Helena, foresaw, and recognized, the future femininity in her daughter. And she believed that through dance, singing, and, yes, girls' gymnastics, in the manner and with the means by these things pursued in those modern times, practice and training would see to it that her body and voice matured, and a womanly soul also (or vice-versa: with softening, by a beautiful and melodious shaping of the soul, Flora's still boyish body would form and develop, this body like a young stalk that will, by singing in the Serbian Jewish Choral Society, leaf out, developing its buds and flowers.) Thanks to her mother's stance on these things, Flora grew up in relative freedom.

In contrast to other girls from their neighborhood, the *mahala* in the lower part of Dorćol known as Jalija, she went alone into the city, and, furthermore, unaccompanied to the gymnastics sessions in the *Sokol* building named after Dušan the Great. Less than a year earlier, in May of 1910, when *Sokol* associations from Austria-Hungary (with Czechs, Croats, and Dalmatians, plus Serbs from Vojvodina, Croatia, Bosnia, and Herzegovina) were *en route* to a Pan-Slavic gathering in Sofia, all of them beaming in an exhilarated and convivial Belgrade, Flora had been swept away by enthusiasm and wanted, at any price, to witness the rally at the Kalemegdan, and she threatened to go there alone if her brother Miša was not willing to accompany her. He used the occasion to take pictures of the mass meeting of girls.

Right at the end of 1910, the first ballet school opened in Belgrade; Flora already felt old then. But if at that point she could no longer dance, she could travel. After age eighteen — the sudden drop-off. As if she were standing on the summit of a mountain. Everything else around her was only descent, going downhill. Fog. Perhaps far off, behind the fog, was some higher ground, *terra firma*, but it was out of reach. She planned to enroll in the Women's Upper School — natural sciences, history, geography. She got carried away with the idea of traveling to India, Tibet, but she was a female. She had lots of desires, but it seemed to her that there was no time even for one more of them.

And then she would permit an innocent little song, a sound, the silver flashes of Schubert's "The Trout" ("*Die Forelle*") to pull her into a reverie, after which she would talk her girlfriends and her brother into going outside and experiencing nature, at least as far as Topčider, if not to Avala, and she would daydream about hiking around the countryside with her male and female classmates the way various organizations for young people do it, the *Wandervögel* and the *Jugendbund* among the Germans, and others, trekking along village lanes, dressed simply, sportively, carrying a bit of food with them, sleeping in the haylofts of peasant houses, and earning their meals helping the proprietors work in the vegetable patches and grain fields. Sometimes she would go with her mother to the meetings of the Jewish Women's Association, and she joined in the efforts to arrange help for impoverished kinsmen and kinswomen, but she thought that their organization should concern itself also with the education of girls, to encourage them in their inclinations, their love of exercise, the freedom of body and spirit, rather than limit their involvement to assisting girls to marry (engagements, nuptials, the preparation of dowries).

For her birthday, her father bought her a new edition of *The Great Serbian Cookbook*, which had just been published. In addition to Helena and the maid, there usually wasn't room for Flora in the kitchen — she was the runner between the kitchen and the dining room. But she did bring the new things, hot off the stove, that she created with much desire and a bit less imagination, from Serbian and German sources, the recipes of Madame Helena — and so this gift she understood to be an eloquent reprimand and a suggestion that she abandon her fantasies of perfecting and emancipating her body and embrace its nourishment, the meeting of its daily needs — and she took the gift as an admonishment, yet another one, that it was time to get married.

Flora listened to Berta Pappenheim and wanted in some way to make it known that in this room the visitor had a truly engaged listener. For, obviously, her father had indirectly underscored his expectation that he would hear the guest from Frankfurt speak on some other topics. Berta did not volunteer any information; she showed disinterest and ignorance, lack of familiarity, with those things. Dr. Savić had already acquitted himself brilliantly by telling his story about Sutina, and, in addition, bringing the celebrated Miss Bertha Pappenheim to the house; now he could sample in peace the roulade of goose from the table of Madame Helena, which, by dint of its — the fare's — slightly Viennese, slightly Hungarian-Jewish hints, awoke in him a certain nostalgia for his student days. Helena herself was an adaptable hostess; chatty guests she encouraged with her silence, replete with understanding and interest, and around laconic ones she became a chatterbox. Flora did not inherit from her this very European attentiveness and sense of hospitality. Her face, even against her will, showed what she was feeling, what she liked and disliked. She already behaved like a girl grown too old — although she was barely nineteen — who could allow herself to show her true mood, since she had not passed the exams on how to capture men in the typical way. Nor had she mastered the lesson of a timely marriage. A girl who failed to become a wife in time, who lost the battle for a husband — she fights for women's rights.

The conversation bounced around across three levels. Dr. Savić talked about how Sutina began one morning to speak in an unusual language, articulating with uncanny eloquence some ideas that were, admittedly, a touch unusual or silly, or even totally mad and absurd, but that were expounded in a manner that was strangely eloquent, beautiful in well-nigh literary fashion; he would even say they were polished — if there had not been a certain breathlessness to them, some hysteria or imbalance in their rhythm. He felt confused, and shaken, by this, for it turned out that the distressed young woman presumably had not been born in a brothel, or on the street, or in the ward for venereal diseases, but rather at some point or at multiple points had been dealt a terrible blow by fate, or, as a consequence of her unbridled nature, had been pushed into the abyss by her exaggerated need for love. He attempted to respond to her in similarly clear and coherent language, but she withdrew into herself, or rather it seemed that this unexpected connection to her transfigured or newly found and rightful soul was broken off, and then she fell once more into the stupor and frivolity of an unfortunate, foolhardy streetwalker, and the doctor did not have time to figure out whether or not this was pretense and a lie or some peculiar phenomenon that presents in hysterical women who unexpectedly start to speak in a strange language when they are in a state of morbid ecstasy, popping out of the ambit of their nature and then like cooling steam that condenses on the lid of the vessel of her being, her closed world, returns, dripping forlornly back into the pot, back into her own life.

Flora maintained that destinies like Sutina's exist above all because of the absence of equal rights for women. The Obrenovićes had given equal rights to Jews, but not to women. What happened to the young, unknown women, the impecunious workers, who over the last fifty years tried to gain the dais in our parliament so they could tell us what was holding them down and try to find solutions to their problems? To get higher wages so that they could become independent of men, so they would no longer be their slaves. The emancipation of women and that of the proletariat are inextricably linked. A free life — without industrial or sexual enslavement.

Miss Pappenheim, after briefly reporting on what she had seen and done in her three days in Belgrade, and announcing her future itinerary, went back several hundred kilometers in her mind, northward, and talked about how, in Galicia, there unfortunately...

No doubt the talk of euphoria and syphilitic lunacy in a young girl whose brain had been scrambled by spirochetes, and of the moral poverty of Galician Jewish women, touched Flora, but when she talked it was more akin to taking action. Attempting with a kind of activity that did not come naturally to her to turn Haim's attention her way, she spoke of women's fight for equal rights.

Flora assumed that she herself was interested in women's rights. She tried to spark some of these ideas, this awareness, in her friends, and in the Jewish Women's Association, but in fact, what excited her were the lots in life, most often tragic and poignant, of women who lived their convictions or died because of them: her namesake Flora Tristan ("Sad Flora") and Eleonora Marx. She was especially fascinated by the bitter romance between Marx and Edward Aveling, and her suicide. She began talking about this suicide as if it had just occurred, and to someone very close to her like a friend or a cousin. She didn't know herself why she was going into all of these details: did she mean to demonstrate that every struggle for women's rights and dignity was hopeless and would lead to a ruinous outcome? Or show that the fate of even the most self-aware women was no better than the misfortune of a sick prostitute, or was this simply to draw attention to herself, to alert Haim, to tell him what was going to happen if he continued to scorn her, to hate her on the pretext of hating and disdaining women in general?

Flora spoke of important Serbian women.

And regarding prostitutes, Flora said: "She will not be a prostitute the moment she is a free woman and is accorded respect."

Or: "In order to achieve this kind of psychological state, to reach this human optimum (or something along those lines), women must become free, completely independent in the economic sense, and this by dint of their own labor."

Flora advocated some of Edward Carpenter's ideas, such as:

A beloved person should never, under any circumstances, be allowed to lock herself in a cage; insistence on "free" and "spontaneous" human interactions, although that carries with it the danger of tremendous, fatal suffering.

In Flora's head there was a cocktail of ideas. She heard as positive and attractive the ideas that her brother Miša recounted, mostly ironically or as salacious tidbits, curiosities. He made fun of everything; he did this with things he might have liked as well as with what he scorned; never did Flora know what he actually thought about any given issue. She was awash in his little yarns, anecdotes, superficial flights of fancy, idle chit-chat, and a few relatively serious considerations, his own and those of his friends, about certain ideas. But all of these little scraps, quotes wrested out of context, thoughts — they left their mark on Flora, and definitely left her confused.

Miša Gutman tried to redirect the conversation to painting, which he loved. He spoke of the Impressionist movement, the opposite of Expressionism…

"Some women," he said, "who think and write about women's rights and so forth end up in full visionary mode, in fantasy-land, with transports of imagination about an earthly paradise. They conceive of it as similar to other Gardens of Eden, except with the emphasis on the lives of women. Women liberated, and dedicated to work that they love, financially independent, relaxed and rested and disposed to love, respected by all males. One learned woman who was also a holy fool, and a syphilis sufferer, from Sutina's world, dismissed these hopes as unfeasible. Or insufficiently radical. She held that women should live in isolation, at least a certain number of women, the ones who opt for a free life of a different sort. A small, isolated group of women-suicides, nuns who leave no one behind them as progeny. But in distinction to nuns or female anchorites, they could have, while living and working in liberty, amorous relationships, temporary or fixed ones, with men and also same-sex ones; but they were not allowed to become slaves to their husbands or their lovers, their partners. And they were not allowed to give themselves to others for money, or for remuneration of any kind, not even the skimpiest, nor for gold or precious stones. In this country or valley, or on this island or mountain or whatever else it might be, a great deal would be permitted, but slavery, dependence on men, was forbidden.

"That woman was named Emma Goldman and I know her personally, although I cannot confirm that she has syphilis. A community of the type that you are speaking is not a utopia; it exists; it was founded last year by Rudolf Laban on Monte Verita in Switzerland. It's a kind of dance school, but not for women alone. It is also for men who need to be liberated from the slavery of ruling."

Flora says:

"It's a country in which a woman can dance in the street, or walk, run, sing, and no one can lock her up in a madhouse or a bordello."

Although Flora did not particularly like to sing, not even within the four walls of her home, or while playing the piano, which she did passably well but without enthusiasm, she thought that she might like to do so in this country, in a different life, where something that was slumbering within her now, hidden and latent, could be aroused. In that land, talents of which she had never been aware would awaken in her. She'd be an uninhibited lover for her lover or husband. Flora did not dream of a purely female country, of course, but rather of a country that would awaken the sleeping powers in women, their will, of a country in a special state of electrification, with a distinct atmospheric pressure, where a woman could walk and talk more easily, do more work with less effort, where she could surmount every sort of inertia, beginning with the physical. Some mountain land where it was easier to breathe, where a mysterious and successful kind of communication between people really worked. Where both love and lovelessness, and aversion and attraction were on an equal footing, where the air conveyed without obstruction the vibrations of one's soul, where feelings meshed and harmonized. These feelings could be fervent, tepid, or cold, but they were always that way for both people. So that people, men, women, learn to move about in dance, and not in dance, so that they are in constant complicity, in interaction with others, and also solitary enough. Every woman there will be an artist, and every man too (in a certain sense, at least in their movements, speech, and some things they do in tandem). If a woman is aware of her motions, then stripped of norms she will fill her movement with emotion, meaning, freedom, and in an instant she will extend the liberty into her manner of walking, her life, her escapes, wanderings, and renewed self-discovery... Flora, with her talk of the freedom of dance, truly was trying to provoke, to seduce Haim, but she sensed that it had the opposite effect.

CHAPTER EIGHTEEN
DOCTOR SAVIĆ

All the paths of illness — and healing — in this part of the world led, understandably, through the hospital consulting room of Dr. Savić. He determined the direction, prescribed the strength, upshot, for all of these diseases, all of these migrations, these circulating bacteria that bear dangerous pestilence. People thought of him as a good doctor, and he apparently loved his discipline, and even more so, if one may put it this way—he loved the diseases themselves. Unlike a majority of doctors, he had no fear of working with the diseases, the healing of which was fairly rare and which transcended the powers, motivation, and will of the patients themselves; they were the ones stricken with sexually transmitted disease, but he at least found consolation, and sometimes outright happiness, in talking about them. More than anything, it was because of this that Josef Gutman and some of the other men avoided socializing with Dr. Savić, while women liked listening to him. They felt that he was endowed with some special sense and they trusted this intuition; they exposed themselves as if to the beams of an x-ray apparatus, almost wishing that his intuition, that hard-hearted investigator, would at least discover something suspicious, delicate, small but dangerous, threatening, and thus justify their expectations, providing them with some excitement. In moments of inspiration, Dr. Savić was capable of talking about disease with precision and the plasticity of an artist, and his pronouncements about disease had at time such suggestive power that women who were healthy and strong, listening to him, all at once felt languid, powerless, weak, and thereby became also tractable and more exposed to risk, the games of circumstance, the will of providence, and the skill of the doctor. Although he was not emphatically masculine in appearance or by impression or patent ambition, women in his presence tended to feel like real women. A man who accepts, loves illness, loves infirmity, must certainly be strong.

On the occasion of his regular visits to the Gutmans, the famous Belgrade physician, Dr. Bril, once had taken along a young colleague. The young physician, at that time in general practice, and without any practical experience, took a moment, while saying farewell to Madame Gutman in her foyer, to whisper quietly to her: "I think, esteemed lady, that your little maid might be one of those who has caught that nefarious venereal disease." Madame Gutman was offended, and thunderstruck by these unwarranted suspicions, but after several days passed she did take her maid to the hospital. It turned out that, beneath this girl's unblemished glow on her eighteen-year old cheeks, syphilis was already flourishing, in its second, rapidly changing stage. Himself astonished, but emboldened by this sighting, by his own intuition, the young Dr. Savić then decided that, instead of surgery, the queen of medicine, he would devote himself to her despised daughter, venereology. By the time Berta reached Belgrade, he'd been deemed a devotee, one of the scant few in the Kingdom prepared to talk and write about venereal diseases, prostitution, abolitionism, and similar liminal issues. In the Gutmans' home he was reckoned to be a man of progressive views.

Dr. Savić was a widower, and what's more a Gentile, twenty years older than Flora, and all of these reasons for his exclusion from marital calculations only aroused Flora's determination to persist in her futile, multi-year engrossment. When she first saw him, as a fifteen-year old, or rather when she first heard his voice in their parlor, she vowed: "That is the man with whom I shall spend my life." Later, Dr. Savić would frequently entertain her parents with tales of prescriptions for the treatment of Assyrian princesses or Egyptian mummies from archaeological sites, but also about the subconscious into which civilized, modern man stuffs his discontent and fears, his unattainable desires, his negative feelings, like under a carpet, into a trash can, or an internal pocket, a secret hiding place. Together with her body, in those years Flora's subconscious must have been growing and filling out, expanding into that interior pocket that was her soul because, two or three years later, when Haim proposed to her in the parlor, she was suddenly unable to make so much as a peep; her jaw froze, her tongue turned to wood, and that same evening she was befallen by unusually sharp pains between her legs, along the small axis connecting the three diminutive openings invisible to her eye. And she knew: as a warning and a punishment that pain was saying: she would never marry Haim, nor was she going to have children. If she couldn't have Dr. Savić, then she'd have that pain between her legs, illness as a sign of and seal on her faithfulness. Now, listening to him talking at the dining room table about Sutina, that precious moppet who was eaten up with spirochetes, and who had long since fallen prey to consumption, she realized that she had known for ages, and was already reconciled to the fact, that the doctor would never be able to love her as much as any of his wretched patients or diseases, and that she would be able to gain his genuine affection only at the price of a disease.

CHAPTER NINETEEN
HAIM AZRIEL

In Flora's heart, Haim Azriel was not a worthy rival to Dr. Savić, but he had carved out a place for himself in the Gutman family by persistence and a moody charm. For a short while, he went to school with Miša Gutman, and then he was lost from sight, only to reappear suddenly after several years at the rehearsals of the Serbian-Jewish Choral Society and, with his impassioned baritone voice, create unrest in the hearts of not only the Sephardic but also the outnumbered Ashkenazi women there. He had started studying law in Bern, and then in Prague, only to continue his studies in Vienna, and now in Belgrade he was waiting for his father's finances to recover a bit, while he himself was gathering his strength for a continuation of his academic work, studying some and singing some. Catching sight of Flora at the session of the Choral Society, to which she had gone in an attempt to indulge her mother in at least something, he decided he would fall in love with her, every bit as fiercely as Flora had once fallen in love with Dr. Savić.

Oh, but he was a young man with such strong desires, and such shortness of breath. It so happened that he had expended so much strength in the elimination of the actual and ostensible hurdles put up by the Gutman family around the hand of their daughter and her dowry, that at last, when he had basically won their confidence, or better put, the acquiescence of her parents in the realistic prospects of his finishing his studies and joining Josef Gutman as his legal counsel and partner, even before his studies were concluded, and, despite his Sephardic origins, joining the Gutman family, he abruptly lost interest in the whole set of proofs and conditionals. Conquering these obstacles wore him out, and, all at once he, not grasping what had happened, withdrew, took fright, grew sullen, changed, took to frowning, and at the worst possible moment revealed his immature, cold, and cynical heart.

He shifted the responsibility for this volte face onto his "old friend from the Vienna days," Otto Weininger. But when it turned out that this friendship was imaginary, that he didn't even know Weininger, the unmasking of this lie no longer mattered. He uttered his sentences, particularly those rash, fatefully overwrought ones, and he uttered them as his own; it seemed to him that together with other people's thoughts, he also took over their experiences, unhappiness, and genius. He had already, unobserved, been pulled into the shadow of the unfortunate suicide. But he was not considering following Weininger's example through to the end; he was not thinking of killing himself; he wanted to break through to the essence of things, to the secret of Weininger's brilliance, to the secret of his portentous decision and to secure for him the prominence he deserved. But then Haim, breaking down the obstacles, the suspicion and the aversion, which had protected Weininger's work from the petty bourgeoisie, finding himself eye to eye with his work and his noxious essence, he all of a sudden withdrew, sulked, laughed at his own overkill and his dead idol, and that with a laugh that was cynical and cold, self-mocking, melancholy, and simultaneously winsome, Weiningeresque. Women liked Haim and when Flora for the first time smiled accommodatingly and accepted that he simply had a sharp, slightly mean, backhanded method of conquest, Haim turned around and again quoted something from Weininger.

On the morning of her eighteenth birthday, Flora decided to kill herself. She saw herself standing on the roof of her life, on the highest of its towers, looking with anxiety and disillusionment at the plains. She was on the peak, but she had not experienced, or come to know, anything. She was standing on the roof, at the apex, and it was not even dangerous. Sleepwalkers probably feel safe in this same way. She lowered her legs to the floor and slid them into the slippers with silk piping next to her bed. Upon the peak of her youthfulness, to which she had devoted herself with hope and anticipation, there was naught but dirt, the crumbs of a few leaves, the residue on the chimney. She didn't know what joy was supposed to look like, or happiness, the racking up of supreme fulfillment that she ascribed to that moment when youth bows down to maturity, with a presentiment of the advance of age. After turning eighteen, the life of a woman becomes transparent, regardless of what happens in it, of the bodily secrets that it reveals; it is foreseeable. Forthcoming, if at the rear of the horizon, death only changes its shape, the way a woman changes her dress. True novelty, surprises, real mystery — they exist, but their revelation only occurs before eighteen. Whosoever has not felt their touch before that point, will never feel it.

It was the right moment to make a clean sweep of her feelings.

Somewhere off to her right and her left, Dr. Savić and Haim were still accompanying her, or were merely walking abreast of her; perhaps their presence simply caused her to pick up her pace temporarily, and at times in amazement, displeasure, or unfounded hopefulness she slowed down and faced them, expecting a fatal bullet, headed for her breast, to burst forth from their direction.

That "shot in the heart" after a brief, unbearable zipping sound spread a painful, dangerous silence across the dinner table. The interval between Flora's disappearance with the tureen of leftover soup and her return with the roast chicken lasted a long time. So Miša, veiling the emptiness, softly, but loudly enough for his sister to hear, said: "I read in the newspaper that in London some suffragettes have turned up who are calling themselves 'the women who are silent.' They, it's reported, have found a new way of agitating for the right to vote: they commit themselves to not saying a single word for one hour each day, instead focusing all of their thoughts in that period on the 'big issue' they are fighting for. I guess they hope in that way to use telepathy to influence Parliament."

"Here they call themselves 'the women who cry,'" Flora Gutman said. She defiantly set down the stuffed chicken in front of Haim and ran out of the dining room.

CHAPTER TWENTY
FLORA SEARCHES FOR SUTINA

"Tomorrow I'm going to come visit your patient, Dr. Savić," Flora said. "It's my obligation, as a member of the women's association," she added.

Madame Helena and her husband were of the opposite opinion. Dr. Savić said that such a visit would not be advisable, and not feasible. But any other gesture of charity would be welcome. If Miss Flora wished, she could send the stricken young lady a punnet of sweets, or even better — a warm shirt, socks, and a dressing gown. Along with a few *dinars*.

And when on the following day in the forenoon she drove up in a *fiaker* to the district hospital and requested that the porter call the attendant from the ward for venereal diseases, so that she could take her offering to one of their young patients, the man replied listlessly: "All the ones here are old." But at Miss Gutman's insistence, he summoned the nurse. It was a young woman, with a face at once kind, patient, and fatigued, on which an expression of understanding and forbearance was somehow etched but around her mouth hardened almost to stone.

"Sutina?" the nurse inquired with slight uncertainty in her voice, searching her memory. "Ah, well, she left." She shrugged her shoulders a little. "She's no longer here."

No one knew how Sutina had vanished. Did she flee? Was she released? Thrown out? Died? Was she imaginary?

Josef Gutman says: "That's one of the fairy tales that Dr. Savić tells us."

Miša says: "Dr. Savić concocted it in order to provoke Haim. Sutina is a seed, the embodiment of a spirit, of a madness of art that is spreading across the world. A notion of illness, forcefully manifested. Sutina is an image. An expression."

"If you all contrived her, then I am going to find her," Flora said.

Sutina was for Flora the symbol of desperate escape from misery, death, her own female destiny. She believed that Sutina was the *hidden* disguised Messiah. Flora daydreamed about sick beautiful Sutina, whom she was going to nurse back to health and with whom she would leave to go to the land of women's emancipation, and health. Sutina's potential death served as a warning to her that somewhere, far away, they needed to create a land of rights and healthy life. She decided that she would not marry Haim.

The next evening, while they were walking on foot to a ball, Flora told Bertha Pappenheim, who was breaking her legs on the round cobblestones, a story about another vanished prostitute, this time in Belgrade. Bertha became discomposed — her instincts for searching for people who disappeared immediately steered her away from the women's ball at the Hotel Imperial, which she had not wanted to attend anyway. Bertha told Flora about St. Roch's Hospital in Budapest. They both thought that Sutina and this consumptive Jewish woman were one and the same person.

"Perhaps this Female Continent really does exist," says Bertha Pappenheim. "I don't know geography at all, and for heaven's sake not history — because of that, my travels are full of surprises. But first of all let us find our little Sutina and prepare a surprise for ourselves. It's not out of the question that our two women know each other."

Miss Pappenheim had a ticket for that evening's train, and a whole series of already fixed obligations, but she was definitely not going to miss out on a chance to see Dr. Savić's ward and his little patient. The lady had a firm, even, and yet resilient gait, and she moved swiftly and purposefully, as if in her ankles she had small built-in springs and one only had to adjust something, tighten or loosen it, to make her start taking strides that were seven miles in length. "You'd reach Egypt faster on foot than by train," Flora said, and Bertha Papppenheim smiled and didn't let the other woman hear her heavy breathing. And Flora did not hear it, because she herself was out of breath, out of a desire to tell all that she knew; she marveled at the cultured nations, the Germans and the Austrians, on account of their passion for walking and their endurance, and she was fascinated with the fact that today without a doubt the most magnificent and brilliant scientific ideas are being born on mountain crags and forest paths, in high pastures, below snowy Alpine summits, and on the other hand as far as she herself could conclude the great religions also in all likelihood originated with walking; Abraham strengthened his faith in the one God while going to Canaan, Christ gave sermons and deliberated on his new rules while strolling through olive groves and along the roads of Judea and Samaria, Muhammad went from Mecca to Medina, and there was Buddha, wandering along the banks of the Ganges. As for her, Flora, she was satisfied with walks to Topčider, or even all the way to Avala sometimes. She envied all of those *Wandervögel*, and the members of other youth organizations, …If she were younger, she would sign up for the women's Sokol… Yes, after her eighteenth birthday, she could feel herself aging every day, but she would learn to dance. Here in Belgrade, only last year, a contemporary ballet school opened. She was enthusiastic about modern dance, which permitted, glorified, free movement, contrary to convention, dictated only by the music, and musical emotion. Without emancipated movement, there was also no freedom of thought; she was convinced of that. Women with legs armor-clad in plaster molds could not have free minds. Their thoughts bounced around and spun in a plaster vortex without true amplitude or expression. In a truly free country, a woman would be able to dance on the street, and they wouldn't cram her into a looney bin or a bordello… She regretted tiring out the lady with her unrealistic fantasies, but this brisk walking did her good, as did the crisp afternoon in the company of such a distinguished lady. Miša claimed, though, that all female walking was a kind of withdrawal, striding backwards, while men's was necessarily a form of conquest. Let it be that way, then. Let women's walking be escape, backing down, but there is no reason to stand still. Sometimes the most important thing is to be in motion, striding, ranging about like a crab, traveling, changing locations, life, and also even yielding. But, while walking, not to stop.

Flora, in fact, and for various reasons, expected a great deal from that visit with Sutina. She didn't even know herself what. To resolve dilemmas, anxiety, figure out vague intimations. Haim once said: "All roads to the future pass through the hospital surgery of Dr. Savić." Haim had been envious of the success and good reputation of Dr. Savić at the same time that he was intolerant toward the objects of his efforts — toward women. He noted cynically that women did not deserve such a doctor. "Actually," he said, "sick women are creating the future for Dr. Savić. They see its direction. Syphilitics are twentieth-century witches, prophets. Healthy women sit in their houses or apartments; they make their homes and protect their health. The sick run from their illness, in fact; the sickness in them prompts them to move about and spread disease. Wellness is conservative; *sickness is revolutionary, or imperialistic*, it's the same thing, and it's at the basis of every spread, and every revelation, of all adventures, even scientific ones. Artistic ones, especially. Why would a healthy man climb Kilimanjaro or ache for the North Pole? Wellness does not have the tendency to spread; only sickness does. Therefore a healthy man does not speak publicly about the future. That's a departure from good taste and elegance. The future is only spoken of by the sick, the moribund, and low-lifes. And of course all women, without distinction. Women, with their function of giving birth, are very much slaves to a nebulous future. They think up the future. Their inner organs do. A man lives in the certainty of the present, which with every passing moment is simply confirmed, and lasts. Women taint the world, and they set male minds spinning with talk of the future and that's how they subdue men. The man is only defending what is his. The woman is a little bird that wants to lay eggs in another's nest. But since she doesn't have the strength to displace and drive forth her neighbor, she lays those eggs in the future. All things considered, it turns out that Dr. Savić is not fighting illness but producing so to speak a stronger, more powerful disease; he is the generator, a helper to women in the birth of disease. Illness discovers, creates the world. The discovery of the world, *ergo*, is a sick need: "In fact," Haim says, "Illness is smarter, more cunning, than health; frequently it points out a man's direction."

Flora's and Berta's eyes then fell on a scene easily hidden by the body of the nurse in the doorframe; it was an old woman with a bare bottom who was coming to meet them, crawling towards the door, leaving behind her a wet trail.

"Now where's Anđelka going?" the nurse says, as gently as one would to a kitten.

She looks keenly through the door, at Flora and Berta, and sits down sideways, in an almost feminine way, as if with this one movement she was returning to a human shape, as if her desire for doors, her view, the closeness of the door, the world beyond the door, dictated the humanity of her movements.

"There," the old woman said and pointed ambiguously in the direction of the door.

"Where is the patient?" Flora asked sternly. "This lady came all the way from Vienna to find her and return her to her parents."

Neither Dr. Savić nor the patient was in the hospital. The nurse, Stojanka, a powerful, angular old woman, stood in the doorway to the ward for dermatological and venereal diseases like a great stone wedged into the entrance to a cave.

"Dr. Sandić is the attending physician. He's busy now, doing consultations," she says, "but regarding that patient, the foreigner named Koko, she's not here. Nurse Milana will come on duty only this evening."

"I was told that a foreign woman was brought here and that she was gravely ill." Flora again avoided saying Dr. Savić's name. Since she'd sent a message early that morning, following last night's dinner, by the custodian's son, to the effect that she would like to visit Koko and bring her warm undergarments and some skin cream, and cookies, Dr. Savić was avoiding her. At first there was no response, and then he let it be known that he'd be coming there directly. "She didn't die, did she?"

"There's nobody like that here." Nurse Boulder could not remember whether a very young girl from the public square had been brought in by the police. "It's not written on their foreheads who's really young. All of them here are old. And it's the police who bring in nearly all of them." She was standing in the door, almost taller and broader than the doorframe itself, and there was no doubt that no one would be getting around her alive, not to enter or to leave, not a phantom, nor the smell of a disease, nor the reek of purulent wounds, of feces and urine, it could not wriggle past her shoulders, her hips, and the frame, not the tired moaning, as annoying as the creaking of a door, but at the mention of the word "death" even that impenetrable body like a bulwark of granite, staggered a bit, pulled back and hesitated, folded, and between her muscles and the doorframe Flora saw a gap where all the tedious and difficult actions were being performed: getting people to move around, turning them over, carrying out shovelfuls of excrement, and these sufferings continued in her body, which struggled against the distress of the scene. This nurse in the door, Stojanka the Staunch, used her body to impede sicknesses from beginning to seep through, exfiltrate, mill about.

"There's nobody like that," she says again, adamantly, although it is clear to Flora that a woman like her didn't distinguish between young girls and old women, neither by their names nor their ages, and probably not by their diseases. She just huffed and puffed sluggishly, slowly and carelessly passing out the shovels, lifting and lowering raw and aching bodies, gathering, covering, uncovering, shushing.

Flora saw only part of the hallway, and several doors. Then in one of the doors appeared, on the threshold, a leg, a head, arms. A haggard figure crawled up and sat down on the doorsill. She was wearing a shirt and a wool kerchief. Some silk rags, a petticoat. Her gaunt, wrinkled midsection was uncovered, her left foot was bare, and on the other foot were a pink sock and a silver shoe. From the shoe hung an unlaced corset. Beneath her spread a puddle of water. She looked with terrible seriousness at the guests, as if she recognized them. Her shirt was sliding off of her shoulder and she was continually raising her shoulder strap as if using that motion, that sign of recognition, to greet Bertha. This winking with her strap was her final struggle for life, for normality — the staying of abandonment. To go, or not to go. To live, or not to live.

"Maybe that wasn't her name," Flora said. "But she was very young and seriously ill."

The nurse had no time. Behind the barricade of her body, human figures were squirming, leaning forth, trying to slip past.

"The doctor will be here this evening," she said, sensing that she had exceeded the degree of kindness, cooperation, which her temperament could bear. And, closing the door of the ward before all the misery, disease, and madness could escape, she added:

"She ran away." For she knew that sounded the most improbable.

"Or died?" Flora was as wet as the wall. Then she decided to leave.

To Bertha Pappenheim it seemed, even back in Budapest, that the St. Roch Hospital was a refuge for the mentally ill, and really just preparation for some grand performance in which all of these costumes, this random crazy behavior, would mesh together as parts of a whole one day, emerge as a stage production, and *make sense*.

CHAPTER TWENTY-ONE

BERTHA PAPPENHEIM TRAVELS TO THE SOUTH AND TO THE EAST

Bertha and Flora said their farewells, and Miss Pappenheim promised the girl that she would stay in touch from the road, from Jerusalem, definitely.

It might seem that Flora's decision to travel with Bertha to Palestine was reached in a second, at the moment she ate the last gooseberry (empty bowl, emptied life) but that's not how it was. A feeling of rapid aging, with Haim's distancing himself from her. He changed his spots all right; he turned into a woman, revealed the face of an evil woman (the *vile* O.); Dr. Savić loved her while she was weak, while she was unable to control herself, while she was dependent upon him in her hysteria, and now he loved the little harlot on her death bed. Death, a vanished prostitute...

Her decision did not meet with the anticipated resistance from her parents. The conversation proceeded more quickly and easily than Flora could have hoped. After lunch, she announced her decision to leave forthwith on a journey to Palestine. Helena had relatives in Jaffa. A voyage to Palestine, envisioned for some future date — next spring, God willing — could be arranged expeditiously. Miss Pappenheim was a serious and intelligent traveling companion. It was a good opportunity, because Flora would be able to help her relatives with their spring work in the orchard and vegetable gardens. Mr. and Mrs. Gutman believed that in Palestine, the land of pioneers and enthusiasts, their daughter would find both a husband and work that were good for her soul. And they believed the atmosphere there might match her views on relations between the sexes, were were slightly out of control. Mrs. Gutman was baffled by Haim's appearance and his tantrums, and even to Dr. Savić, on whom they were counting to be their last line of defense, reasonable and mild-mannered man that he was, Haim seemed: disturbed, out of his mind.

Miss Bertha decided, on the morning after missing her evening train, to treat herself to a white coffee and toast in the lounge of the Hotel Paris. That's when she was approached by Flora, attired in a traveling frock.

"I have decided to keep you company on the trip. This is the only sensible way for me to spend part of my dowry," she said, sitting down at her table.

Miss Bertha Pappenheim managed to produce, by means of her energetic intercession with the *Shef de suerte* and other newly forged Belgrade connections of hers, the necessary travel documents, so that her departure from the capital was put off by only one day, and then both of them boarded the train for Sofia the following morning.

Right at the outset of the trip, Flora opened up and talked about how she had tried, the previous year in May, to board at least three trains that were carrying Sokol members from other Slavic countries through Belgrade on their way to the gathering in Sofia. She had felt a tremendous desire to join them.

They immediately agreed on their goals. Flora was in search of Sutina, and all along the way she kept thinking she had spotted her. "The search for Sutina is the search for her own true identity," said Bertha. For her part, she was simply collecting information.

In a letter to Mrs. N., Bertha Pappenheim writes that perhaps she will be the only person to benefit from her trip; it is quite certain that the effort and a few hostile encounters — such was her meeting with the young Haim Azriel in Belgrade and, more than anything, the feeling of powerlessness and futility, the everyday insight into the misery of her people, the female sex, and especially her Jewish kin in the southern Balkans — exactly like Poland and Galicia — triggered tension in her, anxiety, a thickening, a feeling of asphyxiation, which could be resolved only in an uncontrolled attack or in some very serious disturbances, an embarrassing loss of control (temporary). After she, as an eighteen-year old girl, had been Dr. Breuer's patient and subsequently fled Vienna, after her case, known as "Anna O.," engendered psychoanalysis, she mastered the techniques by which she could neutralize or redirect, transform, an imminent attack. Everything pointed to her being able to think intensively, passionately, feverishly about hysteria, engross her consciousness and will, and thus preempt the explosion and in that manner allow for the suppressed unconscious content somehow to be released slowly and deliberatively, instead of bursting forth in a spasm or shriek or being trapped in feelings of deadness and nothingness... Bertha Pappenheim was businesslike, enterprising, efficient on all fronts. Her goal seemed clear. The white slave trade, an inspection of the work of the association, and philanthropic and other organizations. Regarding her emotional life at the time of this trip, one could hardly reach any conclusion other than that she did not much believe in the utility of her mission. In contrast to the pragmatism of everyday life while traveling, the minor risks of a journey, the worries, etc., of a life split off and full of unpredictability, stood the design, planning, and consideration of hysteria, a hysterical being that in its daily relations is predictable, with risk, but in the long run, on the way to an untouched country, in view of life in its entirety, carrying a fundamental uncertainty, an openness...

Her journey down the Balkan Peninsula to Alexandria played out on two levels: the first was utilitarian, pragmatic: it left a trail, could be read in her letters, which were collected in a book published in 1924 by Sisyphus Arbeit in Leipzig, and the other is hysterical and it is, one could say, the journey of Bertha's womb, the final journey on which it, the uterus in turmoil, interrogated itself, summed up its decades' worth of trips...

Bertha Pappenheim journeyed to the south and east and her letters to the north and west.

A quarter of a century later, right after Bertha Pappenheim's death, only one year before the Second World War, Flora read once more the letters that Bertha Pappenheim, from her Balkan and Near Eastern journey through Palestine and Egypt, wrote to her colleagues in Frankfurt, her followers, her "girls," devotees, or subscribers, as she termed them, and which (the letters) she — Bertha — published in 1924, at which point she realized, as she wrote in a foreword to her epistolary journey — that her project, all of her labors, undertaken with the aim of protecting women, girls, and children, and of directing attention to Jewish deprivation and squalor, had not resonated widely; she realized that everything she heard subsequently was just her own voice, isolated and unknown and without effect, impotent. But at least she had spoken up: "To see injustice and remain silent, is to be culpable (*complice*)".

But not even then — especially not then — this trip of hers with Bertha Pappenheim, their mysterious journey, seemed absolutely unreal to her. It seemed unreal how sharply concrete and informative Bertha's letters were: at a distance of a quarter of a century, all of those names, initials, institutions, the whole complex apparatus (doctors, activists for the protection of women and children), cities in passing, on a line from Sofia-Plovdiv-Edirne-Thessaloniki-Istanbul, all of the diplomatic representations, businessmen and prostitutes, women for pleasure, were compressed into in a mixture of dust, sand and fog, a smokey curtain that covered, overshadowed, took captive the true nature of the voyage: an indecisive, unsuccessful attempt at escape, just a half-escape for a woman who still believed that she had something to lose, indeed a person who runs up to the brink of the precipice, to the edge of her continent, but does not have the courage to hurl herself off from there, and moreover isn't aware of possibly wanting to throw herself into the abyss, into the twilight, so that she could see what the finale of a day looks, the setting of the sun, above the invisible opposite shores.

All of Bertha's constant and manifold activity on the trip excluded Flora, squeezed her out, but it disclosed to her how that degree of scrambling, resourcefulness, that much volition, transformed Flora into a blind spot... In the letters to her colleagues, Bertha made no mention of Flora anywhere.

Flora barely remembered only a few of the meetings that Bertha described in detail. Bertha spelled out facts, confronted Flora with them, created superfluous events, and found and thought up redundant people, in order to patch over the true meaning of her journey: Bertha Pappenheim was following Sutina's trail, and Sutina was searching for her continent.

Over the years, Flora had on occasion altered her feelings and memories about that trip. Sometimes it seemed to her like participation in a strenuous game with singing and dancing in a burlesque, or like wandering through the murky streets of a ghetto, sometimes like informative student presentations, occasionally like a tourist trip freely selected, sightseeing, in cities on a tour bus, hightailing it with closed windows through the changing landscape, or asphalt roads and dusty peripheries, and behind the window panes, without logic or order, the scenes of the edifying scenery alternating with cities with sumptuous architecture and groups of half-naked, bleary-eyed and dissolute urchins who pelt the bus with stones or roll about in the dust, with broad, convulsive gestures, clawing up coins to buy bread.

Later, it seemed to Flora that then, on that trip with Bertha Pappenheim, she had been, if not within reach of her goal, at least in a position where the things she had started could have become her life's work. If she had not given up at that time, she would have found little Sutina. If she had only continued her trip, the Female Continent, or city or island, would have become reality at a crucial moment.

Flora knew that ordinary, and even fantastic, ideas are frequently born in the heads of utterly ordinary people. And precisely thanks to the fact that their lives are ordinary, and fantastic ideas begin to live that ordinary everyday life and in that way meet with their realization: this is also their implementation.

The Female Continent (if and when it is discovered) will be, is, an emotional fact — the truth of emotion.

Men's countries are discovered, originate, as the result of an idea. America first existed as a notion about the roundness of the globe, about an India one could approach from two directions. The Female Continent exists first and foremost as emotion. As an emotion that cannot find its object, but rather must open up, exists in the necessity of opening. The Female Continent is or will be a materialization, an embodiment, a grounding of great continental emotion at the moment when a large quantity of feeling and sensation is concentrating, projecting. In the world there is so much unrealized, unchanneled female emotion than an entire continent can be created.

Flora believes that Bertha Pappenheim is also travelling to the Land of Women, but she will not discover it; it is a secret.

"What is the Female Continent?" Flora asks Bertha Pappenheim.

Haim: it's a female garbage dump.

Sutina: the land of convalescence and-or death.

Flora: a country of emancipation and healthy life.

Bertha: is silent.

Who is the mysterious Ana O.? What is hiding behind what, Bertha Pappenhim behind Ana O., or Ana O. behind Bertha Pappenheim?

Is the cipher "O" the code for a woman's island, country, planet, continent?

Why did Haim Azriel, who spoke with aversion of women, metamorphose into a woman?

Will the entire world metamorphose into a woman?

Where is Sutina traveling?

Where is Bertha Pappenheim traveling?

Where is the womb traveling?

Where are the women of Galicia traveling?

CHAPTER TWENTY-TWO
FLORA GUTMAN'S VISION
The Impression

Letter dated April 1, 1911

Dawn materializes in an instant, almost with a bang. It doesn't look like night pulled back to one side, with the sun breaking out on the other, but more like daybreak came with the collision of the two of them, like the first dawn of the world.

The elements are still unaware of themselves and the water and air are wrapped, bluish-green, in misty haze, like a great swaddling cloth.

In fact the small red sun seems like a torch, a flaming cannonball, which simply flew into the night, piercing it, and it seems like a big balloon full of indigo burst, ignited, and burnt up in an instant, and its ashes, gray-blue-green shreds, precipitated, depositing themselves in the newly born, all-encompassing emptiness.

And the day *per se* had still not issued forth; the colors still had not thought up a picture, when into it sailed, moved, the first settlers. In tiny boats, barely identifiable (with every blink of the eye, another one enters), they arrive from somewhere outside the picture and one cannot predict how many of them will be coming over the course of the day. One also cannot see where they are sailing — the view is completely opaque and the only things showing are broken verticals, scarcely noticeable in the blue-green prospect, and one cannot see whether there's a forest or brush or scrap iron in the depths around the docks, nor can one guess what the figures there represent — fishermen, holidaymakers in the early Sunday morning, hunters, or fugitives sneaking along the coast.

There is thick morning mist, but by their outlines, even more so by the tension of the barely discernible shapes, one can make out that those are women in the boats.

The landmass along which the boats will dock still has no name, but over the course of the day it will certainly get one. It will definitely not be easy, for one already has a hunch that in this country not a single shape, color, and maybe no name, will stabilize, that it will be a land of rapid and perpetual change, a land in which along with cheerless colors will disappear every sensation of weight and actual life hardships; but there will be a deep sense of the commonplace, and a beautiful and therapeutic happiness.

No, no one will forbid men from setting foot on this new shore, but a man will simply be afraid, shrink from landing on soil that pulsates in the light, on which the light fragments, shudders, and diffuses the way soil quivers in a weak but continuous earthquake. The soil here flows, the same way water does, and the air in which nothing is immovable, and nothing promises easy and certain eternity. Only women know how to live in a life without a tomorrow, how to relish being on the flickering rim, before the shimmering end of the world...

Letter to her parents (or to Dr. Savić?)

I absented myself from Belgrade, from my home, so that I could muster up the courage to speak these thoughts, the source of which I do not know.

On the road, a person grants herself the right to exaggerate, in an act of freedom of thought. Letters from a lesser or greater distance are a traveler's greatest adventure.

Everything that is excessive, silly, the recipient will ascribe to the unknown surroundings (exaggerations, while covering the distance to one's home/destination seem natural, just as adventure and aggrandizement in novels strike the reader as almost natural — at bedtime). Sometimes I think that men understand only the overly emphatic, exaggerated language of letters from afar. Recently I've been captivated by the ideas and endeavors of some women throughout history that have become meaningful to me. All of the sacrifices, humiliations, which those exceptional women, few in number, suffered in the name of the demand that they be able to live in dedication to work they love, as much as they love their families, and economically independent, rested, and prepared for love, respected by their husbands.

But now I think, in the city of beautiful, humiliated, invisible women, wrapped in their headscarves, that this goal is inadequate, that we should highlight, drive at, impossible demands and set hyperbolic goals, so that the most modest ones, the most indispensable ones, will become obvious.

I believe that women should stop fighting. They need to retreat to a deserted island, to an empty continent about which are whispering, daydreaming, those thousands of syphilis sufferers united in body and mind, I think that women should quit the temporal battlefield, flee, withdraw from history, refuse to give birth. Women need to demonstrate no more and no less than how they can stop, alter, the world.

Formerly I imagined a land in which a woman can dance in the street, and no one will commit her to an asylum or a brothel. A land, a life, which will awaken and liberate the power of women, in communities of the type established by rare, brave people in a high mountain country of truth, where one breathes easier, where the clean air transmits vibrations of the soul, where every man and woman would be artists of motion, movement, life.

Now I know that freedom lies in renunciation, pulling back; the only utopia worthy of our efforts, of life, is a utopia of extreme isolation, the renunciation of a positive utopia. The utopia of a complete solitude.

Formerly I wanted to be a man. To hide, take shelter among men and in that way try out my powers and the possibilities of mind and soul. In that desire for freedom — how would it get here, at the gates of the Balkans? — I was prepared to take any risk. But now I have doubts about the success of women's work. I believe in the defeat of feminist ideas. I realized this when Bertha Pappenheim was at dinner. What remains to me? That I set out after a young sick prostitute who fled from your ward and took the path of other slaves—if she isn't dead. If she did die, then am I to continue on this journey in her place, for her soul, if she was not just concocted, if you all did not concoct that whole story yourselves, for the sake of amusement…

CHAPTER TWENTY-THREE
A DOUBLE JOURNEY

Bertha Pappenheim and Flora sat down opposite one another next to a window in the train. Were they traveling or standing still? Or was one of them traveling, and the other not? An empty womb roams in search of fulfillment. Hysteria is roaming in place, the impossibility of escape. Hysterical optic, the optic of an agitated uterus: through it, with it, everything on this trip could be seen differently. To the ordinary eye, the world consists of indications, hints. The hysterical eye sees closure, rounding off. Fullness can be reached; fulfillment is compensation for half-ness, through hysteria. It also does not satisfy; if it is sufficiently turbulent, it brings a certain temporary assuagement.

In this hysterical trajectory, lines continue, indications begun on the plane of a "real, obvious" journey, encircle, acquire the integral sense of an appearance; details that otherwise would not be clear enough or would have no consequence are conducive to the hysterical interpretation of the world. On the plane of hysteria the scene continues, comes to a *resolution*, an *explosion*.

Wasn't the appearance of the consumptive Jewish girl in Belgrade, about whom Dr. Savić was talking, also a continuation, excessive, undesired, but necessary, a fulfillment of that horror intimated in Galicia and also in the hospital in Budapest?

Hysteria will give this trip another, new meaning and outcome, goal. In terms of what is real, pragmatic, she will go back home to Frankfurt. Her womb's journey will end elsewhere; it will not go back home, because in the life of an individual, of a woman, of a uterus, there is no return, but instead only a pulling away from its beginning. Her womb on its wanderings, its journey, had a goal with which her mind is unfamiliar.

As for Flora, it looked, to judge from the letters she received from Bertha, like she had not even departed. Hysteria is roaming in place, the impossibility of escape. The first letter reached her from Thessaloniki. The description of a beautiful Jewish woman, red-haired and pregnant, in a whorehouse. The beautiful Jolanda irresistibly called to mind Sutina. Was Haim there? Flora stayed — did Haim go? Flora had a feeling that Haim is right there, that Bertha had seen him but wasn't going to say so openly, only tacitly, describing only the girl. Next to the girl, Flora saw Haim and she sensed that his place was indeed there, that he trampled on his true passion out of feigned disgust. Why didn't Bertha Pappenheim describe everything in her letter? Was she keeping it as sustenance for her own hysteria, neurosis, and literary efforts?

The final letter she received from Bertha Pappenheim was from a ship in Alexandria. It told of girls who were not permitted to disembark. Flora began to cultivate her vision as an aspect of escape. The disembarking of the women, like those of Gauguin — but this simultaneously involved those impossible ones, from Warsaw, Galicia, Budapest, and Thessaloniki, Jewish women, yet tanned, cleansed, ready for purification. In the Impressionists' paintings, she saw water, verdant vegetation. She recalled her visit to Paris, or in her black-and-white photographs she animated color and light, fluidity, locomotion, elusiveness of the elements, as if the view and the observer are traveling through the picture.

The Jews' movements themselves produced frightful, mechanical, hysterical images of bodies that move uncontrollably, scramble away from the illness, or drown in it. Through these pictures the image of the Female Continent also pitched suddenly into the subconscious, like down a well.

Some of the available facts imply that Flora did, however, journey to Palestine, but only after the death of Bertha Pappenheim. She toured the towns and brothels that Bertha had also visited. The womb does not recognize time and space; it journeys even when the woman is no longer there.

It appears that the consumptive Jew gets undressed and dressed before traveling and before remaining. As if faced with a dilemma. She goes or she does not go.

She gets ready to go and to stay.

She puts on her clothes and strips down.

But instead of melting, she combusts.

The Female Continent was both "there" where Mrs. Frank was going and there where the women were sailing and "here." It is simultaneously there and here. That's the mystery of a woman's illness. And of the Female Continent.

The fertile fields passed by, fields from which the Morava River had just returned to its channel and left behind soft, sludgy traces of its fury. The feeling of the mythical antiquity of a people was pervasive. She carried on a conversation with people in a mixture of Yiddish and Russian, which she didn't know. The more severe her attack, the more distant, lesser known, was the language she used. And not just the language, but the world, the region, that was opening up before her. Hysteria is quicker than the imagination, as fast as a bullet. It travels, it flies, lethal, like on the wings of the wind, on a thunderbolt itself. A journey is always restoration, mostly painless, slowed down, expounded, the recurrence of the lacerating experience of hysteria, of hysterical flight. A man in a train, on a journey, apparently understands all languages, speaks to others and to himself in foreign tongues in which he's otherwise not proficient; he is in motion and he sees panoramas and stations that normally are not there, in that place, in that form. A woman on a trip is that platonic womb, which is free, freely floating, colliding with her soul and other organs, travels, wanders; and that wandering in the body of a woman provokes tumultuous events. Something of these thoughts, presentiments, passed through the head and heart of Miss Pappenheim while she tapped the window pane. What was this new journey on which she had embarked other than the coerced roaming of a barren uterus eager for fruit and life, and of a great, protracted, enduring, unremitting attack of hysteria, camouflaged as a journey, as life.

Dear Flora,

In Plovdiv there is a Home for Foundlings. One year an extraordinary number of children were found on the street... The proprietress of the Café Chantant in Edirne, Laura, "the benefactor of the Jewish community" — she is mixed up in the white slave trade. Grotesquely fat, she's suffered numerous strokes. Through her, wards of the Home for Wayward Jewish Girls made their way into Turkey. The Home was operated by Rabbi Šašam Braši. His disciplinary methods for the delinquent girls, of whom there were fourteen: if they were not being "smart," he would punish them; he would publish their photographs or cut off one of their pigtails or smear their faces with indelible ink. The rabbi admitted — after I gave him a lecture — that these children — the oldest among them was 17 — regardless of the fact that the Torah provides for energetic punitive measures — these children were more victims than criminals and that he would adjust his pedagogical practices. If he, the rabbi, thinks that there are fourteen of these villainous girls "who are not being smart," and who are on his blacklist, then that means that in Edirne's Jewish population of 20,000 there are at least 1400 who are "unreasonable." One journalist, the head of a newspaper, believes that the wider Jewish population in the city is, on the level of morality, in distinct regression. Nobody looks out for the girls who abandon themselves to the life of the streets at twelve years of age. In the words of Rabbi Šašam, there exists in Istanbul one synagogue for dealers in girls where, during Shabbat services, while the Torah is being read, people buy girls. As far as I was able to ascertain, he did attempt to close down this house of God, but he was unsuccessful. The rabbi reckons that he could operate a refuge for a thousand *florins* annually. Something must be done, and urgently, for these young women. A consul from one of the diplomatic missions there said: "What are you going to do? The Jews sell their own children like chickens!" The affair has been covered up and fifty children have been returned to their parents.

Thessaloniki, April 6

Dear Flora,

Last night I found, in the afflicted "de Bara" quarter, in the brothel known as "Jolanda the Beautiful," a Russian Jew in an advanced stage of pregnancy. I sent round a letter to my "friendship circle" (*Cercle des Intimes*) and the women's section, with the request that they contact me, and help this woman who obviously did not sin by herself but is bearing the consequences alone. If they have no further compassion for this woman, let them have it for the child. I do not know the woman's name, but the *dragoman* of the Austrian consulate, Ješan Effendi, does... The woman has red hair and is quite beautiful...

When Flora received this letter, she identified with the beautiful Jewish woman, red-haired, pregnant in that brothel. She sensed her wretchedness, her feelings of being trapped, polluted, hopeless; suddenly all the unbearable, long-growing nausea coalesced. The world, and she herself, were full of filth; she lived as if at the bottom of a swamp, with a terrible sensation of pressure, as if she were about to explode at any moment; she was in over her head. She felt the need to escape. Above all she thought that she must not say a word to her mother about the letter; she feared afraid that either her mother or brother would recognize her self-identification and that they would see her in the figure of this girl. For they considered her very beautiful. Lovely Flora.

Her brother demanded to read the letter. Flora refused to allow it. She needed to get away, take flight. Her brother said: "That's not a letter from* Bertha Pappenheim, but rather from Haim." Flora burned the letter and puffed into the particles of whitish ash, which floated on a gentle current of air and slowly settled onto the white tablecloth.

The voyage on the H.M.S. Euterpe from Thessaloniki to Constantinople

Constantinople is less dirty than I expected. I mean physical squalor; the moral filth of our compatriots here seems unprecedented. The wife of the Russian consul, an American who takes an interest in the woman question and in prostitution, established, with the help of a little committee, a small shelter to which girls are sent every day, girls who *wanted to break free* — but it no longer exists. Even the pregnant ones, for whom she could do something, were not turning up, for the Russian women simply declare themselves to be Turks. The small sanctuary that took in many Jews is going to be closed this summer, in part due to a lack of means and partly because it's not being used. I am going to overcome my revulsion and attempt to make contact."

April, Tiberias

The women's bathhouse in Tiberias is like the antechamber to hell. Morality there seems to be seriously compromised, especially among the women. There's no brothel, but in the vicinity of the baths — caves, on the route pil-

---

* At this point the text reads "to Bertha Pappenheim," but this seems to have been a copyediting mistake in the first Serbian edition.

grims take to the tomb of Rabbi Meir, which are adapted to this purpose. Among them there are no Jewish women; they are taken into homes. Each girl has only one lover, to whom she belongs; if her paramour stumbles upon a rival, he settles things with a knife. There are no out-of-wedlock children. They get rid of them: they strangle or drown them. Everything happens in secrecy, because the rules of morality and honor are very strict.

May, Jaffa

Dear Flores,

Our co-nationals here behave, unfortunately, as if the country belonged to them. Lack of taste, tactfulness, and culture.

How do Jews lose their homelands? They arrive, permeate, their densely packed ghettos arise, and they develop culture, work, and so forth. *They sense that they are on their land* and become arrogant (or come across as such to others) and then they are slaughtered or driven out.

As soon as they feel, for the first time, that they are on *their land*, they should move away before it's too late. Israel, although it's a special case, is nevertheless just one of the temporary stops, one of the countries, the same way that Birobidzhan is. Jews must find their destiny, character, happiness in precisely that mobility, in a nomadic life, like their forefathers. As soon as they settle down for any longer period and bind themselves to one country, *misfortune arrives.*

HAPTER TWENTY-FOUR
THE FOREST OF THE MARTYRS

At the close of April, 1953, Sara Alkalaj wrote from Israel to her former schoolmate, Olga Rot:

"My dear Olga!

I'm happy to know that you're with our people again in the opština. Cvi and I were at the ceremony in the Forest of Martyrs, and we planted five saplings. A column of buses journeyed out from Jerusalem, and our friends from Haifa came, Naharije and Base. There were about five hundred of us Yugoslavs who gathered; otherwise we rarely get together, as if we were —. Samokovlija came from Belgrade. He gave a beautiful talk; I shed unsightly tears. 'A forest that lives and breathes, grows and blooms, represents the victory of life over death, of the light over darkness.' Other people spoke, too, and when Rabbi Alatarac said kaddish, everyone wept. Afterwards Cvi put a pine sapling in my hand, and he took four of them and led me down the slope where holes had already been dug. The whole time I was adding up how many trees I should plant, including mom's family and dad's, but I kept getting confused, and the sun disoriented me. My brain would stop working and I kept starting over. I was crying. I couldn't stop: in the end when we had set out our trees, instead of five black holes there were five small young trunks standing in front of us. I thought, who all is coming here to plant so many?

I'm glad, dear Olga, that you mustered the strength to help in this magnificent campaign. Otherwise we are fine.

As you can see, I'm writing from Jerusalem. We sold the little house in Azor and came here. Cvi works at the post office. Your sister Ila wrote me that you and Pišta split up. I can't believe it. You two should come here and start from the beginning."

Two months before the event that Dina Alkalaj described, on the day that the start of the planting of saplings in the Yugoslav section of the Forest of Martyrs was declared, the Federation of Jewish Communities informed its members to join the drive, which means paying 300 *dinars* or one Israeli pound per tree, for each member of the family who perished in the war, to which a transplanted pine will be dedicated. This was difficult, for several thousand remaining Jews were supposed to pay for the planting of 60,000 trees. Their payments were taken in through the Jewish community offices. A number of women showed themselves ready to go around to the houses of those who had not responded in a timely fashion, and Olga Rot was one of them. With a pad of receipts in her purse, and her son as reinforcement, she began making visits that did not please those households. What was needed was a little persuasion, encouragement; the old ones or sick ones, selfish or stingy; old Mrs. Štajnicova, for instance, lived from darning socks and a small pension, and for herself as the one survivor she was supposed to pay enough for thirty victims. "For whom?" she asked. And Zonenfeld, hard of hearing, wanted nothing to do with any trees. "I can't hear you," he shouted. His older son was hanged in the summer of 1941 at Jajinci, and the guilt for that death was shared with the human perpetrators by every tree, old or young, alive or already turned into a lamp-post, whatever. Mirko Kon recalled that some other people had already paid for his relatives. For his father and mother — his brother in Rijeka. For her sister and her children — his brother-in-law in Daruvar. But he had no living family members in Rijeka or Daruvar. Magda Rot said at the community office that the whole campaign was actually a misuse of the human faith in the power of symbols, and of course it was just one more confirmation of Jewish ingenuity: how to plant hectare after hectare of the finest coniferous forest in such a way that it costs the Israeli state nothing, and that the people giving the money are supposed to be overjoyed at getting the opportunity to pay for their own lives.

Every ten or fifteen days, Olga Rot would bring home fresh numbers on the contributions in Novi Sad, or, later, for other cities as well. In late April, when the letter from Dina Alkalaj arrived from Jerusalem, in which she discussed the beginning of the ceremonial planting of saplings on the Judean mountain, we, in our house, already had access to the data that in Belgrade, for instance, 1,371 Jews had paid for 254 trees to the tune of 76,400 *dinars*, which is, proportionally speaking, a considerably worse result. It could indicate that the citizens of Novi Sad displayed more of a feeling of duty and piety towards their dead, or perhaps that for each survivor they had a higher number of commitments. And one cannot exclude the possibility that the Novi Sad drive was simply better organized and that, thanks to volunteers like Olga Rot, the collection of contributions was not left to chance, to uncertainty, compunction, or the distracted soul of the individual. In some places, such as Bačka Palanka, for example, the count of members of the Jewish community and the count of payments was more or less in balance, while in Bjelovar, let's say, fifteen survivors registered for 156 trees, but by April of 1954 it was actually up to 658! And among the relatively successful communities one can count Čakovec, Vinkovci, Donji Miholjac, Karlovac, Slavonski Brod, Tuzla, and Daruvar. From Sunday to Sunday, new cities would appear in the ledger, and then their order would change in the imaginary rankings: in the spring Belgrade led in the absolute quantity of trees, understandably, while over the course of the year it was overtaken by Zagreb and Sarajevo; Novi Sad kept pace well, trailing the cluster of the largest cities, until just at the end, in November of 1954, when it suddenly broke off and finished only in the middle of the pack. Until the end, Bjelovar charted the best relative result; the little white city, as opposed to big white city known as Belgrade, simply outdid itself a hundred times over. Olga and Nenad became engrossed in the columns that lengthened and branched out on our dining room table, like the map of a battle.

When the end of the campaign was proclaimed, I was almost sixteen years old, and I felt worn down by the constant counts and comparisons, like I'd grown old beneath the endless homework, the knotty algebraic operations, with their constantly growing number of unknowns heading for infinity. It took me a long time to be able to free myself from numbers, although earlier I had not been interested in them. The forest kept growing after the campaign wrapped up; the forest went out on foot with Olga Rot and other women, from door to door, winning people over, conquering, and walking away with ever more new trees. You demanded that I accompany you on those visits.

It wasn't lost on me that my presence had a positive effect. My presence said: Here you go, dear friends, this is how he would look. He'd be this big now, your son or your grandson or nephew, if he had survived, so how about paying for a tree for him and he can continue to grow. I was a living guarantee that the money invested would secure the return of the disappeared, for 300 *dinars* they get a life, that of their close relatives or their own; *I was a sample of accessible immortality, and in addition I raised the respectability and value of my mother. My presence said: have confidence in the woman who managed to preserve one son. What you are purchasing from her is not just a memory, not an illusion, but life itself.* I must have found this to be in my own self-interest, or found at least confirmation of the certainty that I was alive, some powerful feeling for the world and, with it, of my own importance.

I myself agreed to go along on these visits full of sighs, moaning and groaning, backing down, framed photos, reveries, queries about the life expectancy of Mediterranean conifers and the ancient age and divine origin of the mountains in Judea which are from this day forward into perpetuity renewing the memory that is implanted in them via this little mechanism of payment on some rainy April or June day in Novi Sad. Truth be told, sometimes, their miserliness got on my nerves, that disbelief and suspicion of old age. Mirko Kon, before he finally paid providence for his life and let the three hundred dinars leave his hands, wanted to know exactly where his tree was going to be planted and how he would recognize it if he went there personally, in other words, would there be a little plaque on every tree with the name and surname, like you find in an arboretum on rare, exotic trees or specimens from the plant kingdom. "There won't be," I said, hoping to add to the old man's torment. "The tree is happy enough to be named 'white pine' or 'black pine,' 'golden pine' or the like, in some living language or a dead one, Serbian, English, or Latin, and it doesn't need an additional first and last name. I myself would not wish for, one day, some tree to step out of the forest, come up to me, and say: 'I am Danijel Štern, your brother. You and mom bought me for a pound. I'm yours.' And then he'd want to go home with us.'"

Besides, I knew that forests grow, spread, and propagate themselves around the world less by human will, or in accordance with human plans, and more by the dance of circumstance, of wind and water, and that the trees that you and I are recruiting in all of these dreary living rooms, will sprout wherever fate determines, or where they themselves end up wanting to do so, in dazzling high-altitude landscapes and belts of trees, along the edges of continents, far enough away for the actual holder of the receipt not to see or recognize them anymore.

I went on the visit to the Lebls with a great deal of reluctance and curiosity. Sonja Lebl was my age. She had just finished the eighth grade. We didn't socialize with each other, and we had not formally gotten to know each other, encountering one another in the school courtyard or corridor, we would exchange a more or less meaningful glance instead of a greeting: we were the only compatriots in school, and of our generation, which included Lila Klajn and Joška Tešić, probably the only ones in the city, but we acted like we didn't give that any special significance, and I guess we didn't, actually. In front of other people, whenever

I had the chance, I let it be known that there was nothing between us. It was the way half-siblings behave, a brother and sister of a shared, rather problematic father: they are related, but this does not bring them together, or make them happy; instead it only reminds them of their joint tribulation, discomfort, and shame. However, just as such a half-brother would do, from a distance, from the side, I took care of her. I knew how she was doing in school, who she was friends with, who she was in love with. She was rotund, solid, with olive skin and black, curly hair that fought its way out of a bushy "ponytail" tied with a broad, prim, white bow. I didn't find her all that attractive, but I did indulge other people in their comments at her expense. "Cow," I said once in front of a group of friends from our grade, thereby wrapping up the judging and denying the others their petty reproaches and sarcasm. A few weeks earlier it so happened that Sonja had finally learned that she was not the birth daughter of Helena and Rafael Lebl, but their niece. Supposedly a woman had come up to her on the street and said: "Mr. Rafael Lebl is not your father, but your paternal uncle, and Mrs. Helena Lebl is your aunt. Your father was named Leopold, and your mother Ema. Till the war came, I worked for you all. I thought that God would hold it against me if I failed to tell you."

Rafael Lebl and his wife weren't members of the Jewish *opština*, the Jewish community, and they couldn't understand right away this talk about a payment and trees. "Ah, if some memo came,' Rafael said, then in the next few days my wife and I will drop in at the *opština* and pay it. In the Lebls' living room the air was stuffy, and the windows were closed so that the little green parrot they'd let out of its cage would not fly out into the street. One could hear from the next room a rustling sound on the parquet floor, the creak of a wardrobe — probably Sonja. I didn't want to ask whether she was at home. We apologized for coming by unannounced, and they apologized abashedly for costing us time on account of their carelessness. The hostess brought out a bottle of homemade sherry. Rafael recalled that your husband might have known the famous Radoslav Mijuški, a pre-war attaché in the Serbian government, a diehard supporter of the MP named Cveta Maglić, of the Radical Party. After liberation, he had a position in the Social Insurance Bureau, but he was soon arrested for some kind of speculation and got a three-year sentence. After his release from prison, he went on with his lucrative dealings. He made stamps and seals for imaginary companies, and used them to validate orders to various enterprises in Zagreb, Sarajevo, Skopje, and other cities. "Do you remember, Mrs. Štern? *Te-Ko*, *Agrometal*, and many others. The merchandise arrived at the railway station in Sombor, where it was picked up by his trusties. He didn't pay the vendors, but later sold the expensive wares throughout the Vojvodina and elsewhere, at steep prices. He lived the high life, was capable of spending 30,000 *dinars* in one night. On the occasion of a search of his residence, hundreds of kilograms of aniline dye were confiscated, and several rolls of the finest fabric, a lot of cash, and numerous stamps for non-existent firms…"

You listened to him intently, with a furrowed brow, and you tried to remember this famous Mijuški, or Iđuški, whose cavities your former husband probably filled and whose golden bridgework he put in, and then you noticed that the blank, stamped pad of receipts was still lying there wide open on the lace tablecloth. A circle and a Star of David and the letters of the seal spelling "Jewish *Opština* of Novi Sad" were fuzzy, smeared, shaky, and you hastily covered them up with your hand, closed the pad up and dropped it into your purse. What could be done with such receipts — I thought — they can't take anything from anyone, and they acknowledge everything to everybody. I could acknowledge fabricated, fake debts and accuse myself of imaginary offenses. I could sign a receipt for every mouthful I ate in my parents' house. I could in my old age collect my debts and tot up my bottom line. I was afraid that the Lebls seemed to have no trust in us, that they regarded us with suspicion, like traveling salespeople who were selling hundred-year old fog or Himalayan mountains, or forests and lakes in the desert, and who had come to poke around still more in their heartbreak.

She came into the dining room right as we were making for the foyer. To enter at the end of a misplaced, misfired visit could not have been an accident. It was, rather, calculated for a certain effect.

"Good day, Mrs. Štark," she said with affable earnestness. "Hi, Nenad." Never before in my life had she addressed me. She greeted us with the attentiveness of a gracious hostess and immediately got to the point:

"Mama, why wouldn't we contribute a tree immediately for each of my late parents? I have some money saved up. I'll get it right now."

Her hair was bunched in the nape of her neck, but not in a "ponytail" but in a quietly depressed badger or doggy tail. Her courtesy was cold, artificial; she believed that overnight she had become a woman and that she was game for any and all gambits to prove it. Was this because of what she had learned about not being her parents' daughter? It's true that I also had the sneaking suspicion that maturation and growing up were a succession of blows, unexpected acts of cognition that wash away, peel, reject childhood, shake it off like mud caked on your pants after a fight.

But she didn't bring out her savings. Instead she invited me into her room to show me the album with stamps that remained from her parents. There were triangular stamps from Mauritius, and Madagascar and the Jewish Autonomous Region of Birobidzhan. It turned out that the album had been here for ages, but only now had she found out that it was her property. She urgently needed to do something with it.

"What do you think? What should I do with this album? Rafi says it's a valuable collection." She now called her father, Rafael, by the name Rafi. "Should I add to it? Don't feel like it. Should I sell it? They'll rip me off. If I keep it — what would I do with it? The people who collect stamps are cranky old enthusiasts, cowards with their heads in the sand. Do you know anything about stamps or philately?"

"Do you want me to sell it for you?"

I had decided this: if Sonja mentioned her own situation, then I could talk about it now too. I am going to tell her: "You see, I survived, but my brother Danijel, the first-born, didn't. Why? How? Because I agreed for them to separate me, to betray my parents, but Danijel did not. Because in '44, just before the deportation, without saying a word, I stayed with people I didn't know, a certain Katica and her mother, understanding even though I was not yet four, in contrast to my brother, that this was the only way to survive, and Danijel, who was six, decided not to agree to life on those terms. He clung to mother's hand and would not agree to let it go for anything in the world. I failed and broke faith with them; Danijel didn't. You don't have this kind of problem. Besides, it's important that you are loved..." And here my voice would suddenly descend to masculine depths, and from this source of new and manly strength I would put forth this message: "...and that you found this all out as a mature person, and not, for example, in the most sensitive years of life, when it would be..." and so on, and then I will at any rate ask her what's true: that the former housekeeper stopped her on the corner of Zlatna Greda Street and related her story, or is the true account the one where she only by accident discovers the whole thing in the streetcar, when she, bringing back home from school some testimonials and documents, for the first time in her life looks at her birth certificate, which she had already taken back and forth to school several times, and she read the name of her parents and her adopters; she threaded her way through the crowded streetcar up to the driver, yelled at him to stop, and then charged out the door.

"Do you know your way around with stamps?" she asked me, but I didn't know what to say.

"Look, I'm..." I started, but Sonja grabbed me by the hand, pressed her face to mine, taking care though not to touch me with her full duck-like breasts, and decisively set her lips to mine. Simultaneously she also took my other hand, preventing me from either embracing her or pushing away. Although lacking previous experience, I immediately inferred that there was no desire in this kiss, no tenderness, and no invitation to conspiratorial sympathy, or challenge, trust or spite, temptation. It's like she was kissing me to give me the flu, a cold, and thereby giving me a reason to stay home from school; more than anything it was a show for the people outside her door, for her fake parents and the other folks out there in the living room, a challenge directed at them, a nonverbal invitation to open the door casually and find an indecorous image of disobedience and protest. The kiss was cramped: it seemed like in those few seconds we were using our mouths and teeth to hold up, stretch out the lowered curtain of some little amateur home theater, so that the audience would think that behind it something existed, that behind it was some touching plot, about to unfold.

When the kiss began to abate, and our lips drew apart, I moved after them and it was only in Sonja's unexpected retreat that I saw the desire that had not been in the approach and the kiss itself. The lips that had distanced themselves no longer belonged to that clumsy, aggrieved schoolmate who had just now offered them up, but to the girl who was just being born in that ungainly body.

And a short time after our visit to the Lebls', Sonja metamorphosed into a big-bosomed young woman, developed almost fast as lightning, into an adult, the way a hunk of clay on a potter's wheel becomes a vase, through the narrow waist of which, between rounded breasts and hips, the stem of a flower from the garden will scarcely fit. Her face cleared up, its light fuzz receded behind her temples, and her eyes, earlier bashfully close together, each settled into its rightful place: in a word, she grew up all of a sudden, turned out to be beautiful, and — forgot about me.

For me, though, that kiss has retained a different meaning, a special significance; it gave form and name to my problem, which tormented me like a scab. I also was not the birth child of my parents! Sonja forewarned me with that kiss, notified, burdened me, branded me, betrayed, pulled me after her: she let me know that I had also grown up in a lie, and maybe I wasn't who I thought I was. I was supposed to take away from that kiss the message that perhaps I was taken, adopted as a substitute for Danijel, something like that tree of his that will represent him on earth. I felt no need to check. Despite the documents, and every possible attestation from Katica and her relatives, about how they concealed me and looked after me and ultimately returned me safe and sound to my parents after liberation, they only reinforced my conviction that I was also part of parallel actions, campaigns for both afforestation and dissembling.

Why would my fate be any different from Sonja's? Death is always more likely than life, the lie more probable than truth. In those months, the newspapers were writing, and in our house there was a great deal of talk about, the search for the Finaly brothers, a pair of Jewish boys from France who, during the Occupation, after the deportation of their parents, were entrusted for safekeeping to a French woman who raised them as Catholics and after the war refused to give them back to their aunt, after their parents had perished in the camps. The boys' trail was simply lost;

all of France was searching for them, in a great hubbub just like in the movies. The accused person in question, Mrs. Antoinette Braun, at first hid them in French monasteries and then in a Spanish one, where their trail was lost. Millions of people were dead, and everyone was howling, including your sister, at the Catholic woman Antoinette, as if she were hunkered down in the next room, eavesdropping, but I rooted for her. I pulled for the boys not to be found and returned to their kin; I wanted them to remain in some dark, mysterious monastery, so that some sense of illusory justice would not be established, or the victory of the lie of consolation — the truth should be shown, the cruel truth. And when it was announced at last that Robert and Gerald had been found, thanks to an intensive campaign and the activism of Jewish organizations in France, I felt defeated. I realized that graveyard justice had vanquished risk and adventure and that Robert and Gerald had not been able to evade the lie of a half-happy ending, of the return of lost sons, to the ceremony of an overall soothing operation of replacement. I wanted the true state of affairs to be shown. There is no successful exchange, no consolation; let everyone waste away, starving and stuck in their monastery-prisons.

Danijel, dead, was riding high. He had his bust in the bedroom, his tree at 900 meters above sea level, his love, and me, alive in the exchange. The entire world reverberates with his name: *dan-dan*! The bell on the cathedral, the *Saborna crkva*, every hour, at the cemetery chapel, the bell on the fire engine, on the streetcar, on old-fashioned carriages, school bells at least ten times a day, before and after each class, the bells on boats and barges that chug along the Danube in both directions, on the Adriatic and distant seas, all the world's alarm bells, the rattles on the necks of rams and cows, the bells on the necks of lepers and half-wits, all bells: *dan-dan-dan-dan*. That's the way my brother Danijel chimes in and responds; he's recognizable in picture after picture, noise after noise, bell after bell, sound after sound. He calls me, challenges, irritates and holds back and dodges. We were not equal. He ruled the world in which I was trying without success to find my place. He, the unreal, was your real son; I, the real, was the indistinct, incomplete, unacknowledged replacement. It would be easier for me if I had tangible proof that I was yours by birth. In a grove by the Danube, not far from the playground, I selected a willow from which I intended to hang myself when the time came. That hour was supposed to strike in May of the following year, 1954, on the tenth anniversary of Danijel's death. Meanwhile I wanted to finish my sixteenth year and prepare everything that I'd planned out; I wanted my suicide to be the expression of my free will and maturity. But I planned too much, so much that I was not able to do everything. And also Luka required too much of me: the whole book on the grammar and orthography of Serbo-Croatian, plus *War and Peace* and *Dead Souls*, which weren't part of the required reading. Thus, when the designated day arrived, I was not ready. Nonetheless I made my way out to the grove, to the chosen tree, resolved to leave my mark, until further notice, in it with the tip of my pocketknife. The weather was nice, the sturdy trunk was covered in smooth bark, and when I carved the first vertical of my initial into it, the bark began to detach and I heard the tree say "NO." I recoiled, but then the blade itself, below this, carved the word "YES." We were logged in, both my brother Danijel and I, I who refutes and the one who confirms, who agrees. I didn't give up. I only deferred. The tree should remember that.

"Well, do you want to pay for your relatives?" I asked, in order to mask my embarrassment. True, it sounded stupid, as if I had asked her whether she wanted me to buy two tickets to the movies. And maybe that thought was in the back of my mind. They were showing *Forbidden Games* by René Clément and even though I would otherwise never have gone to see a film like that, I imagined that a girl like Sonja should see it — that is to say, it was a film that a person could watch with her.

In March of 1954, Eva Berger unexpectedly returned to Novi Sad from Israel. She had left here with the first of the expatriates.

"Look at me, back home. I came back home!" she said, tumbling out of the express train that had brought her from Rijeka into the arms of Olga Rot. "I thought I was never going to wake up."

The two friends cried in the *fiaker* almost the whole trip, all the way to Olga's apartment. When the coachman unloaded the luggage on the frozen lawn, Olga Rot, losing her strength, sat down on the biggest suitcase: "I'm happy that you have returned," she wanted to say, but her voice failed her.

"Here I am. I've come back home" — there was something intoxicating in the sentence that Eva Berger kept repeating when she'd meet old acquaintances or her few remaining relatives; in the beginning it was with excitement, warmth, and joy that she expected from those to whom she was returning, later with ever more reluctance, uncertainty, and a feeling of guilt, shortening the sentence quite a bit to "Here I am." She was here. That was the one thing that was beyond dispute: whether she had come back home or she had just left home was a question that only history could answer. Those who had not, in their day, had the decisiveness and courage to move away, now they held it against Eva that she betrayed their mutual dream about the promised land, and secretly, surreptitiously, they were themselves grateful that she had returned. Their fear of the new hardships and a new beginning in a new land — was justified.

Olga Rot was the one person in her day who tried to dissuade Eva from emigrating. But back then nothing could hold Eva back. From that moment in September 1944 when, with a bullet in her side and broken ribs, she had regained consciousness in a pile of dead bodies in Bergen-Belsen, she did not cease fleeing from one dream into another, or better put, from one awakening to the next. When in the spring of 1945 she found herself in the baths in Palić, walking naked out of the disinfection stall, she said: "I thought I would never wake up." Only four years later, at the crack of dawn, after a Mediterranean night with no moonlight, as the Greek ship approached the harbor at Haifa, Eva, standing on the tips of her toes so she could glimpse at least for a moment through the giddy mass of emigres a little piece of bluish Mount Carmel, she said the same thing: "Lord, I thought I was never going to wake up." Eva couldn't explain why those four years that she spent in Novi Sad after the war had become a nightmare, just as now she could not explain why she had run away from Netanya. Life in both postwar Novi Sad and postwar Israel began in the radiance light of morning, but they depleted themselves quickly, sank below the horizon, condensing into heavy, obscure slumber. And so now, every shoulder onto which she fell, seeking welcome, was just a shade darker than the previous one, and maybe she was not even going to make it four years there, and then in some third location she would rub her moist eyes and whisper in the ear of some random, uninterested visitor: "I thought I was never going to wake up."

* * *

On the slopes of the Judean mountains, renewed life took root. Neither the cloudbursts and freshets of winter, nor the drought of summer, nor winds of the desert will ever be able to dislodge it again.

In the late autumn of 1954, however, after more than four years of silence, Sara sent a long letter. The handwriting was hers, but upset, stormy, agitated; it had not changed, but it skidded, grew shaky, leaned first to one side and then the other, and the rows of writing, detaching themselves from the lines on the thin paper, slid hopelessly, fell and settled in the bottom right corner like a pile of dried branches, fallen from the narrow paper page of the letter, scuttled to the side.

"I knew it," whispered a flabbergasted Olga.

"A new scandal! The Finalys!" — exclaimed old Zonenfeld, holding the *Bulletin of the Jewish Opština* in his hands. "The thirteen-year old girl for whom people had been looking for years, a young Jew named Anneke Beckman, whose parents were murdered during the war, had been spirited away to a monastery near Liege. When the court authorities came to take the child, she disappeared along with the nun to whom she'd been entrusted. Now there is a search for them and to that end warrants have been issued. Also in the Netherlands there was a similar case that also ended well. Namely, three times a little Jewish girl was found, and three times she was hidden in various monasteries. This was the case of the thirteen-year old Rebecca Melhada, whose parents were gassed in Auschwitz. You see, Olga, our children are coming out of their hiding places, turning up in the light of day."

The Zonenfelds didn't have children. His brother had had two, and lost one, and never even read the papers anymore. The news did not interest him. Before the war, when everybody had children, Mrs. Zonenfeld wouldn't talk about "our children," because they belonged to other people. Now, when nobody had children anymore, all of the children who had not survived, who no longer existed, whom no one had anymore, were also hers. Old Zonenfeld, bound to his wheelchair, in contrast to his nephew, the one surviving relative who decided to live with him instead of with his own father, read all the news that his nephew brought him. He was the translator and followed all the current events; about the Finaly brothers he knew everything by heart, from A to Z. he also knew the numbers of men and women in the group of Bulgarian Jews that passed through Belgrade on their way to Israel, and how they got there. He knew how our people in Israel were getting along, and when the Šterns from Sombor "had twins" or when Gaon Lunenfeld was killed in Jaffa at the door to his house. People brought him newspapers and reading material and carried it away. His living space did not extend further than the railing on his terrace, but he knew everything they were reporting on in the newspapers. And more.

That had been a decade of habituation to life; it took ten years for that miracle to be accepted as fact. But exactly in that time, those small, individual wonders of salvation, after getting used to all-encompassing emptiness, to universal absence, of everybody and everything that comprised their earlier lives, all at once had the tendency to spread. As if that decade of habituation and acceptance of emptiness and nothingness never even existed, after the appearance of the first returnees from stories and from their refuges (finally little Marko Anaf dared to come out of his hiding place in the attic) there suddenly followed universal anticipation. That was the moment when miracle revealed itself as a general rule.

Through the room of Samuel Zonenfeld, but also outside of it, people expounded upon reports of the large transports of Jewish children and women whom the Germans by arrangement with one of Hitler's close viceroy and American Jews handed over to the Russians to take them via the Trans-Siberian railroad into a country in the Far

East. Another, even less credible story, had to do with reports of the dozens — later it proved to be hundreds — of huge sailing ships loaded with rescued children that were plying the South Seas, stocking up on food and water on uninhabited islands in the Pacific, like the Solomons.

Life, after many years, appears to be a succession of stories. Some are true, others are contrived. At that time, the campaign for the "Forest of Martyrs," the adding up of the dead, felt like one of those stories. Every tree was confirmation that a person had been found, had eluded death, preserved him- or herself, and was going to return.

"Look at this, Olga" — he went on, obviously indifferent to Olga's pallor as she read the letter — "this is what Leon Leneman is writing in the French journal *Evidences*: '"Very much unexpectedly, people again began to speak of the 'Jewish Autonomous Region of Birobidzhan.' In an official communique in the Moscow newspaper *Pravda*, it is reported that in the elections of March 1954 Birobidzhan will pick five representatives; at the same time, the *Birobidzhan Star* reports that in the coming months Jews who are coming from Russia, Belarus, and Ukraine will take up residence in Birobidzhan. And that's not all. Here the radio station of the autonomous territory recently reported that Birobidzhan is expecting a sizable number of immigrants who are moving there at the expense of the local authorities." There you have it! And I watched an interesting film in the House of Soviet Culture called *The Land of Happy People* that talked about this. The screenplay was written personally by our compatriot, the journalist Isaac Babel. This isn't propaganda. It's real."

"I knew it," groaned Olga, even more softly.

"Dear Olga," Sara Alkalaj wrote, "I am extremely unsettled by something that happened yesterday. I wasn't even capable of telling you about it right away. With friends of mine who'd recently bought a car, we set out to see how the trees are coming along at Yaar Hakedoshim. We haven't been there since we planted them last spring. Cvi has been wrestling with health problems, and we were constantly putting it off, as if we had a presentiment of something bad. I still had in my mind the memory of the luminously green gardens and orchards in Beit Zayit and in Motsa, which we saw last spring from the bus. They appeared before my eyes whenever I thought about our Forest in the intervening months. But now, in fall, immediately after leaving Jerusalem, a heavy downpour cut off our route, fell in front of us like a lead curtain, and as we went down the zig-zagging road, it was like it was going ahead of us, leading us. We weren't able to punch through it, even though we could see clear skies just a stone's throw away.

I know for certain that we turned right off of the main road approximately twenty kilometers from Jerusalem and continued over a substantial summer track going uphill. I remember clearly the signpost at the intersection, and the sign and its inscription. Cvi remembers it, too. Yesterday, however, although we were very alert, even after the rain stopped, we couldn't find either the sign or the signpost. At the spot where they were supposed to be, sure enough, a road split off. I was convinced it was the same one we'd taken six months earlier, although the humidity, mist, and fall colors changed all sorts of things, including the sharpness of the slopes and the height of the mountains and the direction of the roads. We drove uphill like last time. Around the curves emerged the bare, stony mountains like last time, and the flattened summit on which we stopped and the peak of the neighboring mountain and the valley that yawned between us and the little village on the third mountain behind us — it was all like last time. Everything, my dear! And the mountains of Judea were bare like last time, even here and there covered with underbrush — like last time. Nothing had changed. Our saplings were nowhere to be seen. Nowhere the pine trees, nowhere the Forest of Martyrs! Cvi blamed himself for having taken the wrong turn off of the main road, but I was sure that we'd taken the route we should have, and that we had arrived at the place we'd had in mind. Our friend, who hails from Bratislava and supposedly climbed Triglav in his youth, felt the need to tell us how according to the reports of some mountain climbers, within reach of some inaccessible places in the Andes, there appear, like mousetraps waiting to spring, optical illusions that manage to hold up even the most persistent and best prepared alpinists. In those baleful places, namely, whichever mountain pass a person surmounted, up whichever rock face one climbs, the next landscape presenting itself to him is the same as the one he had just passed through. However much he walks, the same view always opens up before him. And so he constantly climbs the cliff that he already climbed, and beyond every pass he descends into the gorge out of which he just came. In addition, the thin air renders his progress difficult in the extreme. The final step before the goal is repeated endlessly. The mountaineer collapses into the already traversed path, until he either gives up or perishes. We arranged to go back in two weeks, but I don't want to.

Maybe I am ill. Here everybody is more or less sick; I know that we reached the place for which we had set out; it's just that the forest was not there. Across the slopes we located holes, half filled with rocks, debris, and dust like the abandoned dens of desert foxes. What happened to the forest? The whole day long Cvi tried to calm me down but I'm not the problem — it's the force that wants to wrench out my memories, pull up my entire life by the roots. This power drew me here four years ago — I had abandoned myself to it — and now it has again taken hold of my heart and is pulling me to some third realm, who knows where, into madness I guess, and it won't allow me to be soothed or to collect my thoughts. This force is so strong that it can even tear a tree from the soil, and move entire forests from place to place. My dear Olga! The trees you set out with your own hands have vanished! The forest has fled. What's going to happen to us?"

"Oh, God —" Olga cried out, letting go of the letter. She was shaken, although for some time she had already had a presentiment: after the sighs, the thoughts and people and the Forest were going to start for the East, along some long ago sanded-over caravan route, towards a destination which History had mapped out. Just a few years after the war, when her *kolektiv* was visiting the steelworks in Smederevo, she watched the Russian barges, riding low in the water beneath their loads of wheat, corn, and sunflowers; they chugged along, down the Danube, and the long freight trains were lost to sight in clouds of steam and flour as they rolled from the riverside fortress to the horizon. "All this is going to those Russian Jews in their Bidzha, or whatever the fuck they call that new country," the host whispered to her. He was an elderly, toothless painter and did not know that she was the only Jew at the rally.

Imagination, a dream world, needs food the same way people do. Thus the entire world will direct a portion of its wealth to the East, to the place for which the forest has departed. If anything exists for certain, it's that Birobidzhan, the land to which innocent reveries had been turned, is now swallowing every memory, life, love. It is where everything is remembered or forgotten. It's the duty of every Jew to contribute to this idea, to pay his or her debt to the Unrealizable. Wherever they plant trees, at least one branch will leaf out in Birobidzhan; wherever they lay foundations, at least one wall will rise in Birobidzhan; and much of what moves along the Danube will float on into Birobidzhan. The person and the pain that disappear, as if removed by a human hand, will surface and resurrect in Birobidzhan. And look — behind the ships pine trees have now set out, and behind the pines will come fruits, step by step, root after root; heading there will be trees with lemons, figs, oranges, olives, and ultimately also eucalyptus and cacti embedded in stone.

It could be that no one other than Olga Rot was prepared at that moment to believe Sara Alkalaj. But in those years, forests were still capable of emigrating overnight. When Providence decides to indulge the reveries of unhappy women, elemental disasters will be visited on the world, along with geological shocks, biological revolutions;

mountains will move, the desert will come back and devour the forests of the craggy hinterlands, and on earth will originate new islands of happiness, and the evil, rotten continents will tumble to the bottom of the sea, into oblivion. For if a woman wanted to keep at bay her suffering until the end of the world, the distances will distance themselves still further, space will elongate, attenuate, and finally pop like a string on a musical instrument; if on the other hand she wishes to reach unattainable dreams, propinquity will draw even closer, all goals will become feasible, crossing *terra firma* and the ocean a matter of a few strides, every Birobidzhan real, and the world will contract until it curls into a cone that can stand upright upon the palm of a woman's hand.

THE END

AFTERWORD: THE BELGRADE CONNECTION

This novel is a challenging and bracing exploration of movement. Its movements are multiple, maybe even legion, and they are tied to bodies and brains, ideas and ideologies, and countries and conflicts. *The Road to Birobidzhan* is a feminist novel, but it is also a medical novel, a Jewish novel, and a political novel. It is a profound statement about alterity in history and the fragility of memory.

Who Was Judita Šalgo?

Judita Šalgo was born in Novi Sad, a large, cosmopolitan city in northern Serbia (then Yugoslavia), on February 6, 1941. Her family suffered grievously in the Shoah. She studied world literature at the University of Belgrade and worked for decades as a literary editor at various institutions and journals. She married Zoran Mirković (1937–2015), a medical doctor and a writer, in 1967, and they had two children. She won several major literary awards before dying of cancer on September 12, 1996. She is buried in the Jewish Cemetery on Doža Đerđ Street in Novi Sad.

Today Šalgo is considered a very important figure in the evolution of Yugoslav feminism, as well as in the development of experimental prose and poetry in the cultural capital of Serbia's northern province, the Vojvodina. She spoke and worked in Hungarian as well as Serbo-Croatian (the language that is today know as Serbian, Croatian, Bosnian, or Montenegrin), and, like her husband, identified primarily as a Yugoslav, although her heritage also contained Hungarian, Serbian, and Jewish elements. Towards the end of her life she was active in movements for peace and national reconciliation in war-torn Yugoslavia.

The Plot of the Novel

The forward progress of this novel — its plot, although that noun would need to be understood as a hybrid of history, micro-description, and conversations, compounded with the movements mentioned above — is strongly informed by geography. There are, broadly seen, major journeys or motions in the book that run in intersecting directions: a north-south journey, involving Bertha Pappenheim, Jewish populations (especially women who have been sexually enslaved or otherwise trafficked), and a young woman from Belgrade named Flora Gutman; the east-west journey, or axis, involves opposite ends of the Diaspora: Jewish immigrants to the US and Jewish settlers in Soviet Birobidzhan, a province for Jews created by the USSR, along its border with China, in the 1920s. The city of Belgrade is at the intersection of these two journeys. Powering much of the movement in the novel is the phenomenon of hysteria, brought to modern prominence by the Viennese psychiatrists Breuer and Freud but depicted here as a pillar of Western patriarchy and medical science dating back to Classical Greece. Sometimes hysteria is supplemented by Jewish characters' quests for the Lost Tribes or for a Promised Land, or by more secular utopian aspirations. But hysteria is such a huge factor in the novel that its repeated invocation by Pappenheim and others could be seen as an effort to "take the term back," to reappropriate and repurpose it into a search for a "female continent," or a more just society for women. Perhaps it resembles, in this function, the self-identification of British activists, referred to several times in the novel, as "suffragettes." One can think of other examples of "reclaimed" epithets in the popular culture of our own time.

What the novel is "about" is a question that one could attempt to answer, at the simplest level, with the terms hysteria, Holocaust, and homeland. The novel shows a wide variety of people in a number of countries "on the move," sorting through competing ideas about utopia and justice, often against the backdrop of Nazism and Hungarian fascism, the Shoah, the Soviet dictatorship, and the Cold War.

Contexts

Any reckoning with this powerful novel must encompass the language, style, and form in which it is written. Šalgo's writing is demanding. Novels by poets are often rigorously composed, either in terms of their compression or their lyricism. Since Šalgo's work on *The Road to Birobidzhan* was "interrupted" (a term that people close to her prefer to "unfinished"), it is possible that the text contains some repetitions or inconsistencies. Still, the main reason this text is demanding is because Šalgo wanted it to be that way. A complex subject deserves a complex treatment; or, put another way, form can reinforce function (or message) in beautiful ways in art. It was not a goal of this translation to "spare" the anglophone reader, or to tidy things up; at times, adding a comma or a period, or clarifying the relationship between competing clauses in a long sentence, seemed like a reasonable concession to readability. None of this can disguise the fact that there are many moving parts in this work. There are so many of them that readers must be prepared to fight for their understanding.

Part of Šalgo's style, or part of her postmodernism, are the elements of the *nouveau roman* and magical realism in her prose. The use of so many historical figures in the text, from Rothschilds to Rosenbergs, from Bertha Pappenheim ("Anna O" of Viennese renown) to real-life poets and presidents, of course reminds one of a "historical novel" (but aren't all novels historical?), except that these elements are mobilized and deployed in a thoroughly modern, playful, and poignant way that does not dally in "romance" or "cultural literacy." Šalgo makes her own marvelous compound of all of this, while telling a unique story. At times, perhaps unexpectedly, except that they, like many other parts of the book, are lyrically inspired and satisfying, descriptions can rear up mightily, towering over the text, accumulating like lessons in baroque imagery, as at the very end of the book, when a factory full of people building Tito's socialist Yugoslavia becomes aware of the existence of distant Birobidzhan.

While academic studies and literary criticism of *Birobidzhan* have thus far focused on its feminist message, and rightly so, there are signs that other facets of the novel are also meeting with critical appreciation. Tijana Matijević, for instance, has pointed out that the novel marks, in periodization, the beginning of a unique form of post-Yugoslav literature, while a number of scholars are examining the range of ways in which Šalgo's writing is emancipatory. And then there is history. Not the history behind or of the book — what I mean here is history itself. We meet it in Šalgo's novel. Very early on, one character is seen "expounding a comparative history of the world based on arson and bonfires" — an undertaking more modern than topical in its sensibility! Elsewhere there is a reference to a history of what are essentially epidemics of love. And other characters refer to the "open waters of history," which are the scene of great adventures and sufferings, while others seek alchemical interpretations of contemporary events through literary hints and personalities. Individual malice can turn a "hangover into history," by clouding judgment and creating victims. And what if history is actually chained to words, to characters and letters, and humans are speeding it up by writing so many things down?

Every author, or even every longer literary work, has a set of frequently-used words that jump out at a translator or other close reader. In Šalgo's case, these words provide an opportunity, or even the necessity, to translate individual lexica in various ways; as I see it, varying translation (through close synonyms) is a nod towards the honest recognition of polyvalent vocabulary; no one benefits from a translator refusing to make a tough call on a word or phrase, however, and of course repetition for emphasis or lyricism needs to be captured and conveyed, but alternating between commonsense translations of frequent word in a text can also be an embrace of the openness and possibilities of expression within and between languages. The words that seem to recur most frequently in this novel are terms related to *grč* (spasm or cramp), *mučan* (painful, nauseous, tedious), *tok* (course or duration), and all shades of words signifying journey; tracks or traces; miserable or wretched; to scream or to shout; and to intimate, suspect, and intuit.

There are puns — always hard to translate — and straightforward humor as well. Presenting the reader with the interplay between "home" and "gnome" in a speech, or "*banja*" (spa) and "*banovina*" (a unit of territory akin to a state or province) are little stretches of cool shade in a text that sometimes feels ready to overheat. Some examples of Šalgo's humor would be the out-of-control dinner party where the master of the house threatens to throw pastry at an obnoxious guest, or the sarcasm of a student in the late 1940s grumbling over being assigned *Dead Souls* and *War and Peace* in a society already saturated with death and Russians, or the cringe-worthy *faux pas* of a hostess at a salon; Šalgo also uses French, German, and Hungarian words in characters' thoughts and speech to convey authenticity or emphasis shared European context; in the Hungarian case, some of the terms almost seem to be meta-comments, or notes to herself about what she was trying to convey in the Serbian text.

Conclusion

The world needs more Judita Šalgo. Let us hope that this novel will only be the first of her books to appear in translation. There is no doubt that the growing list of able and motivated literary scholars looking at her work will present us with new techniques and unexpected interpretations. As for this translator and historian, I can confirm that Šalgo's writing is as rich as it is rigorous. Little did I expect how much the poet was going to analyze the mechanics of history as discipline and its construction as text. Those of us who write and teach about bad ideas and failed projects know (as we are all coming to realize nowadays about conspiracy theories) that "this history leaves in its wake indisputable tracks and marks, even if its sources are dubious." But in particular I leave this translation inspired by Šalgo's perspicacity, hopeful that a sense of the historical beyond the episodic, even in the century of Auschwitz and the atomic bomb, is actually possible.

John K. Cox
Fargo, ND (USA)

SELECT BIBLIOGRAPHY

Works by Judita Šalgo in Serbian (Serbo-Croatian/BCMS)

Novels

Trag kočenja (1987)
Put u Birobidžan (1997)
Kraj puta (2004)

Poetry

Obalom (1962)
67 minuta naglas (1980)
Život na stolu: pesme (1986)

Short Story Collection

Da li postoji zivot? (1995)

Essays and Other Texts

*Jednokratni eseji (*2000)
Hronika (2007)
Radni dnevnik: 1967–1996 (2012)

Works by Judita Šalgo in English Translation

Story

"The Story of the Man Who Sold Sauerkraut and Had a Lioness-Daughter," translated by Alice Copple-Tošić, in Agata Schwartz and Luise von Flotow, eds.,
The Other Shore: Women's Fiction from East Central Europe (2006).

Poems

"Dictionary" and "Dictionary of Breathing, translated by Snežana Žabić, in Biljana D. Obradović and Dubravka Djurić, eds.,
Cat Painters: An Anthology of Contemporary Serbian Poetry (2016).

"Life on a Table," translated by Biljana D. Obradović, in Biljana D. Obradović and Dubravka Djurić, eds., *Cat Painters: An Anthology of Contemporary Serbian Poetry* (2016).

"Six Interpretations of Poetry," translated by Vladislav Beronja, at www.harlequincreature.org (2019).

Essays (translated by John K. Cox)

"Comments on Television" on www.apofenie.com (2021).

"Ferenc Fehér Square" at www.pescanik.net (2021).

"Paper Pictures" in *Dalhousie Review* (2021).

"What I Wrote About" in *North Dakota Quarterly* (2022).

Works about Judita Šalgo

Božović, Gojko. "Umetnost i stvarnost" (1998).

Đerić, Zoran. *Upotreba grada* (2014).

Djurić, Dubravka and Šuvaković, Miško, eds. *Impossible Histories: Historic Avant-Gardes, Neo-Avant-Gardes, and Post-Avant-Gardes in Yugoslavia, 1918–1991* (2006).

Dražić, Silvia. *Stvarni ii imaginarni svetovi Judite Šalgo* (2013).

Gikić Petrović, Radmila. *Tokovi savremene proze* (2002).

Ilić, Dejan. *Inhabiting the Zone of Uninhabitability.* The Open University, PhD thesis, 2002.

Marićević, Jelena. *Legitimacija za signalizam.* (2016).

Matijević, Tijana. *From Post-Yugoslavia to the Female Continent: A Feminist Reading of Post-Yugoslav Literature* (2020).

Mirković, Zoran. *Filozofija ljubomora* (2012).

Pavković, Vasa. *Neočekivani pesnici* (2015).

———. *Pogled kroz prozu* (2006).

Rosić, Tatjana. "Autopoetika kao antiutopija. Motiv 'nove zemlje' u romanima Vojislava Despotova i Judite Šalgo" (2006).

Todoreskov, Dragana V. *Tragom kočenja: prisvajanje, preodevanje, iiraslojavanje stvarnosti u poetici Judite Šalgo* (2014).

Tucakov, Ljubica Šljukić. "'Bezgranično carstvo besmisla': jedno tumačenje poglavlja 'Istočni greh Nenad Mitrovića' u roman *Put u Birobidzan*" (2015).

Tucić, Vujica Rešin. "Judita Šalgo u zlom i potkupljivom svetu" (2019).

TRANSLATOR'S NOTE

It is a great honor to translate the major novel of the late Yugoslav writer Judita Šalgo (1941–1996). Long held in high esteem for her experimental poetry, she also wrote noteworthy prose in a wide variety of genres. Her essays, which can be politically engaged, magically quirky, or autobiographical, are a delight, as are her highly inventive short stories that lead the writer into unexpected juxtapositions and insights on modern society. As scholarly interest in Šalgo's work continues to grow, mostly in Serbia, translations of her work into various languages are also gradually increasing in number. In addition to the indisputable *avant-garde* and feminist hallmarks of her oeuvre, her writing reveals a very heterogeneous set of influences, debts, and modes. As complex or unusual as her writing can be, readers (and translators) can take heart in the observation that Šalgo's creations are never very far removed from the concept or act of creation itself: by individualizing and annotating history through a variety of chronological and lexical, not to mention geographical, devices, the author leaves us with a sense of almost limitless possibility, even in a century of extreme political actions and unprecedented human costs.

The textual basis for this translation is the volume *Put u Birobidžan*, edited by Vasa Pavković and published in Belgrade by Stubovi kulture in 1997.

The challenging nature of this text and the unusual route to posthumous publication of the "interrupted" (but not unfinished) Serbian original present the translator with the joyous task of thanking even more people than usual for their help with project. Nothing would have been possible without the friendly and generous cooperation of Šalgo's daughters, Ivana Mirković, and Tamara Mirković, and without the sage advice of Vasa Pavković.

In addition, my heartfelt gratitude goes out to:

Bojan Babić, Dušan Bogdanović, Milan Bogdanović, Jasna Dimitrijević, Miloš K. Ilić, Dragana Mokan, Marijana Nedeljković, Darko Tuševljaković, and Dennis Vulovic, for beautiful Serbian words;

Vladimir Arsenijević, Gojko Božović, Dubravka Đurić, Irena Javorski, and Melita Milin, and Jeff Pennington for materials and information;

Krisztina Kós and all the other fine folks at CEEOL Press Verlag for the courage to take on this book;

and Danica Vukićević, Dejan Simonović, Nenad Milošević, and Srećko for moral support.

This translation is dedicated to Tijana Matijević, a scholar of South Slavic literature and a very sensitive reader of all sorts of things, for her friendship and intellectual support in recent years.

PRESS

Frankfurt am Main. 2021

CPSIA information can be obtained
at www.ICGtesting.com
Printed in the USA
BVHW042129100422
633918BV00009B/264

9 783949 607042